FOR THIS TO END

Jannicke Howard

Also by Jannicke Howard:

The Hemo 10 Trilogy
Only One Way
For This to End

ISBN: 978-0-9934120-0-4

She staggered into the hallway. Her shoulder hit the wall and she slumped to the floor. Her fingers were stuck together, damp and klibby. When she parted them, there was a film that would stretch so far before pinging apart. The stench of iron was nauseating. She looked down at her body. Her forearms were plastered in congealing blood. Her face was splattered, grim, streaked through with blood. Her drenched hair clung to the back of her neck. She did not feel comfortable in her own skin. She would have run, but there really wasn't anywhere to go. So she sat crumpled in the hallway, certain that despite everything, she had never been more exhausted.

"Naomi?"

She looked fearfully through fingers peeled open. Karen had just closed the door. The once beautiful Karen. The never fazed Karen. The practical, forward thinking Karen. Neither dared to speak for a minute or more. Naomi became aware that the noise has stopped.

"She passed out," Karen whispered.

Only a respite, nothing final yet.

"What...?" Naomi started, but she couldn't finish the question, couldn't think of anything she actually wanted to ask.

Karen stepped away from the door, and Naomi saw her hands shake. It was not a slight hint of movement, but a proper shake, as if she was a hardcore alcoholic coming off the booze. Karen dropped to her haunches beside Naomi. She would have cried, but her body was too drained. "I'm sorry, you shouldn't have had to..."

Naomi held up her hand. They had the same thought, but she didn't want to have to face it head on. She didn't want it verbalised.

Karen leant forward, terrified of the truth she would impart. "I don't know what to do."

Naomi's face was blank. She didn't know what to say. Only that she could hear groaning from the other room. The break was over. She couldn't let Karen go back in there alone. Soon the screaming would start.

This is the world now. Destroyed. Civilisation gone. Global communication ceased months ago. We live in the Stone Age, in more senses than one. The first few weeks, months, some countries muddled through with martial law, but one after another we fell. Electricity supplies failed, the gas was turned off. Internet servers and telecommunications collapsed. Food supplies waned and fizzled out. Peaceful army control wasn't working, and with everyone forced to self-sufficiency, diseased urban populations fled the cities. The countryside couldn't support such a high nomadic population. It certainly didn't need the mobilised spread of disease. In desperation a number of particularly heavily infected cities were fire bombed. And with the electricity off, the mobile phone batteries dead, everything suddenly went quiet. Just the screams of the inflicted, the terrified, at night. Suicides and murder at first as anarchy grew in power and the killer statistic rocketed. The disease ravaged regardless. After a couple of months starvation took its place in the poll table of killers. People were either too stupid to feed themselves, or simply unfortunate enough not to have access to any food. No one knew how the rest of the world was coping. Perhaps there was nothing more alive beyond what you could see. No one knew how or when all of this would end, only that when, or rather if, we ever got a handle on the disease, we were never going back to the comfortable, apathetic lives we had led before.

Of course, this was all a year in the future, a year ahead of when we first drove into Thixendale in the Yorkshire Wolds, Northern England. I still think about that day, even now, after everything that has happened. I think about how stupid we were, that we didn't see. And how close we'd come to the end – we really could have been killed. Even in that first week I began to understand how really I had more to fear from the uninfected, than I did from the diseased. In times of great trauma, it's so easy to let the brain go back to its Stone Age basis. Just to get the essentials covered. Animal desires and needs. Survival of the fittest. Destruction of the weakest. And now there is barely anyone left, *between the deaths, the infections, and the noble, well-intentioned but ultimately naive striving for the better of humanity, we're making ourselves extinct. Humanity. If this disease won't tear us apart, we'll do it ourselves. I wonder if we're really worth saving.*

Dawn was groggy, grey and begrudging that morning Richard, Naomi and Ed drove into Thixendale. Running on adrenaline, wired and exhausted, eyes flitting like the nervous heads of small birds. Always watching for the predator.

It had been a long, slow drive over rough terrain, getting out of the city of York and cutting cross country away from sprawling villages. Eventually they'd gotten into clear terrain. They'd left the flat expanse of farming land and climbed up into the Yorkshire Wolds. The off-road route wound around the steep valleys, quaint designs left on the earth from ice age glaciers that had cut and ground through rock. Now there were steep grassy banks, glittering becks at the bottom, and sheep fields on all terrain. On the tops of hills large productive farms grew wheat and barley in chalk-riddled fields. Tiny villages were tucked away in the folds of the landscape, hidden by the patches of woodland and the steep protective curl of the valleys. Single track roads led down steep inclines, looking like no through roads easily missed from the main route, miles away to the east. It was a perfect place to hide.

The village was a collection of thirty or so buildings and outlying farms along a single main road like a rope laying in the bottom of a valley. It had been a settlement in one form or another since the Stone Age. They'd entered from the east, driving down a seemingly endless rough single track road that twisted along the base of the narrow gully of a valley. The dawn sun attempted to creep up over the hilltops, breaking in through the tree branches cutting apart the base of the skyline. The road was lined with green grazing fields to one side, steep wild meadow grass banks to the other, wire fences and scrubby shrubs, the occasional passing place for traffic they hoped they wouldn't meet. Pot holes ate away at the tarmac. It would be decades before they were fixed again.

Naomi bounced and rattled with the Land Rover, slumped in the passenger seat, watching the scenery with dry gritty eyes and thinking about her abandoned home in York. They'd fled the northern city in the small hours of the morning, sneaking down back roads and across fields to evade notice. There was a complete ban on movement. Army road blockades set up at all the key points on the ring road made sure most never left. It was a national attempt at disease control. She supposed they were just as bad as every other selfish person who pushed against the rules, bullying through with their car, trying to escape. Only that they had quietly departed, and unlike most other people, had been successful. And in a way they had a right to this, at least that was the logic she tried to console herself with. Richard, who was silently driving, headlights off and relying on local knowledge, didn't actually live in York, but in the village of Thixendale they were fleeing to. He had been visiting his younger brother, Ed, who was now sleeping in the back of the vehicle, and had the misfortune to be locked into York. So really they were just relocating to Richard's actual home. They wouldn't try to move again. At least the brothers could use that defence. Her own reasoning was thinner. She was only a neighbour across the road from Ed Stilton, who had been offered a place on the escape route.

She hadn't left that much behind in York other than personal possessions. She only had a rucksack of personal items with her. Naomi lived in a pokey one roomed flat. Since the outbreak all she had was solitude and the big unknown of what horrors the next day would bring. York had not seen the worst of the pandemic to date, but she had witnessed people attacked, ripped, stabbed, murdered... and then last night on the escape she'd seen a huddle, like stray dogs, eating with their hands out of a corpse. She closed her eyes. Why did this have to happen?

The Land Rover came around a corner, Richard muttering that they were almost there. He let off the accelerator. Naomi felt her stomach crunch as she saw the road ahead was blocked, and still the hamlet wasn't in sight. A hefty log, with rudimentary legs nailed on had been set across with the road, with a few coils of barbed wire for good measure. A couple of figures holding heavy work tools stood behind the road block. More worrying was the dug out on the bank by a tree, already with a rough wall, over which someone with a shotgun watched.

One of the men on the road flapped an arm angrily. "Fuck off back where you came from."

"Shit." Richard let the Land Rover slow to a halt a few metres shy of the road block. The engine idled, embarrassingly slow in the quiet, tense morning. "This has started a lot quicker than I thought it would."

The men looked jumpy at the fact the Land Rover made no effort to reverse back up to the last passing place to turn around. One of them gripped the garden hoe with both hands and stepped around the end of the road block. "There's no space for you. Fuck off back where you came from."

Richard wound his window down and stuck his head out. "Is that you, Chad?" he asked, the light still hazy. Over the difficulty to focus, the surreal nature of the situation and the out-of-character behaviour made him hesitant. Chad was a farm labourer. He still lived with his parents in the village and was very much a live-and let-live kind of person. A hulk of a man, probably put here for appearance rather than any real determination to keep people out. Richard doubted this road block would have been Chad's idea.

Chad paused, surprised by the sound of his name. It disabled the menace in his threatening demeanour. He glanced back uncertainly at the man behind the rock block.

"For crying out loud, it's me," Richard said, wanting to kick off, but forcing his temper down. He was quite aware that they could still get thrown out. Collective fear made people do stupid things. "Richard Stilton. I live here. Of course there's room."

Chad's shoulders slumped, relaxing. "It's only Richard," he called up to the figure with the shot gun. The firearm's aim was redirected to the ground. The other man stepped right up to the road block, still suspicious. "He's not alone," he pointed out. Everyone knew that Richard Stilton lived alone. There were newcomers here, because aside from Richard, all other local residents were already accounted for. "Who's with you?"

"Naomi and Ed."

Chad went back behind the roadblock and there were some low discussions.

Naomi bit her lip and looked over at Richard. "Are they not going to let us in?"

"Sure they are," Richard drummed his fingers on the steering wheel, not sounding completely convinced by his statement.

"Power's gone to their heads a bit, that's all. That's vigilantes for you."

Naomi closed her eyes. All she wanted to do was sleep. This continuous uncertainty was a permanent background nausea. She doubted these people had even seen the disease, as isolated off from the towns and cities as they were. Yet they were behaving as though Armageddon had already happened.

"It'll be fine," Richard looked over at her, giving her shoulder a slight push as if to buck her spirits. "We'll get past these and my house is at this end of the village. We can get some rest. We're almost there."

After an age, Chad and the second man picked up one end of the roadblock and slowly dragged it around, so that if Richard drove on the verge, he'd be able to squeeze past and enter the village. Naomi gazed out of the window as they passed by. The man Richard had called Chad raised a friendly hand up at them. The other man, older and more cynical, perhaps with good reason, watched them suspiciously, his face without expression, as three more people, three more mouths to feed, went into the village.

The moment they had passed the road block was back in position.

Richard's house was one of the first buildings they came to in the village. It was bested only by a farmhouse and farm buildings. The village was grey and cool before the sun blasted the base of the valley, caught still by the steep sides of the gully. A clump of trees, then a rough road swinging steeply back off up the hill, and the first private residence appeared. The home of Richard Stilton. It was a two storey house with a neat but low maintenance garden at the front. The valley sides plunged up to the skies directly where the back of the house ended.

Naomi got out of the Land Rover, her legs a little giddy from the adrenaline ride cross country. She stared up at the house. It looked like a quaint family home in the country. Part of the second floor formed protruding windows from the sloping roof, reminiscent of chocolate box scenes. It was surely too much for one man. Although hadn't Richard at one time lived with a woman who was a potter? Perhaps a large house had been necessary for the studio.

Ed slunk off the back of the Land Rover and rambled over to the front door as Richard unlocked it. He muttered something about sleep before pushing his way past and disappearing into the house.

Naomi remained on the short driveway, gazing down the road into the village. The quiet sleeping properties were all set back from the single through road. Carefully tended gardens separated road from house. The land of the stereotypical English, the country life, peace and quiet and good, healthy living. Bad things didn't happen in a place like this. It was difficult to line this up with what she had witnessed in York. It almost felt like a ridiculous, hysterical reaction: fleeing the city and coming here to hide. Perhaps she had been foolish. Richard wanted to come home; Ed needed a break from the city with Emma's death so painfully raw. But Naomi? She was just a girl who lived across the road. Just someone they happened to know. Why was she here?

"Naomi?"

She turned, looked to the house. Richard stood, one hand on the open door.

"Are you all right?"

"Yes, I..." She didn't even know how to finish the thought. "It feels like I've just woken up from a nightmare."

"Bit surreal?"

"Would the people living here even believe what we've seen?"

Richard shrugged. "You saw the road block."

"I guess."

"Do you want to come in?" he tapped the door open a little further. "The travelling's over. You might want to take a nap."

"Are you saying I look rough?"

"Understandably rough."

She smiled lop-sided, approaching the house. "Flattery's not your strong point."

"I can be charming when I need to be," he told her as she passed by and walked in through the doorway. "I'm just not firing on all cylinders right now."

Naomi woke at noon. She'd slept in the spare bedroom. As she sat up out of slumber, she was surprised to consider she had managed some sleep. The adrenaline had been so thick in her blood, her body giddy in horror. Relaxation hadn't seemed possible. Despite the sleep, she didn't feel rested. She was drained. All the incredibility had been slapped out of her. She held onto a dull relief that hopefully they had reached somewhere safe. It was the security felt when hiding under blankets to fight a fear of the dark. Perhaps they would escape the horrors.

Richard was at the kitchen table with a large cafetiere of coffee and his laptop glaring at his tired face. She suspected he hadn't bothered to sleep but had been scrambling away at the computer ever since they had arrived. There were some printed papers at the end of the kitchen table. She glanced down before he noticed her appearance. They had been printed from PDFs on the internet: the unofficial guide to the HEMO10 virus. As soon as the country had gone into lockdown the government had issued hastily written information leaflets about the pandemic. The tone had been calming, vague and suitably avoiding all the nasty details of what was really happening. As soon as those leaflets hit people's letterboxes, unofficial guides telling the bitter truth had appeared on the internet and gone viral. Suddenly everyone was a documentary film maker, a journalist, a social commentator. Social media had never been so active. We're all going to die, and the world has given it a big thumbs down. Just in case anyone had been in doubt.

Richard glanced up as she sat down opposite him. "Help yourself to coffee."

I will, Naomi thought, filling a clean cup. "You don't look like you've slept at all."

"I've not tried." He returned to silence, reading something on screen, before dragging his dry eyes away and giving her his full attention. He smiled lop sided. "My brain's buzzing. I can manage."

"Has it been like this whilst you've been out on assignment?"

"The hours at least. It's never been this scary." Richard was a wildlife cameraman. He'd worked all over the world, out of the country for months at a time. "I don't know how much they know here. I don't suppose they've seen an actual case in the flesh. They need to know the truth." He looked over to the print outs. "We've got to go and see the colonel."

"What?"

"It's not as bad as it sounds."

"We have to check in with the military?" Naomi put her coffee cup down. She didn't own property in Thixendale; she had no relatives. What if they threw her out and sent her back to York?

"He's a retired old colonel, just heading up the village effort. The army's so stretched that they can't leave any personnel at little places like this. We're on our own. Chad was by just after you and Ed had gone upstairs. As soon as Ed's up we'll go over and check in."

"This sounds a little draconian..."

"Naomi, he's an all right old fellow. Don't worry. I don't think he's the type to let power go to his head." He leant over the table and held on to her forearm as if that was all the reassurance she needed. "It'll be a chance for you to meet some of the people who live here."

"They're not going to throw me out of the village?"

"Of course not."

There was a creak of movement above them. Presumably Ed, Richard's younger brother, was moving. Naomi drained her coffee. "I'll just nip to the bathroom, then we can go and check in."

She locked the bathroom door, and stood and looked herself in the eye in the mirror. Tired and wan. Someone sickening for something. "I just need to sleep," she whispered to herself, already thinking she'd be glad when checking-in, whatever that entailed, and meeting the locals was over and she could come back to the house and hide in Richard's spare room. She looked back at herself. Her lank red hair that could have done with a wash. Maybe later. For now she took a hair band off her wrist and tied back her hair into a scruffy bun. Brushed her teeth with toothpaste on her finger, splashed her face with a little cold water and went to the toilet. That would have to do for now.

There was a thump on the bathroom door.

"Just a second, I'm almost done." Naomi unlocked the door and opened it. Ed had his forearm against the doorframe, propping up his slumping body. He looked even more shattered than she or Richard did. He had good reason to. It was only yesterday that his girlfriend, Emma, had finally succumbed to the infection. Naomi had not lost anyone she cared about. She didn't suppose she could really understand that kind of grief.

Ed's breath was rank, and made her flinch. She glanced uncertainly at him. "You all right, Ed?" He looked at her, a stare that brought nausea in the beholder. His eyes were blood shot to the point the whites were almost perfectly scarlet. He ran a hand over his face. "I just need to..." he let the thought hang incomplete, and tumbled into the bathroom as Naomi slipped out. The door shut, and she waited in the corridor. Was this paranoia, or had she seen something they did not want in the village? She mentally worked through the hours: how long they had been in the village; how long they had travelled. When was the last point at which Ed, dare she even think it, could have become infected? Twelve hours. What had the unofficial advice stated? Five to ten hours and symptoms would appear. If Ed was infected, he would be behaving worse than this, surely?

Naomi wandered into the kitchen. She stood in the doorway and watched Richard. He was unaware of the observation. She didn't want to suggest that his brother might be ill, but if she didn't say something and he was infected, they would all soon follow.

"Richard," she started uncertainly. "About Ed, you've not..."

"Ed? Is he up yet?"

"Oh. Yes. He's just in the bathroom."

"We'll head off as soon as he's out." Richard switched off the laptop, pushing the screen firmly down against the keyboard.

Naomi hurried up to the kitchen table. "His eyes were red."

"Whose eyes?"

"Ed's."

"I don't suppose he's sleeping too well." Richard got up and took the cafetiere to swill out the coffee dregs in the sink.

"No, I mean they're really red." Naomi glanced down at the print outs of unofficial advice. Point three: Haemorrhage of sclerotic arterioles: i.e. reddening of the eyes. "Beyond bloodshot. You know it says that it's a sign of..."

"Ed's grieving," Richard snapped. "You're being paranoid, looking for it where there isn't any..."

"Isn't any what?"

They both jumped at the sound of Ed's voice, as if they'd been caught in the act. What act would Ed have disapproved of? Naomi couldn't quite think. Was suggesting Ed might be infected a disloyal trait? Ed looked dishevelled, his suit slept in. He wore his sunglasses, making it impossible to tell who or where his gaze was directed.

"It's not that bright out," Richard muttered.

"I've..." his sentence was broken by a deep sigh. "Fucking headache."

"Here," Richard threw his brother a box of paracetemol. "We've got to go see the colonel now."

Naomi watched as Ed walked heavily over to the sink, filling a glass with water. He fumbled with the pill packaging as if his fingers were leaden sausages. Clumsily, he eventually popped more tablets than he needed out of the blister pack. Downed the whole glass of water in one, wiped his mouth with a tea towel on the side, then slopped off to the front door where Richard was waiting. Naomi gazed down at the tea towel that had been tossed thoughtlessly into the sink, her eyes transfixed by the smear of damp blood on the fabric.

"Are you coming?"

She pointed at the tea towel. This was very wrong. "Have you seen..?"

"You're being paranoid." Richard was terse. The lack of sleep was starting to show. "Bring those print outs and let's get going."

"You really need to see this."

"Fine, catch us up."

Richard stalked out of the house after his brother. Naomi loitered indecisively, moving to pick up the tea towel, then changing her mind. Richard had been so level headed and realistic, ever since this health crisis had started. If this was something to worry about, he wouldn't be dismissing it as he was. She left the ambiguous evidence, and stepped outside. She closed the door but left it unlocked, assuming they didn't need to worry about thieves in villages and times like these.

The Un-official Guide to the HEMO10 Virus

Yesterday the government released an information leaflet that was distributed by the army to all homes in the UK. We have read this leaflet, and feel that it is a misleading and watered down version of what is actually happening.

The government do not want you to panic. People are already panicking and some people have seen what this virus really does. Everybody needs to understand exactly what happens to a person when they are infected. We want you to be scared. You need to be, because if we don't all pull together and work against the spread of this disease, it will be the end. You need to appreciate just how important it is that you don't get infected.

What is the HEMO10 Virus?

This is a completely new disease. We do not fully understand it yet. There is no vaccine and no cure. We do not know where it originated from, which makes it even more important that it is isolated and destroyed as soon as possible.

It is a violent and aggressive virus. It is a hemorrhagic fever: this means blood loss in layman terms. It works far more quickly than most viruses, including virulent types such as the Ebola Virus, Borna Virus and Marburg disease virus - three virus which it shares a few traits with.

How does HEMO10 spread?

The government leaflet tells us:
The virus particles are spread through blood, bodily fluids, saliva, vomit and diarrhoea. If any of these substances from an infected person get into your system through eyes, mouth and other body openings, open cuts and wounds; then you will contract the disease.

This is all correct, yet may make you complacent. Please consider how easily this will work. If someone spits in your eye: you are infected. The most common method of infection we have had reported to date are as follows:
1. Prior to signs of symptoms: kissing
2. After signs of symptoms: biting

What are the symptoms?

5 to 10 hours after infection, the following symptoms will appear and will continue to intensify until death (occurring between 3 and 10 days later):
1. Headaches, paranoia, slurred speech leading to loss of speech.
2. Fever and nausea – following by vomiting, including blood.
3. Haemorrhage of sclerotic arterioles: i.e. reddening of the eyes.
4. Petechia – red or purple spots on body.
5. Hypovolemic shock – i.e. decrease in blood volume; coupled with increasing hunger.
6. Diarrhoea and bloody diarrhoea.
7. Delirium, violent outbursts in increasing frequency; psychotic and psychopathic tendencies. This is seen to culminate with the increased hunger in a single-minded

"hunt, kill and eat" behaviour pattern. Cannibalism is not uncommon.

8. Cell death leading to major haemorrhaging and multi-organ dysfunction. Upon death, the abdomen will explode, spreading infected blood and decomposing body tissue across an area.

What should I do if I or someone I know has been infected?

Immediate isolation. Official government instruction is to contact your local army post for collection. We cannot tell you what to do. We can only point out the following facts:

1. There is no cure or treatment.
2. The mortality rate is 100%.
3. Euthanasia is illegal in the UK.
4. Murder is illegal in the UK.
5. Manslaughter on the grounds of self defence may well be a grey zone, especially in the current medical climate and military control.
6. When the infection fully takes hold, your nearest and dearest will lose their minds. They will not recognise you and they will attack. This is an aggressive virus that kills its hosts relatively quickly, so it needs to jump to its next host fast. This is the weak point we have to take advantage of if we are going to stop this disease.

Disclaimer: We are not promoting murder or euthanasia. We are not **telling** people to take the law and/or the isolation and destruction of disease into their own hands.

"You need to distribute these around the village, if you've not already done so."

"Oh, yes?" The colonel, a man of some seventy plus years, military issue broom moustache and a tweed suit, gave the sheets of printed paper a polite but unconcerned glance as he set them to the side of the table. "I understand there have been confirmed cases in York."

"It's a little worse than that."

"Of course, of course. We're lucky here in that there has been no infection. You'll have seen in York the military rule of course. There's not enough of our boys these days to look after everyone, so we've formed a council, and we're doing the job for them here. The ban on movement is for a damned good reason. Our roadblocks are up to stop anyone trying to sneak out of the towns and look for a place to hide. One has to think of the common good. Why, if we all panic and run, this infection will be spread right across the country in no time, and then we'll all be ill."

Naomi lowered her eyes. This felt like a telling off at the headmaster's office. They were in the village hall, which had been turned into battle headquarters. The colonel's field office was positioned at the head of the hall. Walking in, she could see that the regular army had been by. There were government issue information leaflets and posters, stacks of issue rations, a field radio, and an ominous locked cupboard. In one corner there was a collection of garden tools intended for more threatening purposes: hoes, spades, shovels, bats, crowbars and sledgehammers.

"No one's going to survive long term in the cities," Richard said. "This is much worse than you can realise."

"It wouldn't be if everyone did as they were told," the colonel interrupted, his face reddening. He didn't like insubordination. "But you're here now. It's something that you managed to get out of York and all the way up here. And as you are a local, we'll let you stay. We could do with a couple more pairs of hands. We've got road blocks up at all entry points into the village. We'll get you all on the duty rota for manning the posts."

If you're going to stay, you will be expected to work and fit in. Circumstances necessitated the action. Naomi wondered if this was the future, seeing a disintegration of personal choice and liberty. How good was survival going to be? Still, she was no longer in York. She wouldn't have to hide indoors, and she wouldn't have to worry about coming into contact with the infection. She would just have to look at this as her new job. Quite frankly, her old job and life hadn't been particularly exciting.

"Now, let's see who we've got here," the colonel appeared to calm down, appeased by the thought of a larger army of men and women to command, if only by three more people. The appearance of a form to fill in was a reassuring sign of the old law and order. "Richard we know, of course," he said for no one's benefit, writing something down. "And you, my dear," he looked up at Naomi. "I don't believe we've met before."

"Naomi Ellerbeck," she said weakly. "I'm from York. I've not been here before."

"And are you a relation of the family?"

"No," she started. Was she going to have to provide suitable credentials in order to stay? "I'm just..."

The colonel looked from Richard to Naomi. "Not to worry, my dear. Tell me, what do you do? What did you do before this?"

"I just work in an office." This was sounding worse. No family ties. No useful profession.

"Naomi's also an archer," Richard offered. "She's taken down one of the infected."

If this was supposed to sell Naomi as a valuable member of the village, it didn't work. The colonel looked horrified. "Do you mean killed? That's no way to treat the ill. It's just an extreme variety of influenza. We've never stooped so low before. Why, even with the Spanish flu..."

"This isn't the flu," Richard interrupted. He leant forward in his chair, hands gripping the front of the desk as if he were going to shake it, upset the arrangement of stationary and paperwork, to impress a sense of gravity and urgency. "This disease turns people into psychopathic murders..."

The colonel chortled. "I hardly think..."

"We have seen innocent people being hunted down and bitten by the infected. We saw people eating from a corpse out in the street."

A very obvious silence filled the hall. There had been a handful of other people in the room, pretending to go about their business whilst keeping an ear on the conversation. All pretence of work had stopped, and they were openly watching the desk. No one had been outside of the village, or witnessed firsthand what was happening. A couple of people had still got access to the internet and had watched some amateur films, read some articles, some blogs, and experienced the horror the way someone watching a zombie film in revulsion might do. In an age of computer generated imagery, violence for entertainment and taboos broken, it was difficult to truly appreciate that this was real. The world as they had unappreciatively abused and taken advantage of no longer ruled.

"You need to read what I've brought you and pass it out around the village," Richard told him. "It's been written by healthcare professionals on the front line. People need to understand what's really going on. They need to be prepared for how bad things are going to get."

"There's no need to cause a panic."

"A panic will start when the uneducated have to deal with this. Prepare people and they will be ready."

"I will look at this and deal with as I see fit." As if to underline that he was in charge and would not be dictated to, the colonel picked up Richard's papers and put them in a drawer. "Now, back to what we were dealing with. We have yourself, Miss Ellerbeck, and your brother, I understand."

On cue, they all looked to the front of the room by the door where Ed was slumped on a bench, his shoulders shrunk back into the form of his jacket, his sunglasses still covering his eyes. He raised a hand half heartedly as if to say hello, but made no attempt to speak.

"Ed Stilton." The colonel peered at the younger brother. "Is he quite well?"

Richard shot Naomi a look before answering. "We're all tired, but Ed's had a rough week," he paused, lowering his voice a little. "His girlfriend died of the infection."

This news seemed to soften the colonel a little. "Terribly sorry to hear it. Doctors couldn't do anything for her?"

"They can't do anything for anyone." Richard said flatly.

They never got a chance with Emma, Ed's girlfriend, either, thought Naomi. Ed had been delusional, thinking he could nurse her back to health. As she'd deteriorated, he'd kept her out in the garden, tethered and chained up so that she couldn't hurt anyone. Like a rabid dog that he was too cruel to put down. The virus was so aggressive that no host had been known to last any longer than a week and a half at most after initial infection. She wondered what had happened to the body. Had Ed buried her, or left her corpse out in the air in the back garden?

"Right," the colonel said decidedly, setting his pen down and snapping Naomi out of her thoughts. "Village meeting at the church at four o'clock. Make sure you're all there."

Richard and Naomi stood up. "We will."

They were dismissed.

Ed was behaving like a party animal getting over the night before. Hung-over, tired and possibly suffering from sunstroke, he stomped out of the village hall, grumbling that he was hot and shattered. He even sounded drunk. Informing Richard and Naomi he was going for lie down somewhere cool, he sloped off to the church in advance of the meeting, to sprawl in the graveyard amongst the shady yew trees. It was an unsettlingly fitting choice.

"Ah, Jesus." Richard ran a hand over his face.

He knows, Naomi thought. Deep down Richard had realised that somehow Emma infected Ed, before or after death. The virus was so infectious that it wouldn't need much. A mere drop of blood splattering into an open eye would be enough. Perhaps he had been with Emma when she had finally expired, when her abdominal cavity, expanded with the gases of decay, had exploded in the disease's final desperate attempt to reach its next host.

"What are we going to do?"

Richard looked at his watch. "We've only got a couple of hours before the meeting. I could show you round the village, so you get your bearings."

"I meant about Ed."

"Let him sleep it off."

"Sleep it off?" She could have laughed and would have if being infected wasn't quite so terminal. She pulled on his forearm. "He's not going to get any better."

Richard shook her off, and wouldn't look her in the eye. "We'll walk down the village; I'll show you where the pub is. That's probably where everyone is at the moment."

"But..." Her arms dropped impotently to her sides as Richard started down the village. She didn't know what to do. She could tell someone, perhaps the colonel, but the people here didn't appear to appreciate what the virus was. They'd probably just give Ed a box of tissues and prescribe plenty of bed rest.

A guided tour of the village was over barely after it had started. It was built along one road, following the baseline of a steeply sided valley. There were three roads in, one at either end, and a third that came twisting downwards half way along by the side of the village hall. At the opposite end of the village to Richard's house there was a very short side road with a couple of buildings, leading to a tree-lined field. It was on this no-through road that the pub stood. The Crossed Keys was a white-painted building with a small stack of metal beer barrels piled outside. The front door was propped open and the general hum of banter drifted out into the dead end road.

There was a woman just inside the main door with shoulder-length styled hair and a snug fitting dress that looked like something a fifties sex-icon might have relaxed in when casually expecting guests. Her face brightened with surprise when she turned and saw Richard. "Richard?" she said rather loudly, the mention of his name hushing down conversations. "Chad was just saying you'd come back."

He nodded briefly at her. "Karen."

Eyes shifted from Richard to the unknown woman Chad had also been telling them about. All conversation stopped and Naomi felt like a bug under a microscope. She glanced around the room, the unfamiliar faces looking ashamedly back, lacking in expression. She couldn't tell whether she was welcome here or if they begrudged having another mouth to feed. She recognised Chad from that morning, now sat at a table with another man she'd not seen before. The second man who had been stood at the road block that morning was at the bar. There was something cool and angry about him, not obviously directed at any particular person or situation. Rather it was a general malevolent attitude towards the world and how it had done him wrong.

"Right, everyone," Richard started. He'd never known such an atmosphere in the village. It felt as though he'd just strolled into a saloon in the Wild West; everyone's hands hovering over their holsters, waiting to see who'd draw their guns first. "This is Naomi. She and Ed came back with me."

"Chad was just telling us," a man stood right behind Karen said. "You managed to get out of York. I thought people weren't supposed to be travelling."

"Yeah, well. I didn't want to stay in York."

"Understandable," the man at the table with Chad cut in. "Cities are not the place to be for the long haul."

The man beside Karen snorted. "Storm in a teacup."

The landlord reappeared behind the bar, having been outside to change the barrels. "Richard," he exclaimed. "Good to see you back. Get over here and tell me what's going on."

Richard stalked over to the bar. Naomi hung back in the doorway, feeling distinctly unwelcome.

There was silence, then people looked at one another as if to shrug their shoulders and say, we might as well get back to our conversations. "Naomi," Chad leaned back in his chair. "Do you want to join us? Come and meet John."

"John Settle," the other man smiled warmly at her. He had been the one to make the comment about not wanting to be in a city. Only perhaps forty or so, yet he looked more world-weary and tired than she would have normally expected from someone of his age. His curly dark hair was broken up by white lines. The events of the past couple of weeks could age anyone prematurely. Elsewhere people would be nervous wrecks. Here they still lived a charmed life.

"I'm up at Hill Top Farm," he continued, "just up the track up past Richard's house. What brings you to our part of the world, other than getting out of York?"

"I live across the road from Ed. Richard offered to take me with them."

"Very wise, get out before the main exodus."

"Sorry?"

Chad laughed, not entirely convincingly. "John's our doom and gloom man."

"John's the realist man," the farmer corrected, as if they were talking about someone out of ear shot rather than himself. "Your doom and gloom man is Mark over there." He nodded to the bar where the second morning sentry was still standing.

"I am a realist," John continued. "I see how long this is going to go on for; how much of a change we're all going to have to get used to. We're all going to have to get a lot more self sufficient."

"You've seen what's going on?" Naomi was surprised by this kind of talk from one of the villagers.

John paused, guessing she had witnessed how things were deteriorating first hand. Experience of the blood infection hadn't been the angle he had been referring to. "You ever read John Wyndham, Naomi?"

"No, I don't think I have."

"I'll lend you some books. They should give you a pretty good idea of what I'm talking about."

"He's preparing for the apocalypse," Chad joked.

Naomi felt sick. It had been meant as a flippant comment, and a couple of months ago John would have been the middle aged man taking an interest too far, but now? Today it felt like a reasonable topic of conversation.

There was a flamingo in the stained glass window. Naomi found her attention irrationally drawn in by the pink bird, incongruous with the deathly cold gravity of English Christianity. In the current age church participation was dying out. That might change. People didn't understand the virus, so they weren't really scared yet. They hadn't felt that blind terror that would find most begging God, any god for protection. In the meantime, a village that had always been without a live-in reverend (who was now trapped in another village due to the ban on travel) had little else to do but use the church for meetings. It worked better than the village hall, if only because there was enough seating for everyone.

Naomi was only a couple of rows from the back, at the edge of the pew, but for Richard who had squeezed in beside her. Richard was distractedly fidgeting as if wired on something. He needed to sleep. To her right was an older woman of indiscriminate age – her hair said twenties but her face said fifties – who was rather short so that her feet barely touched the ground when she sat in the pew. She was Anne Douglas, the local shop keeper. Shop was an overstatement for the converted conservatory on the side of her house. She sold things mainly to tourists, with a limited supply of essentials for locals who had forgotten something on the recent online supermarket order.

In the pew behind there was a family. The teenage girl moaned belligerently that she didn't see why she had to attend this boring meeting. The mother flapped and whispered under her breath, pandering a little to the attitude but not budging to let the girl out. Three pews ahead Naomi could see the backs of Karen and David's heads. David was Karen's husband and a rather unsettled man, sticking close to her like a suspicious dog as if every other man in the village coveted his wife and was just waiting for the chance to jump her. On the aisle side of the same row a fat teenage girl in an unflattering blue polka dot dress sat. She looked as though she'd gone to some effort to get dressed up for this social occasion, her blonde hair carefully brushed and set back from her face with a blue hairband. Across from her there were two gangly teenage boys still waiting to grow into their bodies. They were sniggering between themselves, laughter interspersed with crowing at Georgiana – assumedly the rotund girl – and did she think the pew was going to hold out? Watching these proceedings with a mildly disturbing interest was a weathered man with sun-bleached hair, wind-tanned skin and a face like a kicked old leather boot. He cut a weird sailor figure in his sweater of horizontal blue and white stripes. He was a long way from the ocean here. She'd seen him in the pub earlier, and there had been something untrustworthy about him. Every time her eyes had drifted in his direction he had been looking at her, but never meeting her eye.

John Settle, the hill top farmer, was oblivious to what was going on in the church. He was hunched forward and reading a paperback novel with scuffed corners. Beside him were a teenage boy and girl, looking particularly grave and holding hands. Behind them a row of old age pensioners. An intermingled a gathering of unknown faces and backs of heads.

"Thank you for coming, ladies and gentlemen." The colonel had stepped up at the front of the church. Mark Andrews, the grumpy silent one from the road block stood just behind and to the right like a guard dog.

"Oh dear," Anne Douglas, beside Naomi, sighed. "I hope this isn't going to go on too long."

"Before we proceed to the main business for this afternoon, I would like to let those who don't already know that three people were admitted to the village this morning. Richard Stilton, whom as you know lives at the far end of the village; his brother Ed Stilton; and Naomi Ellerbeck, from York."

This set off a fresh batch of murmured conversations, people straining in their places to catch sight of the unfamiliar faces.

"I thought there was a ban on travel."

"What are they doing here? Shouldn't they be sent back?"

A man in the middle of the congregation stood up. "They shouldn't have been let in. We're on limited enough supplies as it is without more mouths to feed."

"Yes, the rules apply to everyone," someone else shouted.

"Send them back."

Naomi closed her eyes. There was something to be said for the old pearl of wisdom that running away from your problems never really solved anything.

Mark Andrews stepped in front of the colonel as if to take a bullet. "They're staying," he said, the tone in his voice suggesting that was an end to the matter. "They're able bodied and will be able to help with the guard patrols and food production. Which is a lot more than some of you are good for."

"Oh dear," Anne Douglas repeated, her voice a saddened whisper. "He wants to throw all non-productive people to the dogs."

One of the retired gentlemen stood up. "I've paid my taxes all my life, I have my rights."

"Ernest," his wife tugged on his shirt sleeve. "Sit down."

"Ladies and gentlemen, please do be quiet," the colonel raised his voice.

The door at the back of the church opened.

"Ah, here we are, Edward Stilton has arrived now. Please take a seat."

Incomprehensible words drifted from the doorway. Naomi twisted around in her seat, horrified to see how much worse Ed was. He was still wearing his shades, which was probably a minor small mercy, because she doubted his gaze was particularly pretty now. His clothes were dishevelled and there was a noticeable amount of darkness down the front of his shirt, as if he'd thrown up over himself. It was probably blood, she thought, but she wouldn't like to say definitively that it was his.

He stumbled into the room, his coordination lacking as if he was heavily drunk. Almost uncontrollably, he hurried up to the pews, and in surprising nimbleness, grabbed a fist full of the teenage girl's hair and dragged her back over the pew, going down on her for the love bite as she writhed uncomfortably, one foot on the seat, the other on the back of the pew in front. She started to scream as teeth broke through flesh. She twisted and pulled like a drowning fish on the line. Her parents were immediately on Ed, trying to get him off their daughter.

Suddenly the entire church was on their feet, shouts and screams of panic, a number running to help, another number trying to get away, and the majority hovering in numbed horror. Only Naomi remained seated, feeling increasingly nauseous.

The girl was released from his grip. Ed ran back out of the church door. The girl tumbled over the back of the pew and landed on the floor with an uncomfortable thud, blood splattering on the cold flagstones. She was screaming, clutching at her throat, blood bubbling up between her fingers. The mother was hysterical, hugging her child and baying for someone to kill that man. People ran out of the church. When Naomi looked up Richard had already disappeared.

Naomi stood up, uncertain of what she ought to do, only that she felt she wanted to leave the village now. York might have been bad, but at least there was some semblance of law and order, some control, someone to turn to. And at the very least, she knew the locality. Here she was an unwelcome intruder. As she moved to step out of the pew, someone grabbed at her arm, the fingers like vices. "Where do you think you're going?"

Karen's husband, David, had a hold of her hand. She couldn't think that she'd ever seen such an expression of hate before now.

"You brought him here."

"Don't be a pratt, David," Karen muttered, hurrying past him to help the screaming girl.

"David, let her go." Chad had joined the fray and had a hold of David's forearm.

"Her and Richard brought that thing here."

"Ed?"

"He's diseased."

"Use your brain. They wouldn't have brought him knowingly. They left York to get away from all of this."

"Let go of that woman immediately."

All three stopped trying to resist one another. Mark Andrews stood in the middle of the aisle. From somewhere he'd gathered a coil of rope that was slung over his shoulder, and a shot gun that was cocked and ready to go. In the background the colonel sat on the steps in front of the altar, head in hands.

"Go home," Mark told David. "You're no use to anyone. Chad, come with me. We've got to bring that thing down immediately. And you," he finally came to Naomi, with a hint of menace. "I'll be speaking to you and Richard later when this is dealt with. Don't you dare leave this church yard."

David stormed out of the church like a sulking child, followed by Chad and Mark, jogging, stern faced, with a mission to accomplish. Naomi went into the entrance porch to get away from the immediacy of the sobbing girl and her desperate parents. Outside it was bedlam, people running in a frenzy, screaming. There was movement in all directions, and yet she couldn't see Ed anywhere.

"Just keep this here and apply pressure," Karen said. "I have to go get a first aid kit so I can deal with this properly."

"Should we come with you?"

"No, keep her here; it looks like madness out there." Karen struggled up to her feet. The pencil skirt on her dress didn't make manoeuvring easy or lady like. She ran for the door, bumping into Naomi at the exit.

"Was that for real?"

Naomi looked over at her.

"You came from York, you must have seen things. That must have been why you left."

"It's the disease," Naomi said quietly. "It turns people into monsters." She looked down at Karen's hands, the fresh blood on her fingers. "It's carried in blood, in body fluids."

Karen gave her hands a distracted glance. "This isn't from Ed."

Naomi looked through the porch inner doorway, back into the church where the mother was holding desperately onto her daughter. "That girl's infected."

"But he was barely on her."

"She's going to die."

Karen opened her mouth as if trying to come up with some contradictory argument. "Shit," she finally said. "I'd better get some gloves. Did they have a cure, any treatment? Is it that certain?"

"She's as good as dead."

Karen hurried out of the church and down the road. Naomi slumped into the side of the church porch, keeping out of the eye line of the distressed parents and crying girl. She should have pushed Richard more, told someone or done something. She'd seen that Ed was infected. Sooner or later he was going to attack someone. They hadn't knowingly brought the disease to the village, but here it was. In less than twenty four hours of their arrival there were now two carriers. The first duplication.

The father was shouting. "How could you have let this happen?" Naomi felt herself unconsciously press her back tighter to the wall. It took a moment before she dared to look back into the church. She couldn't see the little family group; he might have been shouting at her, only that she hoped they had forgotten her very existence.

"You should never have let those people in here."

No, it wasn't directed at her, but it was certainly about her.

"How could you have done it?" the man sobbed. "Look what's come of this."

"They can't have known." The colonel's voice sounded distant, weak.

"What do you mean?!" the mother screamed. "He is a monster. He has bitten my daughter's neck. He was trying to eat her."

"No one would knowingly take such a thing with them."

There was silence bar for the girl's crying.

"Did that really happen?" the colonel whispered. "Could such a thing be real?"

Karen returned after a couple of minutes. Her hands and forearms were noticeably washed and disinfected, the latex gloves – a double pair for the more observant – on her hands. A thin plastic throw away apron over a dress that she would burn later that night. She would regret the loss of a favourite, but did not wish to risk any infection. On her knees, she dropped the bloodied rags onto a bin bag, and started to sew up the ravaged wound more permanently. All tools would be destroyed. The girl whined like a kitten as the needle poked through the skin, stitching up as much as possible and as quickly. The mother cried over her poor ravaged neck. Karen thought that in the long run this rushed job would leave a nasty messy scar, but somehow she suspected it wasn't going to matter.

Karen was just bundling up the bloodied tools, the daughter with a fresh dressing around her neck, when a roar of anguish came from the road. Discarding the bin bag by the door, she hurried out into the churchyard, just behind Naomi. A few people were scattered out on the road. More were nervously watching from their gardens, within sprinting distance of the front door. The particularly horrified looked on from upstairs windows. David, Karen's husband, was holding onto a long pole with a wire loop at the end, the kind of thing used to capture wild and ferocious dogs. The loop was around Ed's neck, the rigidity of the pole a blessing for Ed was thrashing, and it was taking all of David's strength to keep him under control. The two of them did a tottering, graceless circle dance in the road. The villagers kept well back. Mark Andrews, with hard eyes and an emotionless face, was at the side of the road, steadily unfurling his curl of rope. Richard ran up the road towards Mark, shouting and swearing. "You bastard, he's not a fucking animal."

Not a fucking animal. Naomi remembered the end of Emma's days, chained in the back garden at Ed's property like she was a rabid dog. To all intents and purposes she had been an animal, the human part of her long gone. Naomi looked back to Ed. His sun glasses had been knocked off, his jacket arm torn in the scuffles. The side of his head was bleeding profusely, possibly nothing to do with the virus, although the sticky, bloodied excretion down his face from his mouth and nose probably were attempts for the disease to spread. His mouth was an ugly red wound, teeth glistening in the depths, desperate to make purchase with human flesh.

Richard punched Mark in the side of the face. It was a flailing, desperate move that probably didn't hurt much; more about the dramatics than anything else. Mark picked up a shovel propped at the side of a gate to someone's drive, and whacked Richard around the back of the legs, forcing the man to his knees. "Get him out of my way!" Mark roared.

Chad appeared, cutting something of a slightly unwilling henchman. There was a look from David to Chad, as if to question his masculinity. Chad hooked his arms under Richard's armpits and started to drag him away, Richard scrabbling without managing to get his feet back flat on the road. "That's my brother."

"That *thing*," Mark shouted, "Is an advanced case of infection." He strained and lurched up, throwing his rope over the top of the telephone pole at the side of the road, the top catching over one of the metal foot holds fixed to the side. The end of the rope dropped with a thud into the grass verge. He picked it up, the other end of the rope still coiled around his shoulder. "There's nothing we can do about that now. It's too late."

Naomi felt her stomach tighten. Despite the swearing from Richard and the growling and screaming from Ed, the village had become sickeningly silent. Although only a certain percentage of the residents were visible, all eyes were focused on this part of the road. She felt Karen stand up next to her, the woman's arm touching hers, and she could feel it shaking.

Mark nodded to David. David started to approach with Ed pushed ahead of him. Ed was focused on David, whom he could not reach for the strength of the metal pole that divided them.

"But this man attacked a young girl with no provocation." Mark was very close to Ed. He threw the coiled end of the rope, a noose ready prepared, over Ed's head, before pulling on the rope and backing away to tighten the circle.

The girl's mother had stepped from the church, and was a little way back from Naomi and Karen. Her body suddenly erupted. "Kill him."

"There's nothing else we can do." David dropped the pole and ran to the telegraph pole where Mark was already pulling on the rope, leather gloves thoughtfully on to protect from the hard work.

David joined him, and Ed ran at them as the shortening rope brought the three together, before there was a jolt and he was hoisted up off his feet and into the air. There was another determined pull on the rope, and a nauseating crack. Ed stopped moving, his body limply drooping, blood splattering to the ground from his mouth hung open.

"Oh Jesus," Karen turned away from the sight. Naomi had her hands over her mouth, her fingers over her face, barely daring to peer out from the gaps. Could that really have just happened?

Richard's resistance dropped, and he collapsed completely to the tarmac at Chad's feet. No one dared breathe. The colonel, in the doorway of the church, shook his head sadly. This was simply not the way things were done. He realised he had misjudged the situation. Perhaps he wasn't cut out for leading, not in such times. He'd had some warning from Richard earlier, not of Ed, but of what they had to fear. He'd put it away in a drawer and ignored it.

The two men let go of the rope, and Ed's body dropped to the ground in an undignified heap.

Richard stood up. "You'll answer for this."

Mark looked over at him disdainfully. "I think you have a few questions of your own to answer. You'll come back to the church now to explain yourself."

"Fuck you."

"Chad, take him to the church."

Chad looked uncertain. Richard was a pal and Chad was an easy going farm labourer, not someone's mindless bully boy. He did nothing and Richard ran off down the road. Mark gave him a sour look before turning to David. "Go get the truck, get the body loaded on the back."

Turning away from the scene of the lynching, Mark strode up to the church for easier prey, focusing straight in on Naomi. Grabbing her by an arm, he pushed her across the yard and up against a gravestone, roughly holding her jaw and peering into her eyes.

"Mark, stop this!" Karen shouted.

Naomi struggled, kicking him in the shins, and feeling his knee push back in retaliation. He was looking for something, his cold gaze searching her eyes. Not there. His expression wrinkled in disgust and he let go of her, letting her drop to the grass. She wasn't infected. He'd read the leaflets Richard had given the colonel, taken them out of the drawer as soon as the old man had left his desk. He had memorised the symptoms and the timings. There was nothing in the whites of her eyes. She ought to be showing some signs of bleeding by now if she was infected.

"You brought an infected man to the village."

"We didn't know!"

"You'll make it up for this." Mark pointed threateningly at her.

"And what about Hayley?"

The mother's question, out of the background, stopped whatever further threats he'd planned for Naomi. His arms dropped. "I'll take her up to the army rendez vous point. We'll go now."

"I want to come with her."

"No."

"I'm going."

Mark turned, intending to tell the mother to go home. He watched her, blood stained from holding the rags to her daughter's throat. Her hands and arms covered, her face tear and blood stained. Her body shaking. She raised a hand and wiped at her eye with the back of her hand. He watched the skin so close to the eye, the tear dissolving the dried blood to liquid. Fresh smears wiped on skin. Too close. "All right," he said quietly. "You come too."

Mother and daughter slowly followed Mark Andrews down the church path to the road, cowering and clutching at one another like a pair of destitute pilgrims. A truck had been parked up in the middle of the road. Mark opened the passenger door for the two women to get into the front cab. In the back of the truck, covered over with tarpaulin, was the body of Ed Stilton. Naomi watched as Mark threw a shovel into the back of the truck, followed by the shot gun. He and David shared a grim look before he got into the driver's seat. The truck departed from the village.

The front door was locked. She walked the perimeter of the property, to find all windows closed and the back door refusing entry. Naomi returned to the road in order to get a better view of the upper floor. She saw movement at one of the windows, confirming that Richard was inside. She waited for another minute, heart in her mouth, thinking he would come downstairs and unlock the door. Nothing happened.

"Shit," she swore under her breath. It was getting dark and she really didn't feel like sleeping outside. Neither did she want to go back into the village. She could have gone to the village hall or the pub, but after what had happened in the church, she was neither popular nor welcome at present. Not that it was her fault: she hadn't infected Ed; she hadn't bitten the young girl. But she and Richard were blamed by association. Richard had screamed blue murder over the hanging of his brother. It felt as though battle lines were being drawn.

What was she doing here, really? Richard came home; Ed had fled with his brother. She had no real justification for joining them, and the fact that she had now been locked out and was being purposefully ignored only underlined that feeling of being on the outside.

Thankfully the Land Rover was not locked. Her rucksack of personal items was still in the passenger foot well, along with her winter coat. In the current climate it was a little over the top, but thinking ahead, it had seemed a sensible thing to take. It was a creature comfort from times past. She pulled it on and snuggled into the padded fabric, closing her eyes. At least she hadn't taken this into the house.

"How's Richard?"

Naomi turned to find John Settle paused on the road. He had told her that the track to his farm went past Richard's house, so she assumed he was heading home. "I don't know," she answered. "Probably not too good. He's not answering."

"He's locked himself in?"

She nodded.

"He'll need a few days to himself," John commented thoughtfully. "After what happened. What they did to Ed..." he paused, watching Naomi. "That wasn't the way to deal with it. But these things happen when society starts falling apart."

With those few words, she felt distinctly hopeless; worse than before. Of course Richard was going to lock himself away after the lynching of his brother. Of course he was going to need to be alone for some time. She was going to have to leave. She pulled her rucksack from the Land Rover and shut the door.

"What are you going to do? I don't suppose you know anyone else here."

"I'll see if they can get the army to pick me up, get me back to York. It was silly coming here."

"No. I don't think anyone's going to survive in the cities long term. Now you're out, you don't want to be heading straight back." He paused. She looked like an abandoned orphan child, tragic in her winter coat. A classic case of carry or wear it; otherwise it will have to be left behind. "I have plenty of room at the farm, if you want to stay until Richard's got his head back together."

The offer hung between them. Warnings to young children about accepting invitations from strange men echoed from the past. Naomi didn't have a lot of options, and she didn't like the fact that she'd been left to simper outside Richard's locked door as if she was a little lost kitten.

"Sure, thank you," she decided. "That's very kind of you."

I am writing in a dead woman's notebook. I have stolen it. Although the general invitation was freely offered, I am not sure if he realised this was there. This sounds really terrible. But nothing had ever been written in here, and she's not going to be using now is she? Hey, she's dead! Jesus, as if being dead was a funny thing. It's probably the ideal state to be in these days.

I have no access to the internet and I haven't asked if I can borrow the phone. Stupid really. It's not like anyone is going to worry about the phone bill. I've not rung my mother in Scotland. She didn't sound too bothered the last few times I've spoken to her. But I'd like to think she'd worry. We're not going to see each other again. The border is closed, and as far as I'm aware Scotland is still disease free. And then there's the internet. I've not emailed Teresa for a few days, but again she won't be worrying too much. She had the good fortune to be travelling in Australia when all this kicked off, and she stayed put. Australia is also disease free. I suppose it's easier for islands, but then how come we managed to fall so fast?

Teresa's had a bad time. Her brother committed suicide and I don't know what's going on with her parents. Rudi's down in London working on a cure. I'm not holding my breath. I suppose anything's possible, but there isn't a miracle coming. The last time I spoke to Rudi he said it was months if not years away. I hope he takes care. I know there will be high security procedures and all that in the labs, but the risk of infection must be immense. Aside from that handful of people, who else would I want to speak to? Who would care? Work colleagues – I don't think so. Archery buddies... Ross went weird the last few times I saw him so I don't think I'd want to get in touch. Neighbours... my neighbours are all dead. The couple downstairs died last week, as did the old guy across the road. Ed died yesterday. I still can't believe that actually happened. They hung him. Even if he had knowingly murdered someone, that shouldn't have happened. This disease is frightening, but the fear seems to be making worse monsters of those of us who have survived. The long and the short of it is that those names pretty much cover my scope of interaction with the world. This is what being a loner gets you. Being alone.

Of course there's Richard, who is still alive, but possibly nuts, locked up in his house. His brother was lynched. I think anyone would go nuts after that. Hate the world. And yet, the honest truth is, I am really annoyed with him. He brought me to this village, and I just assumed the three of us would all shack up in his house. Now I've been locked out, completely blanked, and I'm thinking, did I completely misread the situation? Ever since the ban on movement came into effect, he's been stuck at Ed's house, waiting for his chance to get out of York. He spent a lot of the past week with me – in retrospect probably just to get away from Ed – but I thought we were friends, or something. I don't know. God only knows what the villagers think. John was tiptoeing around the subject last night, saying I must be really worried about Richard. He must have thought I was his bitch or something... Christ, I can't believe I even wrote that. I'm angry. But I had to set John straight that I am not and never have been involved with Richard Stilton. No doubt that'll get around the village quick, although now that I've said it, I

---

wonder if these times are the safest to be single in, as dumb as that sounds.

Last night I thought I was going to have to sleep in the Land Rover, or the village hall where that creepy despot man will be – the guy who hung Ed. And if I couldn't find somewhere to sleep, maybe I'd start hiking out of the village. I said that, but I don't know if I'd have followed through. I don't know how much of a survivalist I'd be in reality. John, John Settle, lives in a farm on the top of the valley, said I could stay with him. He seems to be a genuinely nice guy. Maybe it had been a dumb move, going home with a strange man; or maybe I shouldn't flatter myself that I'm so incredibly irresistible. It's very kind of him to take me in. And it's so peaceful up here. I'm in the garden just now, the sun is blazing, the birds are singing and I could almost fool myself into thinking that this was all just part of my imagination or a bad dream. But it's not. I didn't sleep too well last night. I kept reliving Ed, the way he went for that girl's neck like a deranged vampire. The blood, Jesus, there was so much blood everywhere. And they hung Ed. Lassoed him like a pig and hoisted him up over a telephone pole. I feel sick when I think of it, the creak, the blood splatters. That girl and the mother were driven off to an army meeting point – supposedly to go to some medical centre to get put down... what else can they do? But... It's just that when Mark Andrews, aka despot, drove off with them, he had a shovel and a shotgun in the back of the truck. Natural tools of defence in this day and age but I just worry that...

"Naomi, there you are."

Naomi jumped, her stream of writing scattering across the page in a drunken line. She had been engrossed in her writing. A need to express her thoughts had come upon her. Just to put her voice somewhere, to someone, even if it only was a monologue of silence. "I was just," she started, not exactly sure which 'just' she ought to be confessing to. Only that she didn't want to share. She was frightened and miserable, and yet felt like an emotional teenager as she tried to pick apart the past day. She closed the blank notepad, a hardback tome with marbled effect covers.

John's eyes flicked to the notebook. "Julie," he said, almost on autopilot.

"I..." Christ, Naomi swore silently. This wasn't exactly subtle. "You said to..."

"Yes, of course. It was empty."

"Oh Christ, I'm sorry," she groaned.

"No, please, it should be used."

"I could use anything for my hysterical female wonderings." John managed a smile. "Is that what you're doing?"

"I feel a need to get it out."

"I'm sure she would have approved in that case. And I did say to help yourself. You can't have come with very much if you just had that rucksack with you."

In some respects she had packed very thoughtfully, sensibly; and in other ways hadn't given a thought to covering the important basics. She might freeze and starve to death, but she'd be doing it in comfort. She had no other trousers but the pair she had been wearing when they'd left, so this morning she was wearing a long skirt from the wardrobe John had offered; the same place she'd found the unused journal. She had a few tops, pieces of underwear and a whole packet of plasters in the bag, so she was ready for blisters. One jumper, her salsa dress, a collection of books, a few CDs (but nothing to play them on), an MP3 player, a stuffed teddy bear, make up – because one had to look good for the apocalypse – a camera, her archery wrist guards, gloves and hat, hairbrush, selection of earrings and a couple of favourite necklaces and an as-was unopened packet of feminine hygiene products. She was relieved to have had the foresight to bring those when she went to the bathroom this morning and had a short lived panic that she was going to die when she saw blood in the toilet. It was a moment of horror before returning to reality. Despite any terror the world could produce, she was still a woman, and the day-to-day run of suffering would continue. The world might be at an end, but Mother Nature wasn't going to cancel the period.

"And you're sure this is ok?" Naomi swung her legs off from the length of the bench. The skirt was pretty. Dressing up was an attempt to reassure herself that all that was good wasn't gone in the world. She didn't need to run here, so she could indulge in impracticable clothing. "I mean, your wife's things..."

"I'm not trying to do a *Vertigo* on you."

Naomi smiled wryly. "That was a good film."

"Agreed. They don't make them like that anymore."

"They don't make them like anything these days."

John sat down on the bench beside her. He hadn't told her a lot last night, only that Julie, his wife, had died a few years ago of a brain tumour. It had been very sudden. The back story explained the dignified, resigned air about him, as if nothing would disappoint again. The weary man. He wasn't neurotically holding a torch for his dead wife, certainly not trying to dress Naomi up in her things to bring her back. Naomi had seen a photograph and there was no resemblance between them. The *Vertigo* quip had been nothing more than a joke.

John tapped the top of the closed notebook. "It's good to have a vent. Especially now. I'm glad it's been used. I don't like waste. I brought you these," he added, passing her a handful of dog eared paperbacks. "They've always been good reads, but I think especially now, they have something more relevant to tell us."

Naomi skimmed over the titles. John Wyndham: *Day of the Triffids*, John Christopher: *Death of Grass*, J G Ballard: *The Drought*. "These are your doom and gloom books?"

He smiled lightly, almost nostalgic, and gazed out towards the valley. "They're apocalyptic novels, but then isn't that what we're in now?"

"I didn't realise farmers could be so deep."

"You need to get out more."

She nodded slowly. "I probably do. But thank you for these. I shall start on them today. There's not much else to do."

"I'm sure Mark'll get you roped into something." John winced at the unintended pun. "I didn't phrase that quite as I meant."

The memory of the creak of the rope sat between them. Ed's bloodied, disease-ridden corpse dangling pathetically from the telephone pole. Roped into something. "I know what you mean."

Mark Andrews, as if having heard his name, wandered up to the farm that afternoon. John had spotted him first, and told Naomi to look over the garden wall. Mark Andrews, at a distance forming a moving shapeless lump on the landscape, strolled up the farm track, some object jauntily slung over one shoulder. As he grew closer they could see that the stick-like item he carried was a rifle, and there was also a pair of binoculars slung around his neck. Naomi and John, leant up against the five foot garden wall, watched the man. Naomi glanced uncertainly at her current host. "Does he think he's going to war?"

John stroked his stubble thoughtfully. "I'm not sure yet quite what Mark thinks is really going on."

"Afternoon." Mark didn't smile as he reached the farmstead. He walked down by the garden wall and entered uninvited by the wrought iron gate. "I've come with this week's rota," he explained, taking a piece of paper from his pocket. "I've only brought one copy," he added, looking at Naomi. "But as you're staying here, you can check your shifts on this."

"My shifts?"

"Everyone in the village has their part to play," he explained, eyeing her coolly as he passed John the schedule. "Everyone able-bodied at least. "I see you're not staying with Richard anymore."

"No, I..."

"Not answering the door to you either?" There was a touch of amusement in his voice. "I've put you down for an evening shift. I hope you're in the right frame of mind for patrol duty."

"Patrol duty?" She didn't remember signing up.

"How well did you know Ed?"

"He was my neighbour."

Mark digested this information, saying nothing as if continuing their discussion by body language; either that or trying to prove a point by making her break first by his silence. Who would be the first to speak?

"I don't think you should put Naomi in that group," John was the one to break the silence, unaware of the challenge Mark was putting to Naomi: if you had a problem with what happened yesterday afternoon, say it to my face now or say nothing at all. "Not with Gordon. Swap her with David and she can join me and Chad."

Mark gave the list a casual glance. "I'm sure Gordon won't be a problem."

"He doesn't understand the concept of personal space."

"Aye, but..."

"He's been stuck in the village a week now. Besides, Naomi's new here and yesterday wasn't handled well."

Mark started to bluster, the heat rising in his face.

"Putting her with a couple of friendly faces would be a good start."

"Very well," the agreement was begrudging. "I'll tell David when I go back. But I can't rearrange every shift." He took the rifle off his shoulder. Naomi didn't know a lot about firearms but it didn't look like the kind of thing a farmer would keep for taking pot shots at pigeons; or a country gent for the clay variety. It looked like something a sniper in an action film would creep about on roof tops with. "Do you know how to handle a gun?" he asked her.

"No."

"Bugger me, Mark, where did you get that from?" John burst out. "I hope you didn't have that lying around at home."

"It's simple to use," Mark continued, ignoring John. "You load it here; bullet into the barrel like so, safety off here, aim and squeeze here."

"You can't teach someone to use a gun that quickly," John started, reaching for the weapon as Mark passed it to Naomi.

"Any idiot can go through the motions of loading it up. Aiming and shooting is the difficult bit," Mark told John. "Now, watch for the recoil of the gun; keep it steady against your shoulder. See the scarecrow over there; see if you can hit it."

It was an unfamiliar weight in her hands. Naomi was in an archery club, or at least she had been before the plague. She was used to target practice with arrows. She had the strength to take the poundage of the string as she drew it back; aiming side on and by sight. Her body tensed up with the bow, focused on the shot. Her arm was an extension of the bowstring. A rifle took away the physical participation. It was an uncomfortable feeling to try and fit her body around it. She was uncertain of the range, and the recoil that would punch after she had pulled the trigger. She looked over at the scarecrow, which was at the far end of the field. She set the rifle to her shoulder. She really didn't know what she was doing, and the bullet went off almost by accident, the back draft ricocheting through her upper body. Out in the field there was a puff of earth as she missed the scarecrow by several metres and unsettled growing crops momentarily.

"Hmm. Not exactly accurate." Mark was watching the field through his binoculars. Disappointed. He wondered how much use she would be. "I obviously got that wrong."

Naomi lowered the rifle.

John looked angry. "Got what wrong?"

He put down his binoculars. "There was an archery set in the back of Richard's Land Rover. I doubted it was Richard's, so I was hoping whoever owned the set had some sense of aim. I'm guessing it must have been Ed's."

Irritated, Naomi stepped up to the garden wall, balancing the barrel of the weapon on the wall and aiming again. If she had been shooting with the longbow she could have taken that scarecrow down.

"Fancy another try?"

Naomi fired again. The scarecrow's mangel head exploded on impact, pieces of fibrous root vegetable scattering up into the air. She put the safety back on and passed the rifle to Mark. She kept her gaze steady, forcing herself not to look away when Mark looked her in the eye. There was something more to this than simple target practice.

"I stand corrected." He took the rifle, hooking the strap over his shoulder. "Probably best you're not on the same watch as Gordon. I don't think he'd stand a chance at close range and we can't afford to lose any people."

"Like Ed?"

"He was a pest that had to be dealt with; not a person," Mark corrected her casually. "I'll see you two at six. And she's taking the rifle."

"Fine by me," John muttered. "It'll get dark and none of us will see a damn thing anyway."

They were silent for ten minutes or so, watching Mark Andrews stroll back down by the field, and out of sight. "What was that about?" Naomi finally muttered.

"I think you just got promoted to sniper squad," John said flippantly.

"And who is Gordon? I don't understand why no one wants to work with him. Is there a problem with him? I don't think I've met a Gordon."

"You'll have seen him yesterday," John said. "He's one of the farm workers, bit weathered looking, forty-ish. He was at the pub when you and Richard turned up. Striped top, looked like a sailor."

She could remember the man he was describing. He watched with an unnerving passive amusement. In the pub every time her gaze had passed by him he had been looking at her. "Not good with people."

"Not good with women," John corrected. "A misogynist in denial who fancies himself a bit of a ladies' man. He used to go to Leeds or Hull every weekend, out on the town, but the last couple of weeks all of that kind of thing has stopped. He made Julie uncomfortable." He drifted off, disappearing into his own memories. "I know Mark has set up the shifts in threesomes," he abruptly continued. "But you don't want to be stuck on shift with him. You're better off with me and Chad."

Naomi felt her hackles rise. Was that meant to be mildly patronising? "I can look after myself."

John broke out into a smile. "I've no doubt. But for better or worse, you're going to be stuck with us for the foreseeable future. Might as well make your time here as pleasant as humanly possible."

The day after Ed's impromptu execution, Richard's house was a shell. It stood as a monument to atrocity, politely ignored by passersby. The windows and doors were locked. No movement was discernible. The building was like a photographic still. The Land Rover remained on the drive. If Richard had left in the night, he had left by foot. John had made a quick circuit of the house whilst Naomi crouched on the front doorstep, flicking open the letterbox to talk to no one.

"No answer?"

Naomi let the letterbox snap back into place. She shook her head. "Do you think he's even in there?"

"Probably."

"You don't think..."

"Think what?"

"Well," she stood, turning away from the door and lowering her voice, as if not wanting to upset the house. "He wouldn't have done anything silly?"

"I don't know. If he has, there's nothing we could do now." John stopped when he saw Naomi's face blanche. He couldn't recall how the subject had come up, but she had told him quite definitely that Richard was just her neighbour's brother. There wasn't any relationship or intimate connection. She was here because she'd gained the sympathy vote and been taken along for the ride. Protestation aside, she appeared to genuinely care, more than a refugee who had hitched a lift. It wasn't just a sense of obligation from the evacuation.

"Don't worry, he'll just be sleeping off a bad hangover. Come on, we don't want to late for patrol duty."

"No, mustn't upset Mark," Naomi muttered, following John up the road. They'd all seen yesterday what happened to people who upset Mark.

John went into the village hall. Naomi waited outside on the road. Georgiana, the overweight teenager mocked by two adolescent boys in the church yesterday, charged up the road and barged past her. The girl was moving at a quick pace, her face red, lips tight and the first tears squeezing out of her eyes. The worst of the emotional outburst would be saved for her bedroom, the door slammed in its place.

"This is for you." John had reappeared, rifle in hand. "You have certainly made an impression."

Naomi took the rifle, not particularly happy with the attention. She didn't want to have to shoot anyone. She ought to have been more forward thinking, misfired and shot into the bushes. Made them think she was really useless. "Where are we to watch?"

"Far end of the village. There's a T junction in a patch of woods. It's all right, and if it rains a lot, the trees keep the worse of the rain off." They started walking again. "We're on till two in the morning."

Her eyes widened at this. "So long?"

Up ahead a couple of teenage boys were hanging out in the front garden of one of the properties, tittering like schoolgirls as they shared a joke. One hunched over his bicycle, his trousers hanging off his arse. The other stood with his hands in his pockets.

"I was only pointing out reality," the one on the bike said.

"Doesn't matter whether half the world's dead or not," the other laughed. "No one's going to want that fat cow."

"Fat heffer. Good for the cooking pot."

They both started up on fresh laughter at this. "Poor old fat Georgiana. Never going to get a boyfriend."

Naomi couldn't help but stare. John seemed to be blind or deaf or both to them. They were just mindless teenagers, and very little they had to say would be of consequence. They wouldn't come up on his radar. Naomi was a little depressed to think even now, people still reverted back to type and tormented each other with petty trifles. Life was so precious and incredibly fragile. Georgiana ought to realise that the opinion of two scraps like these wasn't worth a jot. It hadn't been before the outbreak and it certainly wasn't now. The status symbol of 'having a boyfriend' wasn't important. Although for a teenage girl, it always had been and always would be the be-all and end-all of life. Perhaps there was something comforting in the fact that these little foibles continued.

She and John continued in a comfortable silence through the village. The crunch of footsteps grating on the odd loose gravel chipping that had sprayed out from a driveway. Naomi wondered if Georgiana had a real case to cry about. The world wasn't going to flick back to the normal run of things. Perhaps they'd all had the last of the best, their last opportunities. What were the things that fulfilled people in life? Careers. The modern world of work was over. Industry and business had stopped, the virtual financial world had become nonsensical. Money may never mean anything again. Beauty and clothes, possessions and things: who cared? Love and sex: perhaps she'd already had her last relationship, and that had been over a few years ago. Perhaps they all ought to be crying over lost opportunities. All those thing they would have done, had they known to stop taking life for granted.

"Finally."

Chad sat on a log at the side of the road near the T junction road block. The current watch they were to replace, two women and a man, none of whom Naomi could recall having met before, looked rather bored and eager to be relived. One of the women regarded the rifle on Naomi's shoulder warily. "We're being armed now, all of us?"

"Don't worry, Sheryl," John assured her. "Mark's only making people he's sure can aim carry one of these."

"Oh." She wasn't quite sure how to take his comment: an insult or merely a statement of fact. She looked back to Naomi. "You're the new girl, aren't you? Came in with Richard and..." she faltered, not quite daring to mention Ed's name, as if it might raise anger.

"Naomi," Naomi introduced herself.

"Sheryl," the woman nodded back. "And there's Jean and Donovan here."

"Nice to meet you," Jean said.

"And we're off," Donovan added. "Bloody tedious waste of time. Have a nice evening."

It was like a balloon deflating. Naomi felt overdressed turning up with the rifle. What was Mark expecting to happen? "So we've just got to stand here until two in the morning."

"That's it."

Chad lifted up a large thermos. "I've got coffee."

John settled down in a deckchair to the side of the roadblock, something that would be quickly kicked into the undergrowth should anything or anyone untoward turn up. "Grab a pew," he told Naomi, gesturing to an abandoned stool. "It's going to be a long night."

"Of course, personally I think it will do some people good." Ann Douglas replaced her tea cup in its matching saucer. The world might be going to hell in a hand cart, but she wasn't going to let the little niceties of a comfortable home slip. "Will you have some more flapjack?"

Naomi gazed at the chunky slices piled on a large dinner plate on the coffee table, laden with an assortment of dried fruit, drizzled with lashings of chocolate. "Are you sure we should be scoffing so much?"

"I don't care," Karen muttered, helping herself to a second piece.

"I was just so angry afterwards," Ann explained. "He'd not found my store cupboard, so I made that, just to spite him." She sighed and looked at the produce of her baking efforts. "It's not much of a revenge, is it? But it's the best I can manage."

"Don't worry, we'll eat the evidence."

Ann smiled weakly, and looked at her bandaged foot propped up on the seventies pouf. "Well, do you think it is broken?"

"No, it's just a sprain," Karen told her between mouthfuls of flapjack. "Just keep the weight off it for a few days. I've got a spare crutch at home. I'll bring it over so you can get about."

"I don't suppose I'll be leaving the house now, but it will be difficult to get about. I do live alone." She paused to put her cup and saucer down on the side table by her armchair. "That man is a bully. The way he barged into my shop. All supplies are village property," she repeated one of his lines, her lip curling in distaste. "He told me I could keep the postcards and tea towels as if he was doing me a kindness. He marched straight into my shop and brazenly emptied my shelves. Why, he was worse than a shoplifter; just took my stock. Didn't even try to hide it. Rubbed my nose in it."

"It's because of the rationing," Karen said.

"I thought we already were on rationing," Naomi said. "There were loads of boxes from the army stacked up in the village hall."

"Yeah, but they've found out we're not getting anymore."

"But the local army patrols were supposed to come regularly."

Karen shrugged. "There isn't enough. Not for all the cities, and all the hungry soldiers. I guess they can't spare the time to come visiting the little villages either, so we're on our own. They'll just assume we can grow our own, be self sufficient."

"A little warning is needed for self sufficiency."

"John will already have things on the go. I think Mark was working on rotas for working on the land."

Naomi closed her eyes. The very word rota made her come out in a cold chill at the best of times. When exactly had she and everyone else become an unpaid employee of the Mark Andrews corporation?

"Of course, you'd be surprised how little you can live off," Ann continued, content in the knowledge that she was too old to be put on patrol duty, or any hard labouring. "My mother used to tell me stories about the war. What they lived off, how they all mucked in together. And they survived. People were healthier then, you know. It's like I was saying, it will do some people a bit of good. This will be a good thing for people like Georgiana."

Georgiana the fat teenager, Naomi thought. The girl who cried because she'd never get a boyfriend.

"It makes you think, doesn't it, this self sufficiency thing," Naomi said as she and Karen left Ann Douglas' house and headed towards the village hall. "It's like pot luck, what you happen to have around you when the shutters go down."

"I guess. I've tried not to think about it too much."

"But look at you for instance. It's lucky a doctor lives in the village."

Karen laughed at this comment. "Do you think I'm a doctor?"

"I just assumed."

"I'm the only person with medical training, so I've been lumped with the lot. But in my usual day job I'm a midwife. It's not a profession I'm wanting to practice until this has all blown over."

"No expectant mothers in the village?"

"No, thank God."

When all this has blown over. As if the world would be the same. Flick a switch and it would all return to normal. Naomi was taken to think of Wilfred Coker from the *Day of the Triffids*. He looked further forward than the others, thinking of the longer term when supplies had run out and even scavenging wasn't an option. When something broke, and you needed to fix it, you didn't just need the knowledge to fix the thing, but also how to make the tools to do the job. Right down to nails and hammers. That was what self sufficiency meant. Starting off with the very raw materials found naturally occurring, and nothing else. She didn't think anyone here was really ready for that kind of life. Back to the Stone Age, supposedly an inferior time to the digital age, but how many people today had that kind of practical intelligence to be able to survive?

In the village hall the colonel was hunched over the army radio. Since the lynching three days ago, he had become shrunken and retiring, to all appearances little more than a radio operator, an absent figurehead who hid in the shadows. The father of the dead girl was with him, nervously perched on the edge of a chair, leaning forward as if he might leap across the table and snatch the precious words from the radio's speakers.

Mark Andrews was at the opposite end of the hall, sat in front of a computer. The glare from the screen made his flesh appear sickly. A couple of women were fussing around the supplies, bickering over the way to mark down numbers on the inventory list they had primly fixed to a clipboard.

"I could do with a few more bandages." Karen approached the two women, the request sparking off a riffling through clipboard papers, and the solemn shaking of heads. She was getting through the bandages too quickly, and using them too liberally on unnecessary cases. Old people with sprained ankles and aching joints. Mark had said that she would have to start reusing them. She could boil discarded bandages to make them hygienic.

Naomi idly wandered down the length of supplies. The boxes of army supplies looked unappetising, now a finite quantity as stocks would not be replenished. Towards the end were the spoils of looting: open topped boxes filled with an assortment of food items taken from Ann Douglas' shop, ranging from standard supplies, to locally produced honey, preserves and a box of Kendal mint cake bars. Further on there was a stack of trays of canned fruit, soups, fish. She paused, staring at the disturbingly familiar labels on the cans of pineapple chunks; before looking back across at Mark Andrews. Richard wouldn't have given up the supplies she'd brought with them, surely? Richard wasn't doing anything for anyone. No one had seen him or heard a sound. She and Richard hadn't gotten around to moving all the supplies they'd brought in the Land Rover into the house before that unfortunate afternoon and Ed's execution.

"Thixendale, calling Thixendale, over."

"Colonel here, over."

The static sound of communication, as if direct from an old war film, distracted her from the suspicious food stocks. Naomi looked over to where the colonel and the girl's father were sitting.

"There is no medical centre. Be advised that you must deal with the infected internally. Do not allow the infection to leave village boundaries. Advise how many infected, over."

"None," the colonel bristled. "Advice is not required. Village free of infection, over."

There was a static pause on the radio before the army operative responded, sounding a little confused. "Good to hear, Thixendale. Don't understand the problem, over."

"You need to ask about Hayley," the father hissed, "and my wife."

"Two infected villagers were sent to the medical centre. They were taken to the army rendez vous point three days ago, over."

Static. The husband nervously clawed at the edge of the table. Naomi thought back to the shovel and shotgun Mark Andrews had put in the back of the truck before leaving the village that late afternoon.

"What army rendez vous point? There is no meeting point. All civilians are to stay in their homes. There is to be no movement outside of village boundaries. Repeat, all civilians are to remain where they are. Any infection is to be contained in situ. Infected persons need to be dealt with by the village council, over."

The colonel's hand visibly shook as he flicked back the switch to speak to the army radio operator. "Advise what action should be taken by the village council."

The operator was getting irritated, as if they'd already had this conversation with the village. They ought to know. "We do not have a cure. The infected will die. The council is to contain and stop the spread of the infection, over."

"Advise how to stop the spread, over."

"Terminate with immediate effect, over."

The husband was muttering. No one could really hear him nor were they meant to. He was shaking his head, the movement fluctuating through his body. He abruptly lurched up over the table, snatching the radio away from the colonel. "Where are my wife and child?" he yelled into the apparatus.

"We do not have them. Over."

"Blast you!" the man shouted, the best swear word he could get out, so whipped and coddled by his wife, he'd forgotten what raw, sharp emotion might be. Not in front of the baby, she would hiss. Swear words were a lack of imagination. Apparently. Sometimes blast and sugar simply didn't have the same kick as a motherfucker, but even now his wife's hold over him was complete. "You," he turned, searching out Mark Andrews. "What did you do with them?"

Mark didn't remove his eyes from the computer screen. "I took them to the rendez vous point."

"No you didn't. The army don't know anything about them."

"They're safe."

"They just said on the radio that there's no cure. There's no medical centre." The father marched across the hall to Mark. "They said we should terminate." As soon as he'd uttered the word, it was like a slap around the face. Saying it made it real. "What have you done?"

Mark typed something into the computer, everything running in his good time, before he deigned to look at the man. "Very well. I was trying to spare your feelings. What do you think I did? There is no cure, no doctor, no hospital. Nowhere to go. They were infected, they were going to get sick quickly and turn into deranged cannibals. They'd infect other people. We'd all be wiped out in a couple of days. What would you have done?"

"That's murder."

"It would have been murder to do nothing."

"My wife wasn't even infected!" he screamed. He was red in the face, frighteningly red, as if his blood vessels could take no more. His head would explode, a splatter to break the uncomfortable tense silence that was pulsing through the hall.

"She was wiping blood in her eyes."

"You couldn't be sure."

"I couldn't take the chance."

The man ran at Mark. Even fuelled by grief and fury he did not cut a particularly intimidating figure. Mark calmly stood up and swung a punch, hitting the man neatly, his knuckles crunching between the eyes. There was a gasp and a rush of crimson blood from the man's nose. He staggered back, horrified at the violence. He lost his balance and landed on his rear end. The lights flickered and dimmed, virtually losing all power for a moment. Naomi glanced up at the ceiling. This wasn't good.

"Jesus," Karen muttered under her breath, snatching some wadding off the stock checkers. She hurried across to aid the sobbing man. He was a wretch, shaking uncontrollably. Heartbroken. And this wouldn't end. He would live with this horror until he either starved to death or was killed.

The lights dipped again. Mark sat back in front of the computer. Naomi looked to the colonel, who was staring vacantly at the desk surface. The radio was lying on its side from where it had been knocked over. The disorder didn't seem to matter anymore.

"Fuck it!" Mark Andrews roared as the lights went off completely and there was a whirring thud as the computer died. They waited but nothing happened. The power had gone. "We need to get a generator down here now," Mark stood up, kicking his chair back at the wall. "We must have power."

Naomi stared out of the window. So that was the end of the National Grid? It was a lucky thing summer was on the way. Slipping out of the village hall, she left the haze of swearing and anger. She couldn't bear to listen to the distraught crying, all the time worrying that this was somehow her fault. She had realised Ed was infected hours before he had attacked. She was just too timid to force her point with anyone.

She stopped in front of Richard's house, gazing up at the windows. The only suggestion that he was still alive was the fact that curtains in the upstairs bedroom changed between open and closed. The status had no bearing on the time of day but at least they did move now and then. She wondered about trying the door again, calling out to him, but it seemed futile. Pulling herself up to get a good look into the back of the Land Rover, she was disappointed to discover it had been emptied of all food. A few bags and items deemed useless had been left, along with her bow. Perhaps Mark Andrews had decided to let her keep that, considering her aim. There were a few bags of food that they'd initially taken into the house, but the bulk had been out in the Land Rover. She closed her eyes. They hadn't even managed to pack everything away. There was a certain amount still in her flat in York, abandoned out of necessity. All that stock piling to no avail. She'd started weeks before this nightmare had broken and the travel ban had come into effect. Her old university flat mate, Rudi had advised her to increase her stores. He'd even paid her to do it when she'd laughed at him and said he was being ridiculous. The fact that he worked for the Centre of Tropical Diseases ought to have been a clue that he knew what he was talking about.

Rudi, she thought to herself, suddenly feeling a strong desire to talk to him. She'd ask John if she could use the phone. The electricity was out, but that ought not to affect the phone lines, and she'd seen he had a landline in the kitchen. No cordless reliant on regular charging from the mains supply. She'd call Rudi. He'd be busy, stressed out, but she just needed to speak to someone who had known her before Thixendale.

One final attempt with Richard before she left. She knocked on the door, then crouched and flicked open the letterbox. Ten seconds of silence, listening for a sign of life. Even a sign of death. Nothing. "Richard?" she said, uncertainly, feeling foolish. She didn't know what else to say. "Are you still alive?"

Naomi let the letterbox snap shut. She walked back up the hill to John's farmstead, cutting a solitary figure against the landscape.

It was on the third attempt that evening that she managed to get through to Rudi. After two unanswered calls, she'd decided to phone her mother, who had been glad to hear from her. Considering current events, she was still quite unconcerned. Convinced it was the media making a fuss about very little. The television had always done this with any health outbreak. Swine flu, SARS, bird flu... the world had never ended and she didn't even know anyone who had contracted those diseases. It was easy to be complacent, sitting in virus-free Scotland, blocked off from England on pain of death. The Scots were building a wall, actually building a physical barrier cutting the island in two.

The electricity had not come back on. John had a generator on the farm, but was disinclined to use it unnecessarily, not sure how long they would have to rely on it. He had limited supplies of fuel on his property. Naomi sat on the floor in the kitchen, a candle in a wrought iron holder providing her only illumination. The old fashioned corded landline telephone was propped in the crook of her neck. It was like being a teenager again.

"Who is this?" Rudi unceremoniously barked into the telephone.

He was still alive. Thank god, she thought. "Rudi, it's Naomi."

"Naomi?" the tension in his voice lessened a little. "I've not heard from you for days. Are you all right?"

"Yes, I'm fine. Fine." She gazed out across the flickering shadowed kitchen. She wasn't completely convinced by her statement. "I'm in Thixendale now."

"You got out of York?"

"Yes."

"Thixendale. I don't know it. Is it a small place?"

"Yes. It's just this little village in the Wolds. It's really pretty... not that those kinds of things matter anymore. It feels like the rest of the world doesn't exist."

"That's a good thing. And it's infection-free?"

"It is now."

"Now?"

"Oh Jesus," she closed her eyes. "Ed was infected. We didn't know, honestly, we had no idea."

"Ed is... what, your neighbour?"

"Was."

Rudi sighed. Silence. "What happened?"

"We left York, you know. Me, Richard, that's Ed's brother. He lives here in Thixendale. And then Ed. He must have picked up the infection from his girlfriend. We didn't realise. He was fine when we set off. I mean, he was distraught over her death, but that was all."

"It does take a few hours before the first signs start showing." Rudi paused. "Where is Ed now?"

"He's dead. When the villagers realised, they strung him up. It was awful. They just threw a rope around his neck and hoisted him up. Richard went nuts. He locked himself in his house and we've not seen or heard from him since. He could be dead in there for all we know. I'm staying with one of the locals now."

"That's brutal." Static. What was there to say? "At least he didn't get the chance to infect anyone."

"He bit a girl. Her and her mother were taken away." She lowered her voice, as if she was being listened upon from every door and window. "One of the villagers, this headcase with illusions of grandeur, drove the two of them out of the village. He said he was taking them to the army, but I think he just took them somewhere and executed them."

"I know it's harsh but what else can be done?"

"I don't know, but it's not that great here. He's some self-elected life-is-tough boss. He's got us on patrol rotas, and now we're going to have to be working the fields. There's not going to be any more army supplies. They just took the things you had me stockpiling. They didn't even ask, didn't even tell me. I checked this afternoon and it's all gone. It's like living in some communist farming collective."

"Naomi, this won't be forever."

"You don't know that. You don't know where this will end. We'll work in the fields and do military service, dancing to his tune. And if we are surplus to requirements or don't toe the line, then Mark'll take us out into a field and shoot us."

"Calm down. Come on, don't dramatise. Have you slept much recently?"

"Not really."

"You need to sleep."

"It's not on the rota. I just don't know how this is going to work out. What's going to be left when this does end? You know Scotland's building a wall to keep us out? Leave us here to rot. I just don't know what it will take for this to end." She was shaking, working herself up into a terror. Talking about this with someone from her previous life was not helping quite as she'd hoped. She was reminded of how things used to be, how they would never be again. It made the reality raw. She felt physically sick. She couldn't let her voice rise any higher, or John would certainly hear. "How are things with you?"

Rudi considered his reply before speaking. "Tired. I don't sleep much. But this will come to an end sometime. It will."

"You guys are still working on a cure?"

He sniffed. "We're a long way off that. We're killing it in a petri dish."

"That's good..."

"Not quite the same thing as the human body. This virus is so destructive. Even if you could destroy it before the host dies, how is the body supposed to repair itself after all of that? I don't know. And we still don't know the source, the start, which we really need. All we have are rumours..."

"You can't pinpoint its origin?"

"Possibly Africa. Suspicions are increasing towards a World Health conference. Hundreds and hundreds of delegates from all over the world."

"But if that were the case, why are some countries clear? Some of the islands..."

"Well, that's one point," Rudi conceded. "A lot of island nations are still clear; sadly not ours but..."

"So the big land masses are stuffed."

"Most of us. South America seems to be clear."

"What, the whole of South America?"

"Seems to be. The border between Panama and Costa Rica has been heavily fortified. Guatemala's trying to keep Mexico out. Latin America's basically abandoned Mexico to North America, and refugees from the US, included thousands of infected, have gone over the border. Mexico will end up a waste land. I don't think Guatemala and Nicaragua have had any major outbreaks, but South America as a collective has just gone for the shortest distance to blockade, and Panama is a relatively skinny county."

"So the Americans aren't...?"

"Aren't what? Going to save the day?" Rudi paused. "The president's relocated to Alaska, but I think they're planning on moving to Hawaii soon. Mainland USA is just anarchy. The virus has spread terribly over there. I don't know whether rural communities are coping, but... it's going to end up a nation of farmers, religious fanatics, Alaskans starved of sunlight and not so happy go lucky Hawaiians."

"I suppose it's not so much the virus that we have to worry about, as survival after all of this. We only need a couple of weeks disease free, right? I mean, the infected die after one or two weeks, and there'll come a point where they can't spread it, there's no one nearby to infect or.... eat... they'll die, and we'll be left..."

Rudi coughed. "We don't understand how it's spreading."

"Biting. It's human fluid."

"That is the main way. Well, it's the way. But we've got outbreaks popping up with no previous infection..." His voice lowered. In Rudi's case there was just concern for a fear of being listened to. "There are villages that were closed off, no infection, and then suddenly there's an outbreak. I don't understand it."

"You don't think it's airborne?"

"We can't find any evidence of that, but, just be careful ok. I don't know when this is going to end or what it's going to take. You'll keep in touch?"

"Of course. Do you want this number?"

"It's on the display."

"Of course." Naomi whispered, "Be careful, Rudi."

"You too."

It's now been a full four days since Ed was killed and Richard disappeared into his house. I wonder if he sneaked out of the village days ago. He's worked as a cameraman in some remote places, so I don't suppose hiking off with a rucksack full of the essentials would be particularly daunting. Either that or he's hung himself. John says he's just getting over a major bender. I don't know whether I'm incredibly naive, but can someone drink themselves senseless for that long?

It's been so busy today and it's not over yet. I've spent the day on farming duties, helping John recover an old polytunnel. The metal frame was still in place, but the thick plastic roofing was in tatters. He had the new cover rolled up in the shed, just hadn't gotten around to fixing it. There is more urgency now that we've got to become self sufficient with very little bedding in period. It took six of us most of the day, but it is done. I think the plan is to get vegetables going in there all year around. Tomatoes are the first things to be sown. I don't really know what else. I'm just helping out. Doing what I'm told.

I've got a couple of hours to rest and then it's a night shift on border control. It's ridiculous and so unnecessary. The only people that have ever turned up at the blockades were me, Richard and Ed and they let us in.

Gordon was helping with the polytunnel today. He seems very competent, and I suppose the village rely on people like him. But I can understand why John didn't think it would be good me doing a night patrol with him. Ok, it's perhaps slightly patronising, but nice as well to think that someone's showing a little consideration. I don't like Gordon. There is something distinctly predatory about him. He is hungry, hasn't fed in weeks. Wouldn't leave me alone, kept popping up whenever we had a break or I'd gone to fetch things. Asking questions. Noting I'd left Richard now. Was John treating me well? Said he was concerned about the locals, and I was one of them now. We've all got to look after each others' needs, he'd said. I didn't like the way he'd said needs. Anthony, this slightly gawky teenage lad, was in the barn at the time. I don't think Gordon had realised, and even Anthony understood what was really being said. He stuck to me like my shadow for the rest of the day, which is really rather sweet. He's a nice kid. Was telling me about how he's part way through his A-levels, about what he wants to do at university. I didn't have the heart to point out that those kinds of things don't happen anymore. He probably doesn't want to think about it either, so pretends. Like this is summer camp. Something for the C.V. I suppose we all need some kind of hope to cling to. I'm not too sure what my hope is. I don't know. Maybe this is where I'm going wrong. Anthony wants to be a civil engineer. Gordon wants to shag anything with a pulse. Christ, there was Sheryl at the farm today helping out so it wasn't as if I was the only female. But Sheryl lives with a man. And I am assumed single. I am fresh blood. The whole thing makes my skin crawl.

In a couple of hours it's the night shift, back on the point where I first entered the village. I'm so tired, and so frigging hungry. On a positive note, I'm on shift with John and Chad, so at least I've got good company. John's persuaded Chad to read The Day of the Triffids, *and I've just finished* The Drought, *so we'll have plenty to talk about.*

Naomi was tired. She was hungry. There was plenty to eat. She was living on a farm after all. She was surrounded by all the healthy, natural and organic products she could wish for. But she was craving Chinese takeaway; ice cream and chocolates; popcorn at the cinema; a late morning in her own bed; turning her music up loud and wobbling around her flat, curling up on the sofa and watching a favourite film. Just anything but this. This constant trudge, going from shift to shift. Meaningless totalitarian crap.

They'd come off shift early that morning. She and John had returned to the farm and caught up on some sleep. John was working at the farm that day, but Naomi had an afternoon shift with

Sheryl and Donovan. Mark had told her to take the rifle home and bring it back for her next shift. There weren't that many people in the village able to shoot, and there were enough rifles to go around the able. In other words most residents would be a liability with a firearm. Villages once full of farming and country folk were now outnumbered by the professional rich: consultants, managers, accountants and business people. The country was nice to look at, but they didn't like getting involved in practicalities.

The sun was bright. It bit at the backs of her tired eyes. Naomi felt irritable. Her hair was a mess and tied up roughly at the base of her neck, a headscarf tied over her scalp to cover over the building glut of grease. She was turning into a proper little partisan, marching down the track with a rifle over her shoulder. Dust kicked up at her feet.

She was to patrol the entry road at the side of the village hall. As she started up the bank, Mark Andrews appeared in the hall doorway. He wore a grim expression of concrete as he strode out, followed by Chad. "Naomi, you're coming with us," he ordered, not even looking in her direction as his boots hit the main road.

"I'm supposed to be at one of the blockades."

"Sheryl and Donovan will manage without you."

What now? This would make a change from standing around with nothing to do, she considered as she hurried after Mark and Chad. "What's happened?"

"I don't know. But I don't like it."

She looked to Chad, hoping for a more illuminating explanation.

Chad shrugged. "We're not sure. Jenny Anderson's just phoned us. She was hysterical. Said we had to get over there straight away."

A tear stained woman in her late thirties was nervously hovering at her front door. It was a well-loved family house. Hanging baskets of blooming flowers adorned the front and a child's bike was carelessly left on the front lawn. The family car, recently washed, sparkled on the drive.

"Oh, thank God you're here." She clutched at Mark's arm. "I don't know what to do. I don't know what's happening."

Mark looked unimpressed. "You're going to have to give me a clue."

"It's Mike and the girls," she said, her voice wavering again. "They started to feel rough after breakfast. They're not getting any better."

"They need a doctor?"

"I don't know what it is, but they look like..."

The woman wasn't able to finish the sentence. Chad and Naomi shared a worried look.

"Well, it can't be that," Mark snapped. "We got the infection out of the village days ago. We'd better go in and have a look."

Jenny Anderson seemed surprised by his conviction. Her hand hung on the door handle for a moment, trying to decide if she wanted to follow through. "All right," she said, not convinced, and opened the door to the family home. "Mike's having a nap in the living room; the girls are in the playroom." She led the way down the hallway. The house was uncomfortably quiet. At the end of the hallway there was a sunny opening to the kitchen, and to the right, a closed door. Jenny waved vaguely at the door and muttered something about the playroom.

Mark opened the door. Naomi and Chad were directly behind him, Jenny further away in the kitchen doorway. The girls were in the far corner of the room, out of Jenny's line of sight. Both were under the age of ten. The youngest and smallest lay on her back with her head thrown to the side at an uncomfortable angle. The elder girl was knelt down, her breathing rasping and her dress stained. Her skin was blotchy, with what looked like countless bruises blooming over her body. The smell in the room was distinct, one or both of the girls had soiled themselves. The elder girl looked up sharply, regarding them with bloodied eyes, a snarl on her stained teeth. Her hands were around her younger sister's arm, which she was calmly chewing on, bits of bloodied flesh caught in-between her teeth and dribbling down her chin onto her pinafore dress.

Mark closed the door abruptly.

"Shit," Chad murmured, walking away from the scene, a little weak in the knees, to sit on the bottom of the staircase and catch his breath. It wasn't as though they'd not seen this before. Ed had looked horrendous. Somehow it was worse in children.

"Naomi, take Jenny into the kitchen, get some details," Mark murmured.

"Did you see them?" Jenny chattered, her fingers nervously clutching at Naomi's arm. "I've left them for quiet time for an hour, but I kept thinking about Maddy's eyes. They were just like... just like... you don't think it's possible that they're infected? They can't be. We've not come into contact with anyone..."

"Let's just go into the kitchen," Naomi awkwardly guided the woman back into the room, trying not to be too obvious when she checked the woman's eyes. No sign of infection there. "Oh," she gasped, distracted for a moment when she saw the mess in the family's kitchen. The worktops were covered with packets and bags of food. Bottles of juice, fruit in supermarket bags, individual pots of yoghurt, chunks of cheese in pre-packaged bags, plastic containers of grapes, a large plastic bottle of milk, bars of chocolate. A freezer drawer full of boxes of fish fingers and bags of frozen peas. "What are you...?"

Jenny shrugged, "The power's still off, isn't it. Everything's thawing out. Thought we'd get it eaten, don't want to waste anything." She moved over to the fridge freezer, the doors open, a cleaning rag discarded on one of the shelves. "Thought I might as well give it a clean."

Simple domestic tasks. Every day living. Naomi wondered for a moment if the power had gone off in York. She'd not bothered to clear her own fridge and freezer before leaving. It hadn't even occurred to her. She was hardly the domestic goddess. But then if they were going back to the Stone Age, and the sex roles became more defined, where did that leave her? Naomi looked back at Jenny, perplexed, not just over the fridge, but about bigger questions of womanhood and life as it was to be now.

"Right, let's get this done," Mark was to be heard from the hallway. A door opened, and then there was a loud, reverberating shot. It was surreal. Naomi and Jenny remained as they were for a moment or two, staring at one another as if to question did that just really happen? Naomi felt her stomach knot up. Jenny broke the stalemate. "What have you done?" she screeched, flinging herself out of the kitchen as Mark stepped back from the playroom. The eldest had already broken her younger sibling's neck, so he'd only had to take out one child. Despite his perhaps sociopathic demeanour, infanticide didn't come naturally, even for him. He'd forced himself through a set of actions, knowing what it would mean if this wasn't dealt with.

Jenny was a gasping fish at the doorway. Her first born's skull was splattered on the once prettily wallpapered playroom walls. Another second that seemed to last for hours, no one quite knowing how to react.

"Mike!"

The living room door opened and a tall man in shorts and a rugby shirt staggered into the frame as if drunk. He squinted as if there was bright sunlight or he was suffering from a migraine. He put a hand to his forehead, revealing the tell tale blotching on his skin, ugly on the pale underarm. He'd been dozing restlessly on the armchair. His nose had started bleeding at some point. There was a congealing river down his unshaven face. He saw the revolver in Mark's hand, and perhaps there was enough sense left to understand.

"Maddy!" Jenny wailed at her husband.

"You..." he groaned, "What... whet..." He moved first for Mark then changed his mind, going to take a swipe at Chad but staggering into his wife instead. He caught onto her for balance, one hand clutching on to her shoulder, blood red eyes staring into hers. He felt a fury unknown, fingers curling up and digging into flesh.

"Mike, you're hurting me."

Mark raised his revolver.

Throwing his wife away, Mike fled from the building. Mark fired the gun, but missed spectacularly. Splinters showered from the front door frame to the carpet. All four ran outside, Jenny collapsing into a quivering screaming heap on the driveway. Mark and Chad ran out onto the road, followed by Naomi. Mike was sprinting drunkenly down the village.

Mark turned and looked to Naomi. "Take him out."

Her eyes widened. "I can't..."

"Take him down!" Mark roared. "You of all people know where this is going to go if he gets away from us."

I can't shoot another human being, I can't do it. She stepped out into the road, balancing herself and the rifle against a parked car. On automatic pilot, limbering up, getting ready to take the shot. But I can't do it. She'd killed someone before, shot down a man who had been chasing Emma in York. It had been too late. Emma had already been bitten, but Naomi had taken her longbow, the only thing to hand, and shot the man. Mike hadn't bitten anyone. He was a risk. It was obvious he was infected. He was going to pass the virus on to someone. But how could he be infected when he'd not come into contact with the disease?

"Kill him!"

Breathe. Think of the greater good. This is not murder. Naomi pulled the trigger. The back of Mike's head exploded in a shower of crimson outside of Richard's house. Blood splattered on the tarmac, a brief heavy, infectious rainfall. The body flailed its arms and collapsed to the ground. The legs shook in the final death throes. Then nothing more. Naomi felt her arms shaking. She had been steady for the shot, but she couldn't hit her own shadow now.

"Woah," Chad breathed, his voice hoarse. "That was some shot."

Mark turned away from the scene, furious. "What the hell is going on?"

Naomi wasn't trying to think about it. About the family that had caught the infection as if touched by the devil. About the mother, distraught and catatonic, lying on her side and moaning now and then, but essentially a vegetable. About the random outbreaks Rudi had told her about. The outbreaks with no explanation. When she wasn't avoiding thinking about those things, she was left with a general feeling of disgust. Mark Andrew's little assassin. Hop-to-it girl and do-as-you're-told slave. She may well be disgusted by how Ed was handled, but how much better was shooting a man down in the road like a rabid dog? Mike must have had some of his former self left, because he'd had enough sense to run. If the disease had completely taken over his soul, he would have mindlessly attacked them, raw meat being the only thing his body needed.

"You're very quiet this morning, Naomi."

She pulled the knot taught and glanced up at John. She'd forgotten he was there; in fact forgotten about herself even. Just soaked up into the task at hand, digressed to her thoughts. She was already at the end of the row. They were setting up cane pyramids, the beginnings of wigwams, for bean plants to curl up and around. Naomi had the handles of a plastic bag tied around a belt loop on her jeans; a roll of garden twine steadily unravelling inside. Further back down the row John was setting the young plants in the ground.

Naomi cut off the end of the string holding the canes together. "I shot a man yesterday."

"An intruder?"

"No. Anderson. Mike Anderson. He was infected."

John looked bewildered. He sat back on his haunches. He tapped the base of an upturned plant pot, as if messaging for enlightenment. "I thought the village was clean."

"It was. It is," she corrected herself, looking away in confusion. "Spontaneous outbreak. We went over there and him and his little girls were infected. One of the girls was eating the other one..."

"Jesus," John sounded angry.

"Mark shot the other girl. The father ran out; he was away down the village. So I took him out."

John stared at the ground. "We've all read those information releases. About what the disease really does. There's no treatment. They're going to die. The kindest thing to do is end it early for them." His voice was flat. Logic was easy. The awkward part came when you were considering putting your neighbours down.

"This thing is making heartless bastards of us all."

"Was that the first time you had to..."

"No. It was the second; no, third. There were two back in York. It was self defence." Technically the second had been attacking someone else, but defence had been her key motivation. Then there was been another infected man on the street who had almost taken her with him, had Richard not beaten him to death with a cricket bat. Where was their humanity going? She looked up sharply. "I mean, even if we survive this disease, get through to the other side, how are we supposed to live with ourselves? How will we be able to look one another in the eye, knowing what we've done? Is this something worth surviving for?"

John wasn't sure what to say. He supposed this was the moment for the reassuring pep talk. The world will get better. You did the right thing. Of course she did the right thing, but as someone who hadn't come up to the arena of kill-or-be-killed, he felt as though he was still in the past. That aspect of Naomi's experience marked her as solitary, a survivor. Someone worth knowing, and certainly someone who had proven herself. It also made her a little frightening. And what hope was there? He'd been to desolation after the death of his wife. That blind optimism that the innocent owned had long since left him. He wasn't that sure that things would get better. The silence dragged out. The absence of a response increasingly telling. He looked towards the farmhouse for inspiration, his eyes jumping at the appearance of a figure at the entrance to the field. "Well, there's something I wasn't expecting to see."

Richard Stilton. He was a little worse for wear with the final after effects of a prolonged heavy drinking session filtering out of his system. This appearance marked the end of a six day period of isolation. Only six days, yet he'd noticeably lost weight. He carried a week's worth of beard on his face, and dark circles under his eyes. The light still felt bright, but at least he was sober.

Naomi walked up the field, but loitered a little behind John, as if nervous of what Richard might have become. Six days in itself was long enough, but on top of everything that had happened it felt like an age.

"Richard," John was the first to speak. "Good to see you. We thought you'd done yourself a mischief."

Richard smiled wryly, and they exchanged hearty handshakes and pats on the shoulders, as if he was a lost explorer newly returned to the homeland. Naomi watched, mildly suspicious, keeping John between herself and Richard.

"We did come by a few times," John added.

"Yeah, I did hear." Richard glanced uncertainly at Naomi. "I wasn't in a state for seeing people. I was sat in the front sobering up yesterday, and," he cleared his throat. "Anderson ran past and his head just..." he demonstrated by pushing his hands away, fingers spread in the air. He saw Naomi close her eyes; his guess that she had taken the shot correct. "Bit of a wake up. Needed to get my head out of my arse. This is happening to everyone, and... well... I can't hide from it in the whiskey bottles anymore."

"No more booze left?" John asked.

"Merely a coincidence."

John looked back at Naomi, conscious she hadn't said a word. "Naomi?"

She forced a weak smile. "Nice to see you about again."

"Right, well," John rubbed his hands together. "I think we've got enough canes set up for the number of plants I've got. I can finish up planting these."

"Aye, I'll let you get on with the good work." Richard shifted his gaze to Naomi, loitering in the awkward pause. "Do you want to come for a walk?"

"Oh, I don't think that's a good idea. You don't know who might be roaming about."

"No one, I would have thought." Richard stood his ground. "I'll show you a bit of the local geography. Don't know when you might need to know."

"I can finish this up on my own," John reiterated, to resolve Naomi's indecisiveness.

She didn't really feel as though she had a choice. John clearly thought she needed to make her peace with Richard. Although how did one mark peace when there had been no argument? Richard owed her nothing and yet her feelings toward him had soured. These past six days had started with a distinct sense of abandonment. If it hadn't been for John she would have been left for the dogs. Strange, how a break, a period of silence, could be as uncomfortable to get over as a serious fight.

"If you're sure," she mumbled to John, hoping for a last ditch change of mind that wasn't forth coming. She walked up the field to Richard. As she neared the finer details came in to focus. He looked as though he'd spent a rough week in the dark. His brother had attacked a girl and then been lynched. She ought to give Richard the benefit of the doubt. It was foolish to think anything or anyone revolved around her, and besides which, no one owed her a damned thing. She was lucky to be out of York and in the middle of nowhere. She smiled, a little more genuine this time. "Good to see you again."

"Yeah," he smiled sheepishly. They started to walk towards the farmhouse. "Look, I'm sorry about leaving you on your own first day we got here. I wasn't thinking... it's been all right here with John?"

"John's great. But you don't need to apologise. You're not responsible for me."

"I brought you here."

"Which was a favour. God knows what York's like now."

"No," he sighed. "I wouldn't want to be stuck in any city these days."

They left the farm property and followed paths along the fields, past narrow little valleys. Rough green meadow grass filled the valley bottoms and slopes. Across the tops of the hills where the flatter terrain lay there were ploughed fields. In some of the fenced off valleys cattle grazed, oblivious to the tragedy that had befallen the human race. Bees hummed as they flitted from flower head to flower head. They passed a furrowed field of growing potatoes, the soil riddled with white stones. They walked the brow of an L-shaped valley that Richard said was called Deepdale. The track took in the length of the valley. As the path started to dip down towards the bottom, Naomi caught sight of a small stone church spire beyond a copse of trees. "Are we going to another village?" She sounded a little horrified. "Is that a good idea?"

Richard smiled wryly. "I don't think the villagers here are going to mind. Come on."

The village in question, Wharram Percy was uninhabited. It was a victim of a past disaster and a medieval deserted village. Of the village habitation itself all that remained were marks of old foundations. Grooves in the land demarcated where lanes and buildings had once stood. The shadows in the land were more easily seen from the air. The ruined church and tiny graveyard still stood. Up until now they had been looked after by a historical charity. Such organisations and priorities wouldn't exist anymore. History would have to take care of itself.

At the graveyard a jumble of leaning, wind-worn and lichen coated headstones sprung up from the jungle of lush uncut grass. There was even a boxy looking stone sarcophagus. Beyond the church stood a Victorian semi-detached cottage, with an old train station sign from a local village nailed up on the windowless end. The two buildings were empty, used once by archaeologists excavating the site. As if a token of their presence, the back garden was full of particularly clear medieval house foundations.

"It would be a good safe house," Richard had commented, tapping the walls.

"Safe house?" Naomi had been unconvinced, peering in through a dingy window.

"I mean if we had to get out of Thixendale suddenly," he had explained. "A place to reconvene."

Naomi had looked back at him as he had said this. He had been looking back at the church, unaware of the expression on her face. He was making a presumption that they were some kind of team above and beyond whatever holds the village had. It certainly hadn't felt that way for the past week.

They were now sitting on a wooden bridge. The walkway was covered with chicken wire to prevent tourists slipping in wet weather. The bridge crossed over an elongated mill pond; the first thing they had come to when approaching the deserted village. Apparently it had been restored in the last few decades, and was now something of a wildlife habitat. Naomi sat cross-legged, leaning against one of the railing posts. Richard hung his legs over the edge, kicking at the water.

"You settled into the village all right?"

Naomi pursed her lips and stared down at the water. Settled might not be the right word. "Mark's got me on all the rotas for patrol duty and farm labouring. I'm an able-bodied adult. I am a good little citizen." She laughed dryly, although there was nothing funny about the situation. "I'm one of his little henchmen. I'm actually allowed my own assault rifle."

He nodded slowly. "You do have a good eye. Anderson getting shot in the street..."

"That was me."

"What happened?"

"He was infected and making a run for it."

"Infected?" Richard looked horrified. "They didn't let Hayley stay in the village?"

Hayley, Ed's first and last victim. The diseased and unclean must be driven from the town boundaries. The whole thing was sickening. "No," Naomi sighed. "Mark drove her and her mother out that evening. He said he was taking them to some army rendez vous..."

"Really? I thought they'd given up trying to treat the infected."

"It was just a line. The husband had the colonel on the radio to find out what had happened to them. The army knew nothing about it. I think Mark did them in. I know it's the kindest thing to have done; the only thing really, just as we couldn't have let Anderson run away, but we're turning into monsters."

"You're not a monster."

"The colonel doesn't talk to anyone," Naomi burbled onwards quickly, felling her throat knot up. She didn't want to cry in front of anyone. It wouldn't help. They were all in the shit. She'd come out of things relatively unscathed up until this point. She didn't feel like she had any comparable grounds for complaint. "He just sits in the village hall playing with the radio. He suddenly looks and acts his age. Mark's basically in charge."

"Mark Andrews is a small minded bully."

"He's making the hard decisions," Naomi would give him that at least. In that house it had been Mark who had shot dead the one surviving little girl. He'd not even asked Naomi or Chad, his minions, to do it. He hadn't hesitated. "But there's something brutal about him. I don't feel quite safe with him. It's good that he's prepared to deal with this disease head on, no sentimentality, I guess. But it's the way he's dealing with the uninfected. He barged into Ann Douglas's shop and emptied it; didn't even ask her. I think she found it quite distressing. He's stolen all of my supplies out of the back of your Land Rover. Hasn't said a word about that to anyone..."

"Shit."

"I think if he wasn't worried it'd be a step too far and we'd all rebel, he'd throw all the elderly out of the village. They're not able bodied. Can't help with the rotas."

"This is what worries me," Richard admitted. "Mark Andrews always was a mean-spirited little man looking for a way to prove himself the big man, even before any of this kicked off. Just watch yourself around him."

"I'll be fine."

"And what about the Andersons; how did they..."

"We don't know. I don't understand it. There was no one infected in the village, and it had been days since Ed..." she faltered.

"It's all right."

"We'd have seen the signs before now."

"I know."

"It had just suddenly happened there. The thing is, the mother wasn't infected; just the father and the girls."

"Both of the kids?"

Naomi closed her eyes. No tears. "At least one of them. When we got there they were in the playroom; one of the girls gnawing on her sister."

Richard slung an arm around her shoulders and pulled her in towards him.

"I was speaking to Rudi the other night. He said they've been seeing cases of this; infection suddenly appearing, and they have no idea of the source. What does that mean? Anyone one us could just wake up infected? I feel sick to think about it. I look in the mirror whenever I'm in the bathroom, searching my eyes for the first signs."

"I didn't think it could get any worse than it already was."

"It's like what they say, things could always be worse."

Richard smiled. "Is that supposed to be comforting?"

Naomi laughed, despite everything. She sat up straight. "I don't know. It all seems very hopeless, doesn't it? And I'm laughing like an idiot. We're all doomed. There's no hope."

"I think there are some things to hope for still," he said, holding her gaze for a moment.

Naomi stumbled up, not sure what exactly he was referring to. "We should head back."

"Sure." He languidly pulled himself up from the bridge. "I'll show you a different path back to the village. Doesn't hurt to have a few escape routes."

The farmer stood with both hands folded over the top of his walking stick. His aged, saggy forearms protruded from the rolled up sleeves of his checked shirt. The flatcap was pushed back from his brow so as not to intervene with the view. He seemed unconcerned by the approach of two figures, silently chewing over life as he watched them huff and puff their way up the steep valley side. It was mere coincidence that he stood at the track and they were walking his way. He had decided to wait as he hadn't spoken to anyone in days and was in the mood for some gossip. He'd recognised Richard a good few minutes ago, which was why he stayed. Had they been some of these wandering strangers, refugees, he would have made himself scare. He didn't need any more beggars wanting to stay on the farm. Richard he knew. When Richard was at home he'd often be wandering the countryside in the wee small morning hours, farmers' hours, making films of the local wildlife. The woman he didn't know. She had quite distinctive hair, long and red, a warning flame blowing away from her body. It was a feature he would have remembered. She was definitely not a local.

"You ignoring the curfew as well?" the farmer chuckled.

Richard glanced up at the old man as he ascended the final couple of metres. "I see you are."

"Aye, well," he snorted, a sour look crossing his face. "I've got a farm to run. Cheeky buggers telling us not to leave the house. Who's going to look after the beasts?" He paused, watching as Naomi joined them. "This your new friend, Richard?"

"George Farthing," Richard introduced them. "This is Naomi Ellerbeck. George's is the next farm on from John's."

"Didn't think I recognised you. Where are you from, then?"

"York."

"York?" He raised his eyebrows. "And did you come here after..."

"We both did," Richard said. "After they'd stopped all movement of people."

"I thought they had road blocks up."

"We snuck out."

He digested this information for a moment. "Best thing for it really. Can't feed yourself in a town. They told us there'd be no going out to the shops and no supplies. We're on our own. We'll manage all right. But then, we've the farm. You know the army's confiscated the grain stores out on the main road?"

"I hadn't realised." It didn't surprise him.

"Aye, it's every man for himself. Did your brother get out of York as well? You've a brother there?"

"Dead." Richard didn't offer any more explanation. He was pushing himself onwards through this despair. After the past week he had to at least make a pretence of normality. It was still early and he didn't feel up to explaining just what had happened in Thixendale the day they arrived.

"Oh. Sorry to hear that. Was it this disease? Is it really as bad as they're saying? People have a want to get hysterical, don't they? Mind, I've seen a few strangers wandering the hills; like refugees from the towns. You want to keep your doors locked, else they'll be squatting in your living room."

"Mark Andrews has got all the roads into the village blockaded."

"Mark Andrews," George snorted. "You folks haven't put him in charge have you? The world really is going to hell, isn't it? He built his throne yet?" He shook his head, amused at the mere thought. "Aye, I'd best be getting on. Don't like to stay out too late. Nice meeting you." He nodded to Naomi before heading off up the edge of the field.

"Mark not that popular, then?"

Richard shook his head. "He's wound some people up the wrong way. Come on, we'd better get back. I'll show you another route into the village."

The circular afternoon walk ended down a bank of trees, across a low lying meadow and through a gate onto the no-through road where the pub lay. Sheryl was outside the second to last cottage, heaving a large black rubbish bag into the wheelie bin. She smiled weakly at them, wan and exhausted. "I don't know why I'm bothering, it's not like the bin men are going to be round any time soon to pick this up. I thought I'd tidy up a bit. Seems a shame to waste all this food, but..." she shrugged, letting the bin lid slam shut again as if it were all self evident. She moved to go back into the cottage to continue with her cleaning, then stopped and looked back at them. "Richard?"

Did he look that rough after the past week, he wondered. "Hello."

"I didn't realise you were out and about again. It's nice to see you've not gone nuts."

He wasn't sure quite what to say to that. "Still as sane as the rest of you."

Sheryl put her hand on the door handle, uncertain as if she didn't really want to go back in.

"Why are you cleaning out Julia's cottage?"

"Just seemed like the thing to do. The kitchen was such a mess when we went in."

Richard didn't want to ask. "Where's Julia?"

"Mark took her away." Sheryl looked confused as to why they were asking such stupid questions. "Oh, you've not heard?" She glanced between Richard and Naomi. "Julia got infected."

"Julia got infected? Who did she come into contact with?"

"No one. It just happened." She stepped away from the door, genuinely frightened. "I read the notice you got them to pin up in the village. It was scary but at least we knew what was happening. But I don't understand how, I mean, why Julia went like this. And there was the Andersons yesterday. Mark said you saw them," she added to Naomi.

She nodded weakly. This felt out of control, illogical. As if she was missing something.

"Well, hopefully that's the end of it." Sheryl said hollowly. "I'd better get back in and tidy up. She'd left it in such a mess. Food all over the place. Shame to throw it out, but, well..."

"It's just food."

"I suppose."

"It's just food," Naomi murmured to herself, stuffing her hands into her trouser pockets. It's just food. She started up the road ahead of Richard. She wanted to speak to Rudi. He would point out the obvious in all of this, surely. He had to.

"You been out walking, Naomi?"

Gordon, the man of questionable manners and social etiquette, was sat on the top step of an exterior wooden staircase at the pub. He smoked a limp cigarette, his forehead creased up like the roller doors on a shop front. There wasn't anything appealing on show in his expression. Even at this distance the sensation of his presence was unpleasant.

Like medusa, there was something oddly hypnotic about the man, and Naomi found herself dumbly staring back at him. There was a lurch as something heavily pushed her from behind, dragging her forward like a bar across her shoulders. The moment snapped, and she was walking again. Richard herded her forward, nodding grimly at Gordon out of some instinctive need to keep the peace.

"Richard," Gordon said, almost making the name sound like a joke. "Didn't know you were out again."

"Thought it was about time I got out and saw what was going on," Richard responded tersely.

They walked up the length of the pub and out of Gordon's sight. She was frogmarched away from the bogey man. The pace slowed to something more comfortable as they came out onto the main road.

"Be careful around him."

"I can look after myself," Naomi said tightly. This was rich coming from someone who'd locked her out of the house for six days.

Richard relaxed. "I know. Just remember the police don't exist anymore."

"I can look after myself."

"The police were a deterrent for some people."

They were dancing around an issue, not wanting to spell it out too directly. It came in on a level with looters and opportunists. When the shadow of law and order has vanished, what stops you doing bad things? Morals and conscience? Everyone's ethics were set at different levels, and just because one person was sure the goodness of humanity would win out, it didn't mean everyone else agreed. Naomi thought to the dystopias John had lent her to read. Tales told in ages when society crashed and anarchy took over. Works of fiction, naturally, but an illustration of how people could let fantasies and urges take over. Hey, the world's coming to an end tomorrow; might be the last chance you get. "You don't think he'd cause trouble?"

"I'm not sure. Best not to test it."

"I guess. Are you coming back to the farm? It's John's turn for cooking tonight."

John and Richard were in the living room like a couple of soldiers caught in a tight spot, discussing possible escape routes. Illuminated by candles, for the electricity hadn't come back. It would probably remain down until the current health disaster was over and the national infrastructure could be repaired. John wasn't keen on using electricity from his generator unnecessarily. With summer approaching, they would be living a more natural life. From what Naomi could pick up of the conversation, the two men had read the same books. They had probably already discussed these things in the pub for years past. It would be a little surreal that they were returning to old ground, only that it wasn't theoretical anymore.

She'd left them to it and moved back through to the kitchen to use the phone. There was still something niggling at her about the recent deaths and she needed to speak to Rudi. Someone who she assumed had all the answers, the way people would put their undivided faith in the medical establishment.

"Naomi?"

He must have saved John's number in the phone's memory, she guessed, as Rudi picked up on the second ring.

"Hey. How are things?"

"Pretty much the same. You?"

"Hmm. I'm fine..."

"But?"

She breathed evenly. She didn't want to start panicking. Every time she thought of what she'd seen, her stomach turned over. A man's head exploding on impact with a bullet. Perhaps the next time she was passing a mirror, she would catch a glance at herself and see the tell tale signs of blood in her eyes. "Rudi, you remember last time we spoke you told me about these random outbreaks that were popping up. Did you get to the bottom of that?"

"No."

Not what she had been hoping for. "Thing is, it might be happening here."

"Might?"

She closed her eyes. "It is happening here."

"Oh Jesus," he groaned. "How many cases?"

"Four people, two households. Just in the last couple of days. But there's no one infected in the village. Not since Ed and that was six days ago. Incubation isn't that long, is it?"

"Absolutely not. The first signs turn up in a few hours."

"So how did they get it? They were never bitten. Is it airborne?"

"I don't think so. We've been to a couple of the villages outside London. We've taken blood samples. It's exactly the same virus, no mutation, nothing. And yet we can't understand how it got into their system. Unfortunately a lot of the victims were well gone by the time we got to them. You couldn't ask them. They could barely say anything and I don't think they understood. We ended up having to shoot most of them and get the samples after death. We even brought a couple of bodies back in for post mortem."

"Is that safe?"

"What choice do we have? Anyway, they're dead. They're not going to attack. The biohazard security measures we're taking are unbelievable. Even so, we've already had two lab technicians become infected by accident. The virus population in the blood shrinks, but remains viable in the body for a long time after death, it seems."

"You don't think these people are coming across some old blood splatter and..."

"And what? Licking it?" Rudi didn't sound particularly impressed. He was tired, frustrated. He felt as though the answer was right in front of him, and he was just too dumb to see it.

"How far spread is this?"

"The disease is worldwide, you know that."

"I meant the spontaneous outbreaks."

"I couldn't say exactly. We're in touch with some national health organisations. The Germans and the Swiss are in the same mess we're in."

"So this isn't just England."

"Christ, no. Holland and Belgium have gone down completely."

"What does that mean?"

"There's no authority there. The labs, the army, everyone's infected. They're screwed. France is pretty much heading in the same direction, but they've got a lab in lockdown working on data. We're still in touch with them. Scandinavia's had some outbreaks in the last couple of days, but their centres of population are so spread out they're having an easier time isolating it."

"How about Scotland?"

"Scotland?"

"Are they getting these outbreaks?"

"No, that's the funny thing; Scotland and Ireland are still clean."

"So it could be airborne. But because Scotland and Ireland don't have any cases, there's no infection to spread."

"I don't think so. I hate to say it, but I think the situation would be a lot worse if it were airborne. Besides, the samples we've taken showed no sign of airborne capabilities."

Naomi pursed her lips. Why were some countries suffering, and others disease free? "So what are the ways a disease can be spread?"

"What do you mean?"

"Well, if it's not airborne, and it's not due to biting, the sharing of human fluids, what have we got left?"

"You can have direct contact in many guises. There's water..."

"It can't be the water supply. Only four people in the village have gone down. In one household three out of four became infected."

"But the fourth didn't. That's interesting."

"She couldn't have a natural immunity?"

"Without testing her I couldn't say, but I find that doubtful. The same thing has happened in the villages we visited. Some people weren't infected. Some were living in the same house as people who died. We took blood tests. There was no immunity.

"The other means of transmission are things like insect and animal bites, but we've no evidence that this has jumped the species gap. And I don't think it's been carried that way. Or it can be carried on inanimate objects. Think of the Black Death. And then of course there is food." He paused. "I wonder; could it be something locally produced?"

"This is happening all over the country; on the continent."

"So it would have to be something mass produced. I wonder..."

"If it were mass produced, why is Scotland clear?"

"I'm not sure I can answer that yet, but I have an idea." Rudi went quiet.

"Are you going to share?"

"It's a vague hypothesis. I need to get down to pathology, check the results from the post mortems. I'd better go," Rudi sounded brighter, enlivened by this new theory he was loathe to share. "I'll speak to you soon."

"But..." she was met with the hum of a disconnected telephone call. Rudi had hung up, probably already running excitedly down the corridors, his white lab coat flapping like a superhero cape. Naomi replaced the telephone in the cradle. She wasn't experiencing the eureka Rudi had, but there was something there. Something in what they'd eaten.

She wandered through the house to the living room. Richard and John were slouched back in their respective armchairs, lit by a warm flickering light. John had a glass with a drop of whisky in his hand. Richard was abstaining. Naomi padded in barefoot, and sat down on the settee, curling her feet under her legs.

"Rudi still working hard on a cure?" Richard asked.

"Something like that."

"Does he know why we're having these sudden outbreaks?"

"No, only that it's happening in a lot of other places. They're running tests."

"It's what scientists do."

"He said Belgium and Holland are in a really bad way. I know we're all in a bad way. But from the sounds of things, there's nothing left. No authorities of any description. They're in touch with counterparts in other countries."

A grim silence settled upon the room. The death of a nation felt inconceivable. A virus had brought a country not only to its knees, but had finished off the execution within a matter of weeks. Others, admittedly mostly islands, managed to shut their borders and survive.

"To think a month ago, there were just rumours floating about, but nothing more. Odd isolated cases maybe, but that was it." John mused. "And now nations have fallen." He let out a long, weary yawn. "I'm sorry, I don't mean to trivialise things; only that it's been a long day."

"Aye," Richard glanced at the clock. "I should be heading back. Thanks for the dinner." He stood up and hovered awkwardly, looking to Naomi as if expecting some response. There was nothing. He inwardly slumped a little. "Well, night. I'll maybe catch you round the village tomorrow."

"Yes. Night."

"Night."

Naomi waved Richard off, then went back to running a fingernail along the fabric pattern on the arm of the settee, pondering the question of the source of infection.

"I won't be offended, you know."

Naomi looked up sharply. She'd been lost to her thoughts. "Sorry?"

"You don't have to stay here. I mean, if you wanted to move back into the village, now that Richard's sobered up and is communicating again."

It hadn't even crossed her mind. She wondered if she'd missed a subtle hint. "I'm sorry." She unhooked her legs from underneath her body and sat up straight. John had offered her shelter when she'd been stuck, but perhaps it had only been a temporary stop gap. After all, it was a big ask for a stranger to move in permanently. "I hadn't even considered... I didn't mean to be rude."

John laughed. "I don't mean it like that. It's not a problem you being here, you're very welcome. I quite like the company." He put his empty whisky glass on the carpet by the chair, and leant forward a little. "But likewise I am used to my own company. Don't not go back to Richard's because you're worried about offending me. Because you won't."

There was always something that had to be navigated. Avoid picking up the virus. Avoid causing offence. Prance around the eggshells. She felt like a child of divorce, caught between two parents and undecided where to live. "Thanks. To be honest I'd not really thought of it."

"Things complicated?"

"Nothing's ever simple," she responded vaguely, committing to nothing. She stood up. "I think I'll sleep on it."

"Aye, I'm hearing the call of the pillow," John concurred. "It's been a long day."

Sheryl leant out of the front door like a timid housewife. "Naomi!" she hissed, her voice barely a whisper. The word was too unobtrusive to catch anyone's attention. She tried a short shout. "Naomi!"

Naomi glanced up at the semi-detached house she was strolling past. Sheryl's figure retreated into the shadows of the building as soon as she was sure Naomi had heard her. The open front door was a standing invitation and request. Sheryl's behaviour was a little odd. Standoffish, as if they couldn't be seen in public, but they weren't strangers. In fact she'd spent many hours sitting on patrol with Sheryl, getting bored and wondering how long this was going to continue. A lot of people thought it would be over in a few weeks; a couple of months at the most. Possible, but then hadn't people assumed that the Great War would be over by Christmas?

Naomi, assault rifle over her shoulder, walked up to the house and peered in through the door way. "Sheryl?" she called. "Is everything all right?"

"Yes. Can you come in for a minute or two? You've not got to be anywhere?"

"Not really," Naomi admitted. She slipped into the front hall, closing the door. "Where are you?"

"I'm down in the kitchen."

She followed the voice, finding Sheryl at a square kitchen table. The blind was drawn down to the window sill. Sheryl sat with her head in her hands.

"Got a bit of a headache," she complained. "Painkillers don't seem to be shifting it."

Naomi sat down at the table. "Donovan working?"

"He's taken a walk."

Naomi set her hands on the table. Sheryl hadn't asked her in to tell her she had a headache. She gazed around the cluttered kitchen. It was really quite small, but the houses at this end of the village were smaller than the other country residences. These houses formed a standard rectangle of red brick, a nod to council accommodation. The interiors were not the wide open rooms of interior design magazines. This kitchen was neither glamorous nor carefully laid out. It was full of clutter. There were dishes stacked up by the sink waiting to be washed, a carton of juice, a few empty yoghurt pots, a crumpled tin foil tray – the kind you'd get a shop-bought quiche or flan in, ripped cardboard packaging and a drained milk carton waiting to be thrown out.

"I've done something really stupid," Sheryl finally whispered.

Naomi listened to the clock ticking, not sure she wanted to know. "What's happened?"

"I was cleaning out Julia's kitchen yesterday, you saw me, didn't you? I threw most of it out. She'd been clearing out her fridge and freezer, what with the power cut. There was so much food, so much nice food. Some of those things I can't normally afford to buy. I hate waste."

Sheryl still had her head in her hands.

Naomi said: "You brought some food home." It was a statement rather than a question.

"Yes. Donovan had some of it as well, but he's fine."

Rudi had suggested the virus was being transmitted in food as a secondary route of infection. Food. Julia died yesterday, albeit from a bullet to the head, but she had been infected. Naomi looked over at the food packaging. Headaches. Paranoia. Fever. Vomiting. Reddening of the eyes. The first signs. "Sheryl." She reached over and gently touched the woman's wrist. "Can you look at me?"

"Maybe I'm just being paranoid," she sobbed, looking up at Naomi, tears slowly running from her face. Naomi wasn't sure if they were pink tinged, or whether she just imaged it. But Sheryl's eyes were red, beyond the usual state of a crying woman. Her left eye had a burst vessel like an ink blot beside the iris. Sheryl's expression crumpled when she saw Naomi's face. "I've got it, haven't I?"

"It looks like it."

"Oh god," Sheryl wailed. "Donovan's so scared. He's gone for a walk but he said he's going to have to tell Mark."

At the mention of Mark's name, Naomi felt her bile rise. Mark would come in here, put a bullet in between Sheryl's eyes, get the place cleaned out and be done with it all. Which was effective, but there would be no time for questions.

Naomi got up from the table. "What did you take from Julia's?"

The change in direction threw Sheryl. "What?"

Naomi looked through the kitchen cupboard for plastic bags. "These things?" She asked sweeping a hand over the kitchen work top.

Sheryl nodded. "Yes. Orange juice. A strawberry flan. Yoghurts. Organic milk. And a pork pie." She watched as Naomi pulled on the yellow washing up gloves and gathered the packaging into the plastic bags. She carefully knotted up each bag, before putting them together in a large black bin liner.

"You don't have to start disinfecting the place all ready," Sheryl cried. "I just look a bit rough, but there's nothing wrong with me. I don't want to start biting people. I'm not like Ed." She caught Naomi's eye. "I'm going to turn into Ed?"

"You've seen the information leaflet."

"Oh shit." Fresh floods of tears poured down her face. "And Mark is going to come here and blow my brains out. And if I try to run, you're going to hunt me down. I don't want to die, not now, not like this. I've only got a few hours. I've not got any time to do anything."

She'd never felt quite this useless. Naomi sat back at the table and held Sheryl's hands. "I'm really sorry; I don't know what to do."

"Do you think Karen would have...?"

"There isn't a cure."

"No," Sheryl shook her head. "I didn't mean that. I meant something I could take, you know. I don't want Mark to finish me off."

Suicide. What was the best way of finishing yourself off? "We should go," Naomi decided. "Before Mark gets here."

The two women crept out of the house, Naomi with her bin bag of clues, Sheryl nipping back in for a pair of sunglasses when she realised she couldn't stand bright sunlight. They looked like a pair of amateur thieves. They walked quickly across to Karen's house, trying to look like they were out for a casual stroll.

Karen looked bewildered at her visitors. Naomi was like a guerrilla fighter with the rifle over her back; Sheryl like a rock star just out of rehab, with sunglasses and a generally bedraggled air. "Ladies. Is this a social call?"

"Can we talk to you?" Naomi asked. "Is your husband in?"

"David? No, he's helping up at John's today. What's up with David?"

"Nothing, can we come in?"

Karen led them into the living room. Naomi left her swag bag out in the corridor. Sheryl immediately slumped down into an armchair. Karen sashayed around the room in her slim fit jeans and pretty sleeveless summer top, silver bangles chiming. She offered drinks, which were quickly declined. They were making her nervous. "Okay." She sat down on the settee with Naomi. "What's up?"

Karen looked to Naomi, who looked to Sheryl.

"I took some food from Julia's cottage," Sheryl blurted out.

"Right." Karen sounded uncertain. She didn't think she could eat a dead person's food, but each to their own. Besides, perhaps Sheryl and Donovan didn't keep much food in their own home. "Waste not, want not, I suppose."

"I'm ill now."

"Ill, like food poisoning?" Karen paused, feeling a little foolish suddenly. Julia had picked up the HEMO10 virus yesterday. No one knew where from; that was the frightening part. "You mean the virus is spread in food?"

"Not exclusively, but it might have gotten into some food products."

"Well, which ones?"

"We don't know. No one does. I've got the packaging from what Sheryl ate. I'm going to go through the Andersson's rubbish, see if I can find the common denominator."

Karen stood up. "You mean I could have a can of something in my kitchen that will kill me?"

"I think it's chilled products. Everyone's been clearing out their fridges and freezers since the electricity went off."

Karen looked back at Sheryl, and her eyebrows popped up as if she'd just realised what this had all been leading to. "Oh, Sheryl, I'm so sorry. Let me go get my bag." She disappeared from the room, shortly returning with a black medical bag. Snapping on latex gloves, she crouched down in front of Sheryl. "Can I take a look?"

Sheryl gingerly removed her sunglasses. Karen held her face, carefully prising up each eyelid in turn to see the extent of the bleeding.

"I'm definitely infected?"

"It looks like it." Karen sat back on her haunches.

"I don't want Mark to finish me off."

"Mark?" Karen spoke the name as if she'd never heard of him. "Mark's out there, with Donovan."

Sheryl slunk down into the armchair as if worried they'd see her from the street. Naomi walked up to the side of the window, watching silently. Donovan was talking with Mark, from the body language it looked as though he was trying to reason with him. Mark wasn't listening, instead ploughing on ahead. They went into the couple's home. "They've just gone in your house."

"They're going to realise I'm not there and they're going to come looking for me. I don't want to be hunted down like a rabid dog. I don't want that bastard..." Sheryl was sobbing again.

Naomi looked over at Karen. "Isn't there something you can do? You know, to assist..."

Karen's eyes widened. "I'm a midwife. I've never had to deal with euthanasia."

"Mark's given you access to all the medical supplies. There must be something in there. An overdose or something."

"I can't go and fetch anything now." Karen started to rifle through what she had with her in the bag. Mostly bandages and innocuous drugs that were less than useless. She took out a small bottle of clear liquid. "I've got some morphine."

"Doesn't that have to be kept in the fridge?"

"This is for intramuscularly prescriptions." She caught Naomi's confusion. "Injection rather than IV. I think this is the best I can do."

The two women looked at Sheryl. "What do you want to do?"

Sheryl felt her heart race. This was actually it, the moment of death. She clutched her hands together, visibly shaking, and noticed the blotches on the undersides of her arms for the first time.

"Mark's just come out of the front door." Naomi said quietly.

"All right," Sheryl decided, almost leaping from the chair when she saw Karen take a needle out of the bag. "Not in here," she said, clutching for precious seconds. "Outside. Can we go outside?"

"Sure," Karen agreed, thinking that David would be furious with her if he found out she'd helped an infected woman commit suicide in their living room. "Let's get to the back garden."

Naomi was just closing the kitchen door when they heard the knock at the front door. They shared a look of horror. Karen hurried across the garden, leading the way to hide behind the garden shed. All three pushed into the corner of the garden, up against the privet hedge that separated off the neighbour's garden. Sheryl slumped to the ground and curled up. Naomi stood with her back pressed against the shed, watching as Karen took a hypodermic needle from its packaging.

There was noise from the house, louder because of the open windows at the back. Someone said that they weren't in the house. It was difficult to tell whether it was Donovan or Mark. There was some low noise, then a loud voice, definitely Mark's, shouted. "They've gone to the village hall. She's going to waste our medical supplies on a hopeless case."

Naomi's lip curled. She listened to the sounds of banging doors, the men rushing out of the building.

"Ok, can you roll over and pull the back of your trousers down?"

Sheryl looked surprised.

"Best place for this to go is in your bum."

Injection completed, Sheryl slumped across on the grass, resting her body against the back of the shed. "How long will this take?"

"It'll take about quarter of an hour to start working. Another half hour to really get through your system."

"And it won't hurt?"

Karen smiled weakly. "People don't get addicted to morphine because it's painful." She snapped the bag shut, leaving her latex gloves on, and stood up. "I'll be back in a couple of minutes, just relax." She linked arms with Naomi and walked her across the garden to the garage. There was a door in the side so they didn't have to draw attention by lifting up the main door at the front.

"Was that enough to kill her?" Naomi asked.

Karen tugged at a cord and the light came on. "No, I doubt it. I'm guessing she's not had morphine before, so it won't be enough for a newbie."

Naomi closed the door softly. "Karen!" She hissed. "Sheryl needs to be dead before Mark finds her. Why did you give her the morphine if it isn't enough to kill her?"

"It will stop her caring. Stop her feeling pain." Karen looked distressed. "I deliver babies, do you understand? I don't deal with end of life care. I don't know. All I know is that I only have what I have in my bag, and Mark's not going to let me have any more." She turned to the shelves of bottles and tins at the back of the garage. "We've got to find something here to finish her off."

"Poison her? But that'll make her suffer."

"She's dosed up on morphine," Karen pointed out. "And it's either this or you go out there and blow her brains out." She returned to the dusty bottles draped in cobwebs, taking down antifreeze, rat poison and drain cleaner. She emptied a tub of random nails and screws, shaking out the worst of the dust. She looked back at the bottles of chemicals. "I'll get her to drink these.... or should I inject them?" She looked uncertainly at Naomi.

"I don't know anything about homemade suicides."

"Me neither. Maybe drinking them will be unpleasant. But if I inject, her bum's going to be like a pin cushion."

"I don't think Sheryl's going to care."

Karen's hands tightened around two of the bottles. "I've never killed anyone before. Have you?"

"Mr Anderson," Naomi reminded her. She didn't bring up the others she'd taken out before. "And she doesn't want Mark finishing her off."

"I can understand that." Karen took a deep breath. "You'll help me?"

Naomi would have rather left. She'd had enough of death. "Of course."

"Let's get this done."

In the Anderson's back garden, illuminated by sunshine, Naomi had laid out the contents of the bin bag from Sheryl's kitchen. The arrangement of refuse was set side by side with the contents of the kitchen bin in the Anderson's kitchen. With her yellow rubber gloves on, she sat cross-legged at the head of this rotting banquet and thought to herself, somewhere in all that mess lay the HEMO10 virus. Somewhere.

Sheryl had been dead for about an hour. She'd been away with the fairies, dancing on a cloud of morphine, when Karen had started with the rat poison. Her breathing already erratic, she really wasn't aware of what was happening. She'd stared out at the sunlit greenery of the garden with her ravaged, bloodshot eyes, and gone peacefully as rat poison and antifreeze entered her blood stream. They hadn't needed to use the drain cleaner. It hadn't been a nice death, but out of all the ones she'd seen in the village since arriving, it was the best to date.

Karen had volunteered to phone Donovan to let him know Sheryl had gone. After that she would call Mark and get him to remove the body. Naomi had been grateful she was let off and able to leave before it all blew up. He'd known it was coming, but she suspected Donovan would still be devastated. Mark would be furious about another infection; another stupid infection. It had been preventable, if only Sheryl hadn't taken something from Julia's house. Mark would say they'd wasted morphine on a lost cause. Because they'd made a decision without him.

She looked back at the litter in the garden. It was easiest to take Sheryl's collection and cross reference it piece by piece against the multitude of wrappings from the family bin. They both had orange juice, but different brands. Both had milk. Milk. She couldn't think how the virus could be in milk, but then, she couldn't really think how it could be in any mass produced product. She picked up the final item, a yoghurt pot, a single sized helping with beautiful graphics and a fancy name printed on the side. 'Rêve'. She didn't know what it meant, but the pronunciation in her head suggested luxury, a depth of taste, and a price that meant this would be a treat for a lot of people.

"Rêve," Naomi read out, considering the empty pot. She looked through the Anderson's rubbish and found three empty pots, and one uneaten. On the top of the silver foil, unblemished on the fourth, there were tag lines about luxury and a taste of heaven (was that meant to be an ironic comment?) and something about being probiotic. Good for your gut. Looking at the small print on the side she saw it was manufactured by a company based in France. She put the containers down slowly. They were the only exact match.

She threw the rubbish back into their respective black bin liners and hurried with them into the Anderson's kitchen. She felt hot and sticky, on edge. She ripped off the rubber gloves. She spent a good five minutes scrubbing furiously at her hands and arms all the way up to her elbows before she felt clean.

She picked up the Anderson's cordless phone, thankfully still with some charge in it, and called Rudi. She wandered through to the hallway to sit on the stairs with her rifle. Her eyes drifted to the closed door of the playroom. The bodies had been taken away to be burned, and Mrs Anderson was staying with a neighbour. There was nothing to fear here, and yet there was an eerie ticking silence.

"Yes, who is this?"

"Rudi, it's Naomi."

"Naomi. Is this another number you're using now?"

"No, I think this will be a one off thing. We've had another death today, the third case."

"Did you get to look in their kitchens?"

"I spoke to the woman this morning. She realised early on that she was infected. She'd taken food from the woman who died yesterday."

"Oh shit."

"Rudi, I think it's in yoghurt. It's the only thing that they both had in their bins. I've not heard of it; it's called Rêve. It must be new. It's made in France. Didn't you say they've been hit even worse than us?"

"Yes."

"It's just, if it's in yoghurt, why aren't Scotland and Ireland suffering?"

"I'm not sure."

"It's one of these probiotic yoghurts..."

"I wonder..." Rudi mused. "I'm going to get on to our people in France. See if they can get into the factory. Tell everyone in the village to throw this yoghurt. If anyone's got any of it they've not eaten."

"Do you think it can be that simple, we've been brought down by chilled deserts?"

"If it is, it's just one method of infection. Might explain why some places have been hit so hard despite precautions. I'll be in touch."

"Okay."

She left the Anderson's empty home and headed for the village hall. Mark Andrews wasn't there, but she told the women who were once again checking off the inventory of supplies, to get a message through the village. As a precaution all pots of yoghurt needed to be thrown out. They might not be safe to eat.

Buoyed after the disturbing morning she'd had with Sheryl, she decided to continue her good deeds and go and check in on Richard and see how things were going. She headed down the road towards his house and was just stepping on to the drive when she heard her name. She turned to see Mark Andrews puffing his way towards her. "Naomi," he repeated. "What's this about yoghurt?"

She was feeling more than a little pleased with herself. "We think the infection's gotten into a brand of yoghurt. Rudi's going to check it out, but in the meantime it seems safest to throw any yoghurt out."

"And just who is we?"

Her smile faltered as Mark came up close and she saw his expression. He wasn't happy. "Rudi. He works at the British Centre for Tropical Disease..."

"You have a contact there?" Mark looked torn. A small, sensible voice told him it was good to have such direct channels to the people at the top. On the other hand he was out of the loop. He was in charge. He ought to be communicating with key personal. "And why haven't you reported this before now?"

"Reported it?" Naomi was dumbfounded. "Rudi's a friend. I don't have to report to my private life to you."

"Just who do you think you are?" He was growing red in the face. "What right do you have to order all yoghurt in the village to be destroyed? I don't think that's your call to make."

"But it could be infectious. I can't keep something like that to myself."

"You come to me first."

"You weren't there."

"And whilst we're on the subject, when did you decide to waste medical supplies on Sheryl Conniston? We have precious little here, and I should have been told immediately. I decide what we do; not you."

In the past Naomi might have lowered her eyes, fuming inside but not inclined to be drawn into conflict. It was her usual place in the hierarchy. She knew that she'd let a lot of people walk over her in the past. It was still nerve-wracking, but she forced herself to look at Mark Andrews, his red face, the raised vein on his forehead, the bubble of spittle at the corner of his mouth. This wasn't really about yoghurt or Sheryl. It was about control. "She was terrified," she informed him flatly. "She knew what was going to happen and she didn't want you to come and shoot her like a rabid dog."

"You do not make decisions," Mark shouted. "You will do as you're told."

"I'm not your employee."

"You are a guest in this village at my good grace."

"I think we've heard enough from you," Richard appeared at his front door. "You can bugger off now, Mark."

A rat defending his corner, Mark waggled his finger at Richard; playing up as the angry father. "And you, I hope you're planning on pulling your weight."

"I got your rota, don't fret. Now fuck off."

There was something about Richard's demeanour that stopped Mark. A threat of more potential than Naomi could manage despite the fact that she was the one with an assault rifle slung over her shoulder. Mark backed away onto the main road. "He's a bad influence on you," he told her.

"What?" Naomi scoffed. "He's had nothing to do with Sheryl or the yoghurt."

"I know what's going on," Mark said, determined to have the last word before marching back to battle HQ.

"Yoghurt?"

Naomi turned to him. "What was all that about? I thought I was doing everyone a favour letting them know about yoghurt."

"What about yoghurt?"

"There's a brand that might be infected. Rudi's checking it out."

"Mark's a control freak, a little man, a Napoleon." Richard stopped. He wasn't going to let Mark Andrew wind him up anymore. "Do you want to come in and see my renovations?"

"Renovations?" Naomi was intrigued.

As it turned out, Richard's idea of home improvement didn't look too clever at first glance. He'd ripped out the staircase in its entirety, albeit quite a neat job, Naomi conceded, but even so, it made getting upstairs rather more complicated. He'd even fitted a hatch door on the first floor so that he could separate off the two levels of the house. There was a ladder currently propped up in the open hole. The remains of his staircase were piled up in the utility room.

Naomi stood at the bottom of the ladders and stared upwards. "Why would you do this?" Had Richard gone properly crazy in his week of solitude?

"It makes the place more secure. Even if the house gets overrun, you can be up there, pull up the ladder and close the trap door. No one's getting upstairs."

"If the house gets overrun? This isn't *Night of the Living Dead.*"

"Well, no," he conceded, smiling a little sheepishly. "But it felt better to do this now, rather than wait until there's problem."

"I think you've been reading too many of John's books." Naomi looked over at Richard, who had sat down on a little bench in the hallway. He was smiling rather sadly to himself. He cut a forlorn figure. He'd spent the past week alone in his house, locked up drinking himself to oblivion and removing his staircase. Just because he'd ventured back out into the world, it didn't necessarily mean he was on an even keel again. Maybe she was going to have to move back down here if only to keep an eye on him.

"Look, I know I've already said sorry about the past week," he started. "But I want you to know I'm not going to freak out like that again."

"Richard, don't..."

"What I mean is I'm not going to lock up and keep you out again. John's been really great, and I'm sure he wouldn't have a problem with you staying on there, but if you do want to come back to the village, if you'd feel safer, you're welcome here." He looked up at her. "So you know."

Either that or you're getting bored of rattling around here on your own, Naomi thought. This curfew was probably very hard to take for someone like Richard. He was used to travelling the world on assignments that took him away from home for months. When he was back at home in Thixendale, she guessed he was outside roaming the local area more than he was in the building. When they'd been stuck in York he'd constantly flitted between Ed's house and her flat, as though he couldn't bear to be in one place too long. "When's your next shift?"

"I'm on tonight with you and Chad."

She nodded. "Should be good. You know I'm the sniper girl? You and Chad are just there for a bit of muscle."

Richard smiled at her, his face and body language brightening, relaxing. "I doubt I'll forget."

"I've started growing Chicory in earnest."

John was explaining his latest agricultural experiment. His captive audience, Anna, a blonde twenty-something from an unimaginably affluent background, looked a little bored. Anna had moved to a property in the village to stick the finger up at her arrogant family, only to find herself stuck in the middle of nowhere in the north of England whilst the world collapsed. She was quite sure that it would be over in a couple of weeks. Then she'd be able to drive into town and restock on her diminishing supplies of booze, cigarettes and face creams. Beauty serums that cost more than most people spent on food in a week tended to come in small bottles. Supplies were running low.

When she'd first moved here she said she'd come to the village to get back to reality, get real, be with real people. Real was the buzz word in her prattle. Up until now she had treated the house like a holiday home to doss about in. She didn't work, volunteer, create or do anything useful other than prop up the tobacco and spirits industry. In secret truthful thoughts, she knew that she was bored of the village, and had been planning to leave for good when this damned travel ban had started. She could imagine her father back home in the London flat, swearing about how the country had gone to the dogs. Instead, she was stranded here listening to a tale of chicory.

They were manning the blockade where Naomi and Richard had first come into the village. Naomi sat in the rudimental gun post a few metres above the road. Dawn was creeping up over the tops of the steep valley. Anna looked less than useless, a society girl back from a rave. There was a limp cigarette dangling between her fingers. Naomi wondered if she could shoot it without blowing Anna's hand off. Probably not, her aim wasn't that good. She wished it was, if only to turn off the constant drone of Anna's idiocy. She had talked the whole night through. Naomi had switched off from the discussions a few hours ago. John was bravely holding up his side, still trying to convince her that the world wouldn't go back to what it was, but Anna wasn't having any of it. Deep down she probably knew that the future was the kind of world she wouldn't survive in.

"I used to grow a block of chicory up the side of one of the fields just for the blue flowers," John continued. "But now I've planted out more, I'm growing it as a crop."

Anna snorted like a horse. "How are blue flowers going to save us?"

"They grew it in the war as a coffee substitute."

"Damn, if there isn't going to be any more coffee, we may as well go hang ourselves now."

"Coffee will be one of the few things left. South America hasn't been affected by all of this."

Both John and Anna were surprised to hear Naomi's voice, having assumed she'd dropped off to sleep hours ago.

"Seriously? South America is disease free? Well, that means we'll still have coffee and coke," Anna chortled. "As soon as this travel restriction nonsense is stopped, I'm going to Brazil. I'm thoroughly fed up with all of this. It's just depressing. There's nothing left in Britain."

"Scotland's still disease-free."

"Scotland's fine for a holiday, but I wouldn't want to live there."

"I don't think South America is taking refugees."

"I'm not a refugee!" Anna screeched. "I hardly look like a huddled mass with dirty hair, do I?"

Naomi closed her eyes, thinking, give me patience, and returned to scanning the terrain.

Anna missed the disgust that had flickered over John and Naomi's faces. They didn't try to contradict her. It didn't seem worth it. If things looked to continue in this way, Anna wouldn't last long. "Anyway," she continued, inhaling a deep puff of smoke. "Aside from the coffee, what I really want to know is what you're doing about the tobacco situation?"

"Sorry?"

"I'm down to my last carton of fags. If this really is the apocalypse, what do you suggest I smoke that's home grown."

"Might be a good time to quit."

"Jesus," Anna rolled her eyes. "Abstinence is not in my vocabulary. Although have you seen that fat girl, Georgiana? This enforced food rationing thing is definitely doing her some good. She almost looks human now."

Naomi watched the stick woman wobble with laughter at her own joke. It was cruel. It wasn't even as if becoming Anna ought to be an ultimate goal for anyone. But in the midst of all that bigotry, she had a point. Georgiana was looking better for everything that had happened over the last few weeks. Between the food rations and the hard physical labour she'd put into digging up her parents' back garden to convert it into a vegetable plot, she'd shed a lot of fat. She was blossoming into a healthy young woman. The teenagers didn't call her names anymore. It was depressing that a fat girl could never garner the respect that a slim girl could, but Naomi suspected that some injustices would never disappear, no matter how bad things got.

"You think I could grow tobacco in my garden?" Anna changed the subject back to one of her favourites, stubbing the remains of her cigarette out under foot.

Something out in the field had changed. Naomi raised her rifle, not to shoot but to look through the sights. She felt her spirit sink when she picked up the family slowly trudging through the grass. Shit. More refugees. In the last couple of weeks they'd been increasing in frequency. It seemed heartless to turn them away, but Naomi imagined if they'd let in everyone, it wouldn't be possible to walk up the main road, for they'd all be camped out there in the street. The village would be bursting. There'd be no food left, there's be fights and stealing, sanitation problems, and then the HEMO10 virus would be the least of their worries. In the meantime these scruffy sets of wanderers, people from the towns and cities who had decided to cut their losses and flee to the idyllic countryside, were bounced from village to village, the occasional one getting in. At the moment it was only the brave and the desperate who were prepared to set out on foot. There was some talk that later in the year, if things hadn't improved, there would be great waves of the starving and displaced.

"There's a group heading our way, just rounding the corner in the field," Naomi interrupted Anna's inane babble. "Looks like three adults, two children."

"Oh Jesus, I've not had to deal with refugees," Anna started to flap, picking up a shovel from behind the barricade. "What do I do?"

"Nothing for now." John was watching them through his binoculars. They looked exhausted, walking incredibly slowly. Two kids, could have been either sex from this distance; one woman, two men. One of the men was looking at some folded tattered papers in his hand, probably a map, and saying something to his fellow travellers. At this distance they could make out the sound of human speech, but not the words. The woman stopped, her eye line meeting John's through the binoculars. She was the first to clock them, tugging on the second man's arm, and pointing at the blockade. The children looked relieved, as if they were going to get a hot meal and a bed now. The sight of other people invigorated them, and they picked up the pace.

"Don't they understand what this road block means?" Anna moaned.

John picked up the megaphone. "Stop there," he broadcast to the travellers. "Turn around and go back the way you came."

"We're starving!" the woman screamed. "We need food, somewhere to stay. You have to let us in."

"There's no room." John let the megaphone click off regretfully. It wasn't easy turning desperate people away.

"You bastards!" the woman screeched, collapsing to her knees. They'd probably already been turned away from other villages. The thought of continuing the trek on an empty stomach was too much. One of the children started crying. The men talked quietly between themselves. One of them took a few steps forward. "We can give you money. Everything we have. My wife has a couple of diamond rings..."

"Jesus, what do they think we're going to do with diamonds and cash? Buy ourselves a cure and flights to South America?" Naomi muttered. Cash and currency was meaningless. It couldn't be traded, and the only goods that were worth anything revolved around survival. Diamonds would only be decoration for a grave. Luxury these days was a soft bed and a full stomach.

John lifted the megaphone again. "No. We don't need money. There's no room."

"I thought Mark said he wanted some new people let into the village," Naomi spoke quietly, leaning into the safety of the sandbag wall of her little vantage point.

"He only wants them as single people or couples, young and able bodied," John responded. "No kids, no old people." His face wrinkled in disgust. With the Anderson family out of the reckoning, the mother essentially a broken vegetable, there was an empty house that could provide shelter to a couple more workers. But Mark Andrews only wanted useful people for his little empire. "He's turning us all into his own little bastards."

"It's not our job to feed the rest of the country," Anna muttered.

One of the men had stepped away from the group. "Could we at least have some food?" he shouted to them. "Anything you have to spare. We're starving."

John lifted the megaphone to shout something back, then thought better of it. He looked at the homemade version of a soup carrier he'd brought down with him for the night shift. It wasn't anything glamorous, just potatoes and old onions, but it had kept them going. "Go take them this," he told Anna.

"We can't afford to share our food out."

"It'll only go to waste. There's lots left. You wouldn't eat any. Too many carbohydrates in potatoes, didn't you say?"

"If I go down there, they'll probably eat me, never mind the soup," Anna protested, her voice rising in pitch a little as she grew truculent. "Besides, you know what Mark said."

"And we don't bow down to Mark's opinions without question. Take them the soup." He lifted up the megaphone. "We're bringing some food over," he called to the travellers, making the deal official.

This calmed the group for the time being. Grumbling, Anna picked up the soup carrier and trotted down from the road, climbing awkwardly over the barbed wire fence. Her two hundred pound designer wellingtons looked somehow wrong against the labelled skirt and trim little jacket. The outfit would look fine in a fashionable wine bar, but didn't stand the rigours of work. She wouldn't cut an immediately threatening figure with this travelling family. She'd probably look ridiculously, and they'd assume they'd happened upon a village of rich country toffs who probably hadn't figured out how to peel a potato on their own yet.

The food was accepted and poured out. They appeared to have a little receptacle each. Bowls were held out like poor desperate orphans. One of the men necked his back in what looked like a single gulp, then started walking up the base of the valley towards the blockade.

"Return to the group. You can't come through."

"I'm just going to talk," he rolled his eyes, ignoring John's request.

"Go..." John turned off the megaphone. The man was so close now, by the chicken wire fence by the side of the road. "We can't let you in," he explained.

"We get it, all right," the man said. "If it were winter, we might be more desperate, but it's not too bad sleeping rough, what with summer coming. It's just the food issue that's a problem. None of the villages we've been to will let us stay."

"The countryside may look like food and habitation in abundance, but there simply isn't the space for all the cities to empty out and be absorbed here," John explained. "You should have stayed where you were. The army rations are still being passed out in the cities."

"Sparingly," he sneered. "But you're not getting any?"

"They stopped with the villages almost as soon as they'd started. We only ever got one delivery."

"We had to get out. I couldn't leave the girls in there. They've lost control. You people won't understand what it's like. There are herds of flesh eaters..."

I have some idea, Naomi thought, listening to the conversation. She kept an eye on the family. Anna was guarding the soup container as if she were watching the servants with the family silver.

"Where have you come from?"

"York."

"York?" Naomi blurted out without thinking, the connection back to her home lurching her up into the here and now. She stopped her surveillance and looked at the man. "How is it?"

"Anarchy. A fucking nightmare. They've lost control in the centre. The only thing they're trying to keep control on is not letting anyone out. All the exit roads hitting the ring road are heavily guarded. They started just by shooting the infected, but sometimes people are so desperate, it's hard to tell them apart, so they just get the shits and shoot everyone." He narrowed his eyes. "You from York?"

"Yes, I..."

"I see you got in the village then."

"She was already here before they stopped all travel," John told him sharply.

"That was handy," the man sounded as though he didn't believe them. "Sightseeing, were you?"

"Her partner lives here."

He does? Naomi thought, glancing between John and the stranger. This was news to her.

A scream from the field broke the distrusting standoff. The other man had grabbed at Anna and was threatening her with a kitchen knife. Anna floundered uselessly like a fish plucked from the stream.

"Looks like a few more sightseers with partners need to be let in," the man said. "Or else we'll have to eat more than the soup."

John picked up one of the so-called weapons they'd been provided with, a crowbar – useful in close combat, but at this point harmless. The best he could hope was that he'd cut a threatening figure. It didn't appear to be deterring anyone. "Let her go now."

Naomi ignored the blackmailer at the gates, looking back through the sights at the physical drama at the far corner of the field. She aimed at the soup carrier near the man's feet, and fired. The shot echoed up the narrow valley, a hard whip crack whack, and the soup pot jumped off the ground, its metal side denting inwards on impact. The children starting screaming, the mother visibly panicking, and in the confusion the man let go of Anna. With surprising grace Anna swung around and kicked him in the groin, jumping spritely as if she'd scored a goal for the team. The man dropped to his knees. Anna picked up the kitchen knife, pointing it at the mother, then the man, before grabbing at the soup carrier and scampering to the closest point on the fence she could climb over.

The man at the barricade didn't appear to be daunted. "What, you don't think you're actually going to kill us now?"

"No," Naomi said, surprised by just how calm she was. It probably helped that she was sat down, with the strength of the lookout point to prop her up. Her knees would have collapsed otherwise and she would have been ineffectual on the ground. "But I'll aim to maim. A little flesh wound untreated could soon fester and you'll have a long lingering death to deal with."

"You won't hit them this far off."

"She never misses," John warned the man.

Naomi fired off a second shot at the rucksack on the ground between the man and the woman and children. "I've run out of inanimate targets now."

"You're fucking monsters, you know that?"

John raised the crowbar above his shoulder as if preparing to tee off. "Go back to your family and get moving."

"Rot in hell," the man spat, moving back down from the fence line. "You and your bitch whore." He turned, the back of his neck burning red, and marched towards his cowering band of comrades.

John slowly lowered the crowbar to the road surface, noticing the shake in his hands for the first time. Threats were one thing, but pushed to it, how far would they have been prepared to go; either side? Would he had really bashed that man about the skull if he'd come up onto the road? Would Naomi have started shooting out kneecaps? Would the other man really have killed Anna? And could the travellers have chopped her up and slung her in the pot. "Would you really have shot them?" he asked quietly.

"No." Naomi relaxed back from the rifle, watching as the man rejoined the clan. They gathered up their belongings and started back the way they had come, the woman giving the villagers the finger in a parting gesture. "Thank god they didn't call our bluff."

"How ungrateful!" Anna puffed as she jogged back up the road to her fellow patrollers. "That shows you what a little kindness will do for you. They said they were going to eat me. Can you believe it? Those little brats were eyeing me up like a side of bacon. I bet they would have as well." She dumped John's soup pot on top of the barricade. "Looks like Naomi's ruined your Heath Robinson creation."

John picked it up, examined the dent. There was no hole. Although the pot looked ungainly, it would still be perfectly serviceable. "No worries," he told Naomi. "We can still use it. It'll be a reminder about getting too soft."

It feels as though things are getting better. The last month or so, there's been no more outbreaks. At least not in the village. I don't know about the rest of the world. Who cares? Summer is here, the evenings are long and glorious, it's warm and everyone is feeling positive. We've still got the patrolling and the farm labouring to do, but we've settled into a routine. I manage to avoid Mark quite a lot. He is an obnoxious little shit, but I suppose nothing can be perfect.

We still get the refugees trying to come into the village. It's a steady but sparse stream. I think supplies to the towns and cities have improved lately. The army demands a percentage from all farmers, and as early crops are flourishing, there seems to be enough to go around. We're all living incredibly healthily. I've lost a little weight. I am on a very simple diet. No processed foods. For the most part I have gotten used to it, but there are still some luxuries that I miss. Some evenings I get such a craving for chocolate. And on more mundane issues I am down to my last couple of sanitary towels. Hardly a disaster, but I will need to think about what I'm going to do. Make something I guess, that I wash and reuse. I'll have to ask Karen if she knows what people used to do in the olden days. Not that she's a historian, but as a nurse... funny, you just assume that certain professions have the answer to everything.

I've barely written in here the past few weeks. I've been busy. I'm so tired after my work that I'm out like a light in the evenings. I actually feel happy at the moment. I get frightened if I think too much about how the future is going to work out. It really is a big unknown void, but day to day living goes well. The nights are heavy, intense. We've gone through our troubles and now we've reached peace, and equilibrium. It's bizarre, but it's only now that things are tranquil, that I'm having nightmares. About Ed, about Anderson, Sheryl, and all those refugees we've turned away. I never dream about the virus itself, even though Ed and Sheryl often come to me as diseased corpses. The HEMO10 virus seems a long way away. It feels surreal. Like fiction.

We've had a few newcomers to the village. People Mark deemed fitting enough to allow through the barricades. He needs more able hands to the deck, especially as we lost a few through the yoghurt infections. And depression. Mrs Anderson is with us, but essentially is a drooling vegetable. Donovan hung himself shortly after Sheryl died. That was particularly sad. He wasted away so quickly, wouldn't eat or leave the house. He never locked himself away as Richard did for a week, but he fell harder. There was a time we thought Richard had ended it all. But Richard pulled through on his own. Donovan seemed to drown in the kindness of well-meaning. I think Mark was partly relieved by the man's death. He hadn't contributed to any of the work rotas after Sheryl died. Mark begrudges food to the little children and the elderly, so we've only been Most people are sent away by order of Mark.

There were the three empty houses: Julia's cottage, the Andersons' home and Donovan and Sheryl's house. To replace this sadness, we've taken in new people. There's Jill who's this great outdoors woman. She turned up on her own. She had been backpacking through the countryside and didn't actually ask to stay in the village. She wanted to do a bit of trading as she'd run out of a few things. Won't talk about where she's from or what she's seen, which angers Mark as he's wanting as much news as he can get from all the newcomers. She's got Julia's cottage down near the pub. She goes out foraging quite a bit, and hates Mark even more than the rest of the villagers, but she stays with us regardless. She and Chad make longing puppy eyes at each other when they meet. There's definitely something there. Curious, under the circumstances is it really possible to start a sincere, real relationship under such pressures? How can you be sure it's genuine, and not just a bid to increase chances at survival? But then maybe everyone needs something to look forward to, a little hope where they can find it. Or else what's the point?

In Donovan and Sheryl's old place we now have Rab and Kenny, who arrived together. They were quite happy to move in together, but definitely aren't "poofters", as they so politely put it the first night at the pub. Not exactly politically correct. They were shaking their hands like jazz hands and looking distressed by the idea someone might have assumed otherwise. They're survivors, Ray Mears-wannabes really, who came to the village by accident.

They weren't desperate to move in (it seems that Mark likes these kinds of people best). They said they would camp out in a garden, but then changed their minds and took over the little house. They are quite a funny pair of lads. Rab is a displaced Scot who was living in Wetherby and is furious that his homeland won't take him back. Scotland is shut to the rest of the world. No one gets in or out. Rab's a cliché. He turned up in his hiking boots and his kilt, ginger leg hair blazing in the sun. Kenny's also from Wetherby, although he's not a displaced anything. He's a Yorkshire man. They'd set off from town together early on, seeing the arrival of the apocalypse as they call it. They thought it was a great chance to try out their survival skills and packs. I get the impression they've been planning for this for years.

Finally we got Beverley and Martin, who are living in the Anderson's house. I think Mark regrets letting them in, but he was egged on by the four wheel drive they turned up in, and the fact that they both look like the children of Amazonians. To be fair, they are hard workers. They lived in a rough area of Harrogate, stole the four wheel drive and came across country. Their journey sounds even more impressive than our own escape from York. They're both a bit new age. Beverley is the worst for the crazy ideas. She has this plastic two litre bottle of water she says she took from the spring in the centre of Harrogate. It stinks of rotten eggs. She won't drink it, but reckons it will save her if she ever gets infected by the virus. I did tell Rudi that someone in the village thought they had found the cure, but he didn't sound impressed. I wonder why.

We did get to the bottom of the spontaneous outbreaks. Rudi and the researchers did. It was the yoghurt. The manufacturer in France had produced hundreds of thousands of infected dairy products. Their main customer base was France/Belgium/Holland/Germany, but they'd also been branching out into Scandinavia. And they'd recently decided to take on the UK, so they'd started with England for product release. They'd not started on Scotland and Ireland – lucky bastards – which is why they're still disease free. Of course, none of it was intentional. How can a disease be spread through yoghurt products? Because they're gut friendly yoghurts, full of friendly bacteria that we already have in our stomachs. And these bacteria are put into the products. They have vats of this stuff breeding in the factory. The original source is human. I don't know what it comes from, shit or something. There's a theory that one of the lab workers got infected, who then went to work and infected some of her work mates. More importantly some of that infection got into these bubbling pots of friendly bacteria. Not so friendly after the virus had taken over their cell structure. This is all theory of course, and I don't know whether we'll ever be able to track back the route of infection. So much has been destroyed and too many people have died. Anyhow, because it was all hush-hush with the government at that stage, the company didn't realise what a biohazard they were dealing with. They innocently prepared batches of yoghurts ready for shipping. And the rest is history.

It is all rather grim.

On to more cheerful subjects. Last night was a bit of a boost. Richard cleared out the living room and got this projector and his laptop set up so that he could project onto the far wall. It's been painted white for the occasion. He got the battery charged up off John's generator so that the computer would last out the duration. We had village film night, for moral boosting. Kenny and Rab got this big pan of popcorn going on a little gas burner, and people had to come in and find a space by torch or candlelight. It was kind of a relief that it was dark, so most people didn't notice that the staircase has been ripped out. That's Richard's paranoid security measure. A couple of people have noticed and asked me about it on other occasions. What am I supposed to say? It wasn't my decision! But I am defending Richard like he's some mad but harmless relative. Or I'm deluded.

Staircase aside, Richard seems to be doing a lot better of late. He's lost that haggard, I-want-to-die look and is really quite cheery. He's very good company. I'm living here again, although we do regularly go up to the farm to eat with John. I still feel a little guilty in leaving him, as if I just used him whilst it was convenient. I do feel as though I've done the right thing by moving back to Richard's.

I'm rambling. I was supposed to be writing about film night. The evening was great fun. I think most of the village aside from the poor sods on patrol duty, and Mark came. As it was the first film night, and Richard had set it up, he'd chosen **Lord of the Rings**. There's been a lot of discussion about which film to watch next. We are limited by what films the village already has. It's not like we *can buy any, or download something from the internet. But I hope this is a tradition that's going to continue. And between the village combined, there must be hundreds of DVDs waiting to be watched.*

Anna, the original IT girl managed to get to the evening. She's lost a lot of weight. She was already skinny when I first came here. I've been on guard duty with her a few times, but of late she's been missing shifts. Too drunk to wobble out of the house. She absolutely stank of alcohol last night, looked an absolute mess. I don't know how much longer her body will be able to keep this up. Karen's tried talking to her, and I think Mark's been over to shout at her how this simply isn't good enough, but she's not listening. I don't think she does anything but sit and drink all day and throw paperbacks on the fire. She says she can never get warm. Grim, grim, grim. Mark made a comment the other day to keep an eye open for potential new villagers. There might be another house on the market soon.

From her perch of the edge of the windowsill, Naomi gazed out onto the main road. The height of summer had been and gone, autumn and the harvest approached. With such brilliant sunshine it was hard to imagine the chill would be coming. It would soon be September. She'd lost track of time and had been surprised to note the date on the calendar in John's kitchen the other day. John had been working out when the various crops would need to be picked. Many were so weather dependant, even if he worked out a timetable, the weather would always throw things up in the air.

It would be dusk soon. She'd been in the village over three months now. Six months ago she would never have believed that she could be house mates with Richard Stilton. That she would be living in his spare room, working in a village in the Yorkshire Wolds. It all sounded so farfetched. She pressed her forehead against her bedroom window. She used to sit like this at times in her little flat in York. It had been on the first floor and given a good view onto her street. Not that she was particularly voyeuristic or had nothing better to do than snoop on her neighbours. She'd simply been in the habit of sitting and reflecting on life. Ed's house had been directly across the road from her flat. She'd always noticed when his older brother, Richard had come to visit. Ed was the modern man, city-living, smart and up to date. Fashionable and well-groomed. Richard had been a contradiction, and tended to err to the scruffy side, as if he'd be happier stomping through forests. She always noticed Richard when he came to visit, even back then when she'd had very little to do with the brothers. He'd seemed fascinating, a little wild, earthy; this curious man who travelled the globe filming for nature documentaries. Naomi had felt like a dull office worker who went to archery club on a weekend, salsa dancing so she could say she had a social life. She had generally spent too much time daydreaming about life rather than living it.

"Naomi?"

She shuddered involuntarily, almost falling off her perch. She leant forward without thinking and smacked her forehead on the double-glazed window with a dull thunk. "Ow."

Richard stood in the open doorway. "I didn't mean to make you jump. You looked lost in your thoughts. Anything good?"

"Just mulling over pre-disease days," she sighed, hopping to her feet and wandering bare foot to her sandals. She was wearing one of John's dead wife's dresses. She had purposefully adapted it, removing the sleeves, changing the neckline and cutting off a good four inches from the skirt so that it was a different item of clothing. She really didn't want John looking at her and getting wistful about the dear departed Julie.

"You're still coming to the pub?"

"Yes, of course."

Richard ran his eyes over the room, once a standard empty space that visitors had occasionally stayed in but no one had ever really lived in. Now it was Naomi's abode, her possessions strewn all over. It could almost be a teenager's room, except the lack of posters and the mildly disturbing presence of an assault rifle and archery armoury propped up in the corner. There were some clothes discarded on the bed, including a dress that looked very familiar. It took a few moments to place it. "You wore this when we went to that salsa night," he stated, fingering the edge of the fabric.

Naomi looked wistfully at the dress. "Yes, that was just before the travel ban started." Ed had dragged her along to the nightclub with Richard because Ed had been desperate to chat up Emma, a nurse he liked. Emma had died in York, with all probability infecting Ed. The mood was becoming morose. "Did Kenny get the batteries figured out, then?" she asked, ushering Richard out of the room before one thought followed another and he started brooding.

"Yeah," Richard hung on the landing as Naomi passed, as if waiting to say something but not quite finding the words. He watched as Naomi sat at the stairwell opening, swung her legs onto the ladder and climbed down to the ground floor.

"So you guys figured out how to get into those batteries without maiming yourselves for life with battery acid?"

"Just about."

It had become something of a challenge over the last week. Although it was still light on an evening, the lack of electricity was beginning to tell. There were a few generators available, but with petrol at a premium, the generators were only used for essential tasks. A few people had been reminiscing about music, and how nice it would be to listen to favourite CDs. Kenny had mentioned something about watching a documentary on India where he'd seen them make batteries out of cow shit. They'd actually got a radio running off the thing. That had triggered a slow but steady roll of ideas. There was a group decision that they would recreate the fabled cow pat batteries before the week was out. Richard had even seen it done a few years ago during a trip to India. They'd connected up to the Internet with the last of the energy in Richard's laptop and downloaded a recipe, substituting the tamarind, which no one in the village had, for vinegar. They gathered up empty cans of fizzy drinks, used batteries, wires, and shoe boxes to hold the creations together. The all important ingredient, a bucket full of steaming, stinking cow dung, was collected at dawn. The hardest part had been getting the carbon rods out of the spent batteries. Like a cluster of small boys, Kenny, Rab, Richard, John and Chad had gathered up at John's farm house, filling drinks cans with cow shit and experimenting with the best recipe for a battery. Amazingly they had lined up a couple of shoe boxes of aluminium cow pat batteries that could power the CD player at the pub.

This was in evidence as they approached the pub. The electricity was still off and candlelight flickered from the windows. All the windows and doors were wide open to let the hot air out. There was much chatter, most of the village aside from those patrolling would be here; and the sound of Kate Bush drifted out of the entrance. Since the film night there had been an unspoken understanding that something good in life had to be retained if morale was to be kept up. Life couldn't simply be about Mark's guard duty rotas and enforced agricultural labour.

The pub's population had become so familiar over the past few months, encapsulating Naomi's entire world. Karen, who had joined the party alone as David was on guard duty, was talking to Rab. She had a girlish look in her eyes as they stood particularly close. Chad was showing Jill the batteries with all the pride of a mother hen. Kenny and John were sampling the latest cider, battery brothers in arms. Locals had started brewing their own beer, cider and wine in the recent months. Discarded brewing kits and dusty demijohns were brought forth from garden sheds. Old books instructing on the art wine making were taken down, and lists made of everything that could be foraged from the hedgerows and put to good use. The first vintages were now ready and being served at the pub's musical appreciation evening. Kate Bush was taken off the stereo and replaced with Heart.

"An 80s evening?" Naomi wondered.

"Sounds like it," Richard agreed. "Now, is it the cider or the beer you're going to test first?"

"I thought there was some dodgy flavoured wine to try?"

"Don't think it's ready yet."

"Cider then."

"I'll go fetch you a glass." He brushed around her.

The pub was packed with locals. Naomi was alone in the masses, an unnoticed being, absorbing conversations and atmosphere. Beverly, the hippy from Harrogate and bronzed Amazonian, appeared in her sphere. The woman was wearing a full length maxi dress, something she'd had to lengthen herself by adding a few extra inches to the bottom. None of the spare village clothes were quite her size. Her blonde hair was loose and wild and her forearms armoured by hundreds of clinking bangles. She had a slightly suspicious rolled up cigarette in one hand and a pint of beer in the other.

"Naomi!" she beamed. "Just going outside for a smoke. The ban's still on, you know." She laughed conspiratorially, before winding her way out of the pub.

Someone groaned loudly as the current song got going. "Can't we play something recent?"

Across at the DJ table, for want of a better description was a positive landslide of CDs, all eagerly added in the hope of broadcast. Naomi hadn't brought her music, quite rightly assuming that there would be more than the batteries could cope with. She wasn't sure how much the rest of the village would want to listen to the essential components of her own musical tastes: Suzanne Vega, Fiona Apple, Imelda May, Patricia Vonne, and the Crash Test Dummies. In any case Richard had promised to make her a few cow dung batteries of her own so that she could power his portable CD player at home and listen at her leisure.

"Okay, they've christened this one Burbling Insanity." Richard reappeared with two glasses of cider.

Naomi took hers and drank a mouthful, coughing as it poured down her throat. "Jesus, that's potent."

"The clue's in the name."

"Naomi! Richard!" John had spotted them. He was particularly bright-eyed and fired up. In a moment he was across the room, whacking Richard on the back and giving Naomi a bear hug. His body was elastic loosened by drink.

"He's been drinking like a man from the desert," Kenny laughed. "I think you two have some catching up to do."

The music kicked into the chorus, electric guitars roaring and John's arms were flung up into the air as he rocked to the song, head banging, his body wobbling with the crowds. More people had arrived and the number of bodies swelled. It was standing room only.

"Wow, he's really smashed."

"Aye, but he's happy."

The evening continued thus, glasses drained and refilled, the edges growing more blurred and fuzzier. The music changed from Heart to Elvis to Madonna to Frank Sinatra to Linkin Park to the Rolling Stones to Elton John and onwards to countless other singers and bands. John had Naomi jigging to the Dubliners. It was an awkward dance on the spot for there were so many bodies in the pub but no one seemed to care. It grew dark outside. Inside the warm hug of community embraced all. People's smiles and laughter were lit by the yellow glow of candles. One of the teenagers, who was technically underage, but no one cared, snuck to the CD player and turned off Franz Ferdinand mid-song, replacing them with Lady Gaga, precipitating shouts of protest from some of the older patrons. Despite the complaints the dancing continued, people wedged in haphazardly. It was a puzzle of arms and legs that would be difficult to untangle.

Naomi felt drunk. She could still stand, although she couldn't fall over even if her legs gave up. There wasn't enough space. Her joints had turned to melted chocolate and she rolled and swayed without thought to the underlying beat. She was warm and sticky from the stuffy air. The temperature was ever on the increase from candle flame and sweating bodies. She was dancing on the spot with Richard. They were both laughing like drunken idiots. Richard had a hold on both her hands lest she be cast adrift in the sea of merrymakers. Lady Gaga was the kind of music that the 'serious' music appreciators looked down at and call crude, unnecessarily suggestive and manufactured, but strangely they all knew the words. When the chorus vibrated organically through the villagers, Naomi happily threw back her head and started singing along, a sway moving and undulating through her body. Many others started dancing and they were crushed, apples in the press for the next batch of cider. Naomi was thrust up against Richard as if they'd flicked over to the tango, quite a natural change in proceedings. She continued warbling, her loose hair flopping and brushing against her face. The smells of the pub intensified: malt, beer, sweat, perfumes and deodorants, aftershaves, and underneath it all basic, primal animal scents. No one was holding her hands, and she was left with loose fingers, a vague clasp on the creases in Richard's shirt. She was aware of his hands on the small of her back. She turned her head to look at Richard, a breath away from thudding skulls together. His eyelids were lowered and she couldn't tell whether his eyes were closed or he was just looking down the front of her dress. Then suddenly his eyes were open and he was meeting her gaze directly.

Someone screamed and the moment evaporated. Some started laughing, but an uncomfortable silence and sobriety were sweeping through the room. The volume of the CD was lowered to a barely audible background hum. Someone was sobbing. People's spirits were returning to level ground. Hands were removed from body parts, the party atmosphere broken, embarrassment taking over.

"What the hell's going on?" an angry male voice yelled.

In the porch entrance a sobbing woman, or perhaps a crying girl, leaned against the doorframe for support. She wore a pretty sundress that was streaked and muddy. Her once neatly brushed hair was jerked out of its ponytail and looked like a bush. Naomi didn't like to play to modern society's idea of the beautiful body being thin, but Georgiana had bloomed since she'd lost the excess weight. The quintessential ugly duckling transformation, as the months had toned off the puppy fat. Now she entered womanhood, shaking and crying, wanting to turn back. Blood dribbled down her thighs.

Silence settled over the room. Georgina looked from one surprised face to the next. "He wouldn't stop," she whimpered. "I said no, but he wouldn't listen." Despite the high alcohol proof in the home brews, no one was drunk anymore. "He just wouldn't stop."

Early that morning, still in darkness, after Georgiana had been taken home, sobbing to mother, the pub cleared and solemn faces headed home. Naomi lay awake in her bed, staring at the ceiling and seeing the first crack in the idyll.

Fucking men. In. Bastard men. Push back. I hate men. Pull out. Mark the wanker. In. Gordon should be castrated. Push back. Fuck the human race. Pull out.

She was breathing heavily, so deeply and quickly she could barely keep up with herself. Her face was red from the exertion. The sweat ran down the insides of her arms. Naomi took her cardigan off and threw it over the wheelbarrow handle. She snapped the hair tie off her wrist and quickly bundled her red locks up into a ball on the back of her head, securing in place with the hair bobble. She could feel a couple of loose strands stuck to the back of her neck, the sweat chilled over by the slightest of breezes.

She was alone in the thin field. She stood with her hands on hips and waited for her heart rate to return to something respectable.

She'd arrived at the farm over an hour later than stated on the schedule. No one cared, but Mark had made some snide comment about her poor time keeping. She would have to work twice as hard as overtime wasn't an option, what with there being a meeting this afternoon. Naomi hadn't slept much and was ready to swing for someone, anyone, and it might as well be Mark. John had seen the thin ice in her expression and ushered her to the sheds before she did something she'd regret. Equipping her with a wheelbarrow and a pitchfork, he'd suggested she'd like to go and dig up some of the potatoes. It was a job that didn't require a lot of people, so she could enjoy the peace and quiet in solitude. And calm down.

In the small hours of last night enough had come out so that no one was left in any uncertainty as to what had happened. Whether Georgiana had been leading Gordon on or not was the only debatable point. Even if she had been flirtatious, she was a young, painfully inexperienced girl who had only just started to discover she could be sexually attractive. With the stresses of travel restrictions, isolated village living and a very uncertain future, things had gotten out of hand very quickly. Law and order was otherwise engaged and it seemed as though the only thing that was stopping the villagers turning on each other was their own individual moral values. A lot of people had started wondering: just how much could they get away with? Inhibitions didn't matter, and besides, they may all be dead next week.

Mark, who had thankfully been on guard duty up at the crossroads last night, had seen Gordon walking out of town in the small hours. He had thought something was wrong, and marched the man back into the village. At the pub Georgiana had explained tearfully that she'd been raped, twice, by Gordon. Gordon was currently locked up in the gents at the village hall. No one was really sure what ought to be done. So the village was to have another meeting that afternoon.

Wasn't there enough shit going on as it was? Naomi pulled one of the potato plants out of the ground, giving it a good shake to remove lumps of earth. Had he thought he would get away with it, or that no one would care? Or was he just too randy to think straight? A few people had warned her about Gordon. Of all the men in the village, it didn't surprise her that it was Gordon who had committed this act. But why did he do it? If he was that randy, could he not just have taken things in hand? Everyone else coped without. What made him different?

She crouched down and started to pull the fresh potatoes from the roots, lobbing them over into the wheelbarrow. She worked her way steadily along the row she'd uprooted with the pitchfork, removing all potatoes, no matter how small, and throwing them in. There was a small metallic thud with every extra potato landing in the wheelbarrow.

It was always the men who caused the problems. If there were no men in the world, it would be a much more peaceful, reasonable place, she thought sourly.

"Afternoon, Naomi."

She looked up to see Richard stroll into the field as if part way through a pleasant country trot. He'd been able to sleep until rested, not needed for anything until early this evening. Naomi sat back on the furrow behind her. "I didn't think you were down for working at the farm today."

"I'm not. I just thought I'd come and fetch you for the meeting."

The meeting at four. Naomi glanced at her watch. "It's just gone three."

"What can I say? I'm keen."

Either that or he wanted to do something before. She said nothing, hunched in the soil like an angry child making mud pies. She watched him walk down the field towards her. He looked in the wheelbarrow. "You've got quite a few potatoes in there."

She stood up and gave it a glance. It had filled up quicker than expected. Nothing like a bit of fury to get the job done. "Looks like I'm almost finished," she commented, looking down at her dirty hands, soil stained with dark brown rimmed nails from the compacted earth under her fingernails. "I'm going to have to scrub up before the meeting." She held up her hands to show him. "I could grow my own potatoes in here."

"You're growing potatoes? We could just throw you in the wheelbarrow, and you've picked your quota."

"Hey!" she yelped as Richard scooped her up, the very follow through of the joke unexpected. He wobbled over to the wheelbarrow, at one point almost losing his footing on the infirm earth, and threatening to trip over, crushing them both on top of the wheelbarrow. Naomi instinctively clung on, thinking, don't drop me, I can't have broken bones. He lowered her rather unceremoniously into the wheelbarrow, both of them laughing. She could feel the uncomfortable hard lumps of the potatoes digging into her back and rear end. He didn't pull back; instead they progressed rather naturally from laughing to kissing. Naomi only realised part way through that this was happening and was continuing. Neither suddenly pulled back, awkward and embarrassed, apologising and saying they had no idea why such a thing could have just happened. It just continued.

"Ok," Richard pulled back slightly. "The harvest is gathered. Let's take this back to the farm. Then you need to get scrubbed up." He picked up the wheelbarrow handles as if to start wheeling it out of the field, but the tyre dug down into the soft earth and he let out a puff of breath. "Christ, that's heavy."

"Excuse me." Naomi sat up straight pretending to be offended. "I'm not that big." She rolled up out of the wheelbarrow.

It sprang out of the rut and he started to push it out of the field. "That must have halved in weight at least."

"Worth two sacks of potatoes, am I?"

Richard looked over his shoulder back at her and grinned. "Oh, three at the very least."

Naomi near floated down the village to the meeting at four. She was so happy, she had temporarily forgotten the gravity of what they were communing to discuss.

They'd returned to the house before the meeting. Normally she would have only given her hands a thorough scrub in the kitchen sink. Today the kitchen sink had remained untouched. The shower was thoroughly steamed instead. Thank god the water supply still worked, that they were still able to get hot water. The cubicle hadn't really been big enough, but it wasn't as though they'd been trying to avoid proximity. Even now she could feel the imprint of his hands on her torso under her clothes. There was something special about walking up the village together, casual and to all appearances as before, yet she knew something had shifted indescribably.

Something positive, something good. The world could be a wondrous place. It was easy to be this positive when strolling through the post-orgasmic glow.

Up at the church Karen loitered, hugging her arms around her body. She moved as if to say something as Georgiana's mother marched to the building, but was brusquely pushed aside by the older woman with little more than a glare. Karen slumped back at the response.

"Hey there," she nodded to Richard and Naomi.

"Are you all right?"

She shrugged, as if to suggest she wasn't upset by what had happened. "You've think after the past months, after everything that's happened, people wouldn't be such short-sighted bigots."

Naomi raised her eyebrows, not quite sure what to say. Already she could feel her joy sinking. "Oh."

"Religious arseholes," Karen continued to no one in particular. "Oh, we think that's a sin." She chewed over the facts. Really, she shouldn't talk about anything medical to anyone other than the patient, but the world was going to shit and why should she play the old games? "I am trying to help."

"Of course you are." Naomi had no idea what she was talking about.

"We all know what happened to Georgiana last night. We can't offer her the same services and support as we normally would. But we have to do what we can. I mean, I can't test for any STDs, so we'll just have to keep our fingers crossed on that account. But I went over there with the morning after pill, and I was called an immoral whore. An immoral whore? Excuse me. How is insulting me going to solve anyone's problems? It's not like I'd even gone suggesting an abortion. It's just a little pill. If there is anything, it's only cells at the moment."

"You can't know if she's..."

"Of course not, but I don't want her to be either. She's a teenager who has been raped," Karen hissed angrily. "Why should she be punished any further? I just want to take precautions, because I doubt he did. But the mother says no, and that's the end of it."

Naomi was aware of villagers hurrying past them, eager to get to the meeting, to throw their opinions into the pot. This was liable to get very heated. Karen seemed to have forgotten why they were there, caught up in her own fury.

"She's probably not even pregnant," Naomi said, her voice low, taking Karen's arm to try and get her into the church. "People try for years before they manage to get pregnant, you know."

"Yeah, that's when they're trying," Karen muttered. "Unwanted pregnancies have a habit of cropping up at the drop of a hat. I don't want to be delivering any babies whilst we're living in the age of the living dead." They were up at the porch entrance to the church, villagers behind them waiting to get in. She looked up at the heavy stone building, thinking of what it represented, and wrinkled her nose. Religion had a lot to answer for. "We'd better get this over with."

The first moment through the doorway engulfed them in an uneasy sensation. This was worse than the first day they'd arrived. Worse than the lynchings, the emergency rotas set up by Mark Andrews, the mysterious outbreaks, the shooting in the street. This was setting a precedent for something far more serious and long reaching.

It looks like a courtroom, Naomi thought, as she and Richard slipped into one of the pews. A courtroom in a church. It was all a bit too Old Testament. Judgemental. Karen joined them at the end of the pew. Her husband David sat up at the front of the church like one of the court officials. Mark Andrews was at the pulpit, visibly positioned higher than any other villager. All that was missing was the wig and judge's gavel. Or perhaps a thunderbolt would have been more fitting here. A few of the villagers, possibly the more thoughtlessly reliable, good, easily persuaded types he held no niggling doubts over, were at the front to add to his authority. One of the older women was close by to take minutes. She was the archetype bossy ex-secretary, now in her late fifties. Her time had been and she had grown obsolete, having slid into fat. Held back by the days of plunkety-plunk typewriters, she was utterly baffled by the digital age. Gordon was sat to the side on his own, his hands casually hung between his legs as if resting, but the rope that tied him in place was just visible. The church was packed. Virtually everyone from the village was there. Truth be told, the only person Naomi couldn't see anywhere was Georgiana.

There was a series of three loud bangs. An object was hammered against wood. The agitated chatter lowered. "People," Mark Andrews started. His voice was a little louder than perhaps intended. "We're gathered here today..."

Naomi closed her eyes, thinking of the dearly beloved. This sounded like the start of a wedding.

"To decide what we are to do with Gordon Cunningham, who last night raped Georgiana Thomas."

"Cut his balls off!" someone shouted jokingly.

Mrs Thomas was up on her feet. "I want him flogged!"

One of the retired gentlemen from the old aged pensioners collective was already on his feet. "Has this been proved? We can't decide the sentence before the trial."

Mark rolled his eyes. "We have neither the time, the resources, nor the ability for a trial. There is no law and order so we must make our own."

Conversations with neighbours erupted at this announcement. The older gentleman was incensed. "I beg to differ. This is British soil, and the justice system still reigns. We are not barbarians. There is due course and procedure..."

John Settle, sat in the row in front of Naomi and Richard, turned in his seat. "Edward Ryan," he said. "Retired solicitor."

"...people cannot think that they can get away with crimes simply because of the current problems in the country..."

Mark Andrews looked as though he was losing control of the meeting.

"Had his own firm of solicitors," John continued. "Dealt with the big estates in the area when he was working."

"Every British citizen has the right to a trial."

"We're in a national state of emergency."

"Colonel, you must agree with me."

The colonel, sat near the front, blustered and muttered, but came up with no coherent argument.

"Hang him!" Richard shouted into the fray.

"Richard!" Karen squeaked, before turning to Naomi, nipping her arm as if to emphasis the serious nature of the discussion. "He can't be serious can he? We can't start hanging people."

"He's playing devil's advocate," Naomi told her, before turning to Richard. "You are, aren't you?"

"It's as much as they did for my brother."

Mark Andrews must have heard Richard's voice, focusing in on the point of irritation. "Ed Stilton was infected and already a dead man. Gordon Cunningham is physically fit."

"Get him castrated and he'll bother no one again!"

Gordon jolted up from his seat, having forgotten his tether momentarily. He moved to attack the man who had shouted for castration. The rope strained against his fury. His eyes were narrow, and he swore sour curses and threats. His mental list of enemies was growing. As soon as he was out of this ridiculous situation.

The retired solicitor, Edward Ryan, was bright red in the face. "Judicial corporal punishment was abolished in 1967," he roared, his voice reverberating round the church interior. "There will be no hangings, beatings or physical mutilations."

This final statement sent most of the church roaring to its feet. It was difficult to say quite why the crowd was so incensed. Was it horror that anyone could suggest such hard line corporal punishments? Perhaps there was disgust that fitting retribution was not to be passed out upon the criminal. Everyone had an opinion. No one could be heard.

There was a loud bang, like a gunshot that sent people ducking down, heads hunched into bodies as if they could avoid the path of the bullet. In actual fact Mark had hit a cane against the side of the pulpit in blind rage. "Quiet!"

Edward Ryan was not to be intimidated. He'd dealt with privileged landowners with shotguns and yapping hounds, evicted tenants, protestors and a thousand fools in between. "We must have a trial."

"We do not have the time!"

"Have you even asked the man how he pleads?"

This simple question brought silence to the church. It threw even Mark, who half heartedly raised the cane again as if to give Edward Ryan a thorough telling off, but couldn't think of a word to counter with. He looked to Gordon. "Did you rape Georgiana Thomas?"

Gordon looked him square-on. "No."

"Liar!" Mrs Thomas wrenched herself back from her seat, caught up in the middle of the congregation. She was struggling to go in any direction, grasping at nothing, wanting to throttle the air from the man. "Liar! He's destroyed my daughter."

Naomi glanced uncertainly at Karen. As the midwife and medical representation, Karen was privy to details the general village wasn't. "I didn't think there was any doubt on the matter."

Karen shook her head slowly.

Mark leaned out from the pulpit, examining Gordon with curious disgust. "So you're denying anything happened last night?"

Gordon shrugged. "We shagged. But she wanted it."

"You monster. My daughter would never want a thing to do with a worm like you."

"She was gagging for it," Gordon jeered at the mother.

"I can't believe Georgiana would have agreed to sex with Gordon," Karen muttered, her lip curled in distaste.

"He's taken advantage of her," Naomi agreed. "She's just a kid."

Mark Andrews scanned over the congregation. "Is Georgiana here?"

"She's too frightened to leave the house." Georgiana's mother, Mrs Thomas, called out. A few people close by, sobered by a desperate mother's voice, sat back down in their pews. "She doesn't want to bump into that man again."

"Mr Ryan," Mark turned his attention to the solicitor. "If we're not to exact corporal punishment, what are we to do, according to you?"

"You've not even had a trial; you've not proved guilt."

"We're hardly qualified to do that."

"There's no question of his guilt!" Mrs Thomas screamed.

"I didn't do nothing," Gordon shouted back.

Mr Ryan seemed to be unfazed by the emotions; perhaps this was the kind of thing he'd grown accustomed to when he had been practicing. He did appear to be stuck at a stalemate, without the back up of his beloved institutions. There was no police, no legal system, and no prison, had it come to that. "Defer the trial," he finally spoke, not sounding completely convinced by his own suggestion. "Until this nonsense is over and the country is back to normal."

"You can't let him go," Mrs Thomas protested to the chorus of dissent amongst the villagers.

John Settle stood up for the first time. "We cannot do nothing. That would be to admit that crime is acceptable. It would be to say that there is no crime and anything goes. We have to demand basic morals and decency from ourselves. Otherwise you have to question just what we're trying to survive for."

"We cannot let him go. We cannot flog him. We cannot lock him up, as we don't have the people to guard him. We certainly don't have the spare capacity to produce food for a non-productive member of the village."

"You've not even proved my guilt." Gordon was back on his feet, chest thrust forward like a little rooster. He lifted his bound hands, as if to signify he was ready to be released.

Mark sneered down at him from the pulpit. "Oh, I think there's very little doubt of your guilt. But let's be democratic. Hands up who thinks he's innocent."

Only Gordon raised his hands.

"And who thinks he's guilty?"

There was an overwhelming surge upwards. Even if there had been someone in doubt over the matter, they would never have dared to voice such a controversial opinion. It was a fact that Gordon and Georgiana had had sex last night. It was also a fact that he was a creepy, lecherous man. As to whether it was truly rape, they would probably never know. It didn't matter, the village consciousness was made up, and every person who had not liked Gordon, or who had felt uncomfortable in his presence, had thrown in their lot on the guilty vote.

For the first time since this scandal had broken, Gordon looked genuinely frightened. There was no one to fight his corner. Even the old solicitor, really more interested in seeing the law followed, did not look convinced of his innocence. Gordon knew he'd been a bit rough, a bit forceful with the girl, but she'd been asking for it, fluttering those lashes at him, and joining in with the innuendo-laden conversation. It didn't matter. He had been marked as guilty. He'd seen them hang and shoot the infected. Chase refugees away from the village. The only thing they weren't prepared to do was nothing. It wasn't going to be pleasant.

Gordon stepped forward. "I'll leave."

"Leave the village?" Mark considered the idea. Decreeing Gordon's banishment from this petty kingdom could be a solution.

It would certainly solve the quandary of what to do with Gordon, and no one could accuse him of abusing human rights. No beatings, no mutilations. Gordon could join the thousands of refugees and find himself a new home elsewhere. He could be someone else's problem.

"Very well," Mark made the decision. There was no democracy this time. His word was law. "You'll leave this evening. I'll take you to your house so you can select some supplies..."

"He's getting off scot-free!" Mrs Thomas shrieked. "This isn't a punishment. I want..."

"He is being banished from the village," Mark interrupted. "This is the punishment I see as fitting, and this is how it will be. This meeting is over."

Naomi woke in the early morning. It was chilly. The temperature wasn't low enough for a frost, or to hint at an approaching winter, but it was enough to keep her under the duvet. What date is it, she wondered. Sometime in October. As to the exact date and even day of the week, she wasn't quite sure. She'd have to check the calendar downstairs.

The light through the window was muggy and grey. A twilight of day time. How would it be when they needed lights and heating? The electric had never come back. People had cheerfully coped through the warm summer and long nights. Some houses were heated by oil or gas cylinders, and had a certain amount saved for winter. Others were completely reliant on electricity, and dependant on how much mercy winter would show. When this public health crisis had first started people had said this would soon all be over. Such comments waned as the weeks flicked over. Now people were gathering firewood and clearing out those log burners in preparation.

The lock in the front door clicked open. Richard was back. She listened to him shuffle into the house, kicking off shoes, hanging up his jacket. There was an audible sigh when he saw that she'd left the ladder down. The ladder was to replace the staircase he'd pulled apart. It was an extra security feature that wasn't supposed to left open like this. People kept their doors locked, not so much against thieves, but for the lonesome roaming infected that sometimes passed by. Richard climbed the ladder, pulling it up onto the landing after him. Naomi glanced at her watch on the bedside table. Richard was late. Her watch still working for the time being, but at some point the battery would run out. If only she could read the stars and the sun. Perhaps they would have to make a sundial.

The door to her room opened, and Richard leant against the door frame, peering in. He looked shattered, a slumped figure of defeat. "Are you awake?"

"Sort of," she mumbled, still half-twisted in sleep.

She was in her own room. For solitary nights this was her resting place of choice. It was a warmer room, getting the sun in the morning. It would be a lot better to be in here for winter. "Mind if I come in?" he asked, not waiting for an answer. Barely seeming to move, he pulled off his sweater and T shirt in one, trousers dropped as he stepped, and he clambered under the covers with her.

Naomi hissed. "Christ, your feet are cold."

"You're warm."

Not for much longer, she thought as she felt his body envelope her. "Why are you so late back?"

He grunted, not happily, but as though it was to be expected. "Anna's dead."

Naomi's eyes widened, news of another death waking her up properly. Anna, the IT girl from London had not coped well with being trapped in one village for so many months. She was accustomed to money and privilege, access to all commodities twenty-four-seven. She had never had to work for a living. Idleness was the family motto. She had been fashionably thin when she had moved in. Since the outbreak she had been reduced to a shaking movement of bones, held together by the stench of alcohol.

"It was the booze," Richard said. "Not that I'm a doctor. But you can't drink that much and not pop off. I hadn't realised she had that much stashed away. The number of empty bottles..."

"I suppose the hopelessness got to her."

"People keep saying this will be over, just a couple of weeks more, but nothing changes. It's the same lack of anything on the radio reports. People need a little hope, some point in living. Else it begs the question why bother?"

"Don't be so maudlin."

He glanced across at her and broke out into a grin. "Not like it's the end of the world, eh?"

"Exactly." She shifted in bed as his hands found their way between her clothes at the waist, pulling them up over her head. Her hair was swept over her face. She scooped it back as Richard pulled her onto him by the hips. She'd never known a relationship to be so frequently sexually active, but the initial desire never burned down. There was that steady clinging need to be physically aware that one wasn't alone. To experience a naturally induced high. Perhaps that and the fact that with the trappings of modern living had been removed there was precious little other entertainment. She groaned as she felt him inside her flesh, hands on her breasts, nipples hardening against the creases of his palms. Just take me away from everything.

Later in the day, out in front of Richard's house, Naomi was picking red tomatoes. The plants were virtually dead, yellowed leaves drooping from the main stems. They would have lasted longer had they been in a green house, but some attempt at horticulture had seemed better than nothing. The plants hadn't gotten as big as they'd hoped, but they had been planted late in the year. Apparently. Naomi wouldn't know. She hadn't been particularly green fingered in the past and still harboured a secret thrill that she'd managed to get any edible fruit off plants she'd cared for. John had donated these runty plants to their cause. There had been a few too many even for John's extensive planting regime. Ann Douglas had lent Naomi a book on preserving. She and Richard were going to attempt preserving tomatoes. According to the book, chutney worked well. She'd been making vinegar with George Farthing's wife at their farm a few weeks ago. Mrs Farthing had even let Naomi have a bit of her starter to breed on in a tub so she could make more at home. She was starting to feel quite self-sufficient. Starting from scratch with everything, no nipping to the supermarket for a bottle of apple cider vinegar.

John strolled up from the village hall, heading back to his farm. "Naomi. Salvaging the last of your fruits?"

"Something like that."

John paused at the garden and glanced over the boxes of tomatoes. She had the same problem he and everyone else did with the current glut of vegetables. Some things could be stored, but others simply didn't keep. "What are you going to do with them?"

"We were going to try chutney."

"Ah," he nodded sagely. "That was what the vinegar making was for."

"How do you know about that?"

"George told me."

"Oh. Okay." For a moment she had worried that it was common knowledge. Not that it was a secret. It was just that food had a habit of being taken from houses and gardens. All for the common good, to be ferreted away in the stores at the village hall. Like any system of equality, some were more equal than others. Naomi had yet to see any of the pineapple chunks that Mark had stolen out of Richard's Land Rover all those months ago. "Just don't mention it in the village too much."

John smiled. "Worried Mark'll come and confiscate your hard work?"

"It's more than paranoia."

"Tell me about it."

There was a low, bassline thump in the distance. It was so distant that she could have imagined it. She glanced over at John, who didn't appear to have heard anything. She opened her mouth to say something, but was overtaken by a second thump, a muted boom. This second sound had registered with him, for he looked confused, glancing from Naomi to the village road, stepping back as if expecting to see something.

Richard leaned out of the open kitchen window. "Did you two just hear something?"

"Like a low boom?" Naomi glanced over her shoulder at him. "I don't know what it was."

"I'm putting the radio on." Richard disappeared back into the house.

There was another slight sound, followed by three or four more. It was difficult to distinguish where one started and another ended.

"It sounds a long way off," John said.

"Maybe there'll be something on the radio."

Naomi and John went into the house. Richard was in the living room, hunched over a cow-dung-powered radio. He was tuning in to the government channel. Since much of the telecommunication network had collapsed, and most importantly the electricity supply to many places had failed, television and the internet were not the best means of contacting the country anymore. There were a number of radio frequencies being used to reach out to survivors. Everybody and his mother were on the airwaves. The government and the army broadcast information on permanent loop, advising citizens of what to do and what was happening. It was the filtered, need-to-know version. There were journalists holed up in various parts of the country who couldn't stop doing what they did best. Anarchists and activists transmitted that they were looking to build a new state. Bored teenagers messing about.

Voices came forth from the static crackle, clearer and defined. "... for sanitation purposes. A number of heavily infected sites have been selected for clearance today in initial trials. If successful this means of disease control may be rolled out to other parts of the country. The public are asked to continue following current advice and remain in their homes. There is no need for panic. These will be controlled explosions in infected areas which have already been evacuated of survivors."

The three shared an uneasy look.

A new voice came onto the radio. "And now for some cookery advice. Using a few basic ingredients, you can make a nutritious meal for the whole family from ration pack number thirty eight..."

"Bugger," Richard swore. "We've come in at the end of the information broadcast. It'll be another hour before they get through all this crap and back to the important stuff."

"Try Gillian."

Gillian Nightingale was a journalist hidden away in a small tower just outside of Swansea. She told it as it was, and must have been sleeping with half the army in Wales for the wealth of her information and knowledge was frightening if even just some of it was true. She told more than any of the other broadcasting journalists, and whilst in calmer times it would have been assumed that she was just an imaginative lady who'd say anything for attention, the way the virus drama had transpired made her very plausible.

Richard dialled through the frequencies. Gillian's voice, loud and authoritative, soon came through the static. "It's just past four, so Hull will have started. The Royal Air Force had ten targets listed today, to repeat in order again, sections of London; Cardiff, Birmingham, Swansea, Newcastle, Carlisle – reputedly very heavily infected; Hull, Norwich and finally Middlesbrough. I have contacted what little of the government and army officials are left, but they refuse to admit to the facts. They have lost control, and a recent resurge in the virus has seen infection levels at an all time high. False hopes were raised when the infection started to reduce in the summer. This only worked whilst people remained in their homes. Food shortages have sent people scavenging, and worse, leaving their homes permanently. The infection has increased and spread. The government is cutting its losses and blowing up some of the worst areas, in the hopes that firebombing will eradicate the problem. Let me tell you, this is not working. I am in an undisclosed site outside of Swansea, and I have seen the result of the bomb attack this morning. Swarms of people, biblical herds have fled from the fires. They are a mix of infected and healthy, but the infected are ravenous, and the virus is spreading through these crowds at an unprecedented rate. Although I am not on the ground, I can hear it from my hiding place, and I can see it with the telescope I have here. The wasps nests have been smashed open, and there are waves of people, increasingly infected and insane, being guided by the natural features. They are following roads, filtering through the natural flow of the geography..."

"She sounds hysterical," Richard muttered, perhaps a little disappointed in what had usually been such a grounded, reliable source.

"She sounds terrified."

"These herds will be hitting towns and villages in their paths. This has been the worst planned attack, with no crowd control or regard for cordons that should have been erected beforehand. Hull, the current target, will be emptying as I speak. May God have mercy on our souls."

Richard turned off the radio. "She's hysterical."

There was an unnerving silence. Naomi's eyes drifted to the step ladder, nonchantlantly leaning into the open landing. Perhaps they would be following Richard's safety proceedures a little more thoroughly from now on.

"It's thirty miles from here to Hull," John said quietly.

"Something like that."

"How long does it take to walk thirty miles?"

Richard sat back from the radio, ran a hand over his face. "Depends how fast you walk, how long you go, how many breaks you take."

"Two or three days normally," John said.

"That's if you were doing it as a jolly hike and sleeping every night," Richard added. "Think that a marathon is twenty six miles, and people aim for about four or five hours."

"Isn't the world record just over two hours?"

"But these aren't marathon runners," Naomi interrupted. "They're frightened people, some infected..."

"Herds of infected is what Gillian said," John added. "It sounds like a plague."

"The virus will be rife. By the time they get here..." Richard shook his head. "She was right. If they were going to be that callous and start blowing up cities, they should have gone all the way and fenced it all off, trapped them in there. Oh, they'll get a few with the bombs and the fires, but they'll scare a lot more out. Then they're everybody else's problem."

Naomi stood up abruptly, surprised by how nervous this was all making her. Nervous, after everything that had happened. All that she had seen. This wasn't something new. It had been going on for months. "We'll just have to hope they don't come this way."

There was no direct response to her comment. John stood up. "I'll head back to the village hall; let them know we need to be ready."

"It might not happen."

"I'd rather waste my time getting ready for it." He nodded to Naomi, "I think I'm on guard duty with you tonight, aren't I?"

She nodded weakly.

"Nothing's going to turn up tonight," Richard reassured her. "It's like you said, they're not marathon runners. We've got a day or two. And they might not even come this way."

That night Beverley was sacked. The small, historic market town of Beverley lay a mere three or four miles from the boundaries of Hull. It took the heaviest hit from the plagues of infected. People were torn limb from limb by the hungry in the streets. Hunted down like vermin. The infected, the too far gone, the crazed cannibals, still had enough memory of being human to know how to stalk their prey. Rocks were thrown through windows. Any unlocked door was taken advantage of. Many of the first were caught unaware in their homes, spending an evening around the radio or an early night in bed. Many died, but even the survivors, limping away with broken skin and dripping blood succumbed to the virus' wrath eventually. The army of sickness swelled. Blood and gristle splattered on the hallowed streets around Beverley Minster. People fled screaming into the gathering mists on the Westwood, where the free roaming cattle didn't fare much better than the human race, being attacked by packs of blood-raged beings.

As darkness fell, a number of local army platoons combined to reclaim the city. They attempted to complete the job that the air force had failed to do. Little progress was seen on the ground. Carnage swelled the city to bursting point. There was no organised army or guerrilla target for the soldiers to combat. Instead they faced an array of deranged humans. Thousands of blood thirsty savages. The infected who remained in Beverley were put out of their misery. But many more, driven by a primeval survival instinct, fled to the misty night. With faltering electricity supplies the world had become inky black at night. Even urban centres suffered regular blackouts. Reports suggested the infected were showing herding tendencies. An alarming bi product of the disease created what seemed like an unnerving collective thought. There was infighting within the diseased, a weaker body being pulled apart to feed the walking hoards. However the need to find fresh, uninfected meat, encouraged the sick forward rather than simply turning on one another in a self-destructive last stand.

During the following day, the masses followed main arteries across the Humber and East Yorkshire. They were now split from the panic of army fire. They arrived at the next batch of natural targets: towns of Hornsea, Driffield, Market Weighton and Howdon. They devoured any small village that had the misfortune of being in their path along the way.

It was an ever widening circle, like ripples out from the original droplet of water. As time passed, the swarms would fluctuate, breaking off into sub groups. Some were killed, but new infected people were added to the gathering hoards. Naomi traced a finger up the map, moving from Market Weighton to Driffield. If the dying followed the main roads, they might miss Thixendale. It needed a few turns onto increasingly minor roads to navigate the way to the village. This was a particularly rural area and one might think it wasn't worth the trouble of exploration. Perhaps they would look at it and see no potential food source. Keep moving. Thixendale would be in today's branching out of the circle, but they might escape. Keep on walking. For all roads led to York.

"It's biblical," Ann Douglas, once shop keeper of the village, summarised the current discussions.

Naomi glanced up from the map. She'd become lost to her thoughts, not paying as much attention to what Ann and Karen were worriedly chattering about. They were more alarmist than the people she had just worked the night shift with. Neither of these two women was expected to take part in guard duty. They'd be safely locked up in their houses, hoping no monsters would come knocking at their doors.

"I suppose it is a plague sweeping across the country," Naomi sighed, closing the roadmap and setting it back on Ann's coffee table. "Like a plague of locusts."

"A plague of zombies," Karen muttered. "And nothing happened last night?"

"Not a thing. It was so quiet. We didn't even get any refugees. It's been the most uneventful shift I've done in a while, but I don't know whether I've been this on edge before now," she admitted.

"I suppose they could just head off down the main road to Stamford Bridge and miss us completely," Karen suggested. "We're a bit out of the way."

"I doubt we'd be that lucky. I hope all we do get is just a few lost stragglers."

"When do you think they'll come?"

Naomi looked from one woman to the other. They stared at her so expectantly, as if she had the answers, as if she was the authority on the infected. She just stood guard, held a rifle and hoped things wouldn't be as terrible as anticipated. "I don't know. Maybe tonight knowing my luck. This will drag out for weeks as a lot just roam in circles until they die off..."

"I thought no one was doing two nights in a row?"

"Only people who want to. But I think we're having extra people on tonight."

Ann smiled kindly. "It's so reassuring to know you're all out there protecting us."

It wasn't meant maliciously, but it made Naomi's hands tighten angrily, tendons sharpening. As if they were dispensable, volunteers, glad to sacrifice themselves for the greater good. The old and the young were the ones to be defended at all costs. What use would they be if all the able bodied adults were killed? Ann spoke as if this entire defence rota had been set up for her benefit. Was a non contributory sector was more important than everyone else? Naomi closed her eyes. She was becoming bitter and uncharitable. Tired. Beyond exhausted. She would turn into one of those short sighted whingers from her past life, the pre infection times at her admin job. Moaning about the elderly and the disabled, living off their tax payers' money and doing nothing for it. Forgetting that a society will be judged on how it treats and values its vulnerable. People who moaned black and white about those issues always neglected to consider that every one of us was capable of falling over that line, through age or sickness. Only now the complaint wasn't about money but about life.

"I should head over and find out where I'm going to be tonight." Naomi stood up.

"I'll come with you," Karen offered. "I need to get a few more medical supplies.

Outside there was a map pinned up on the notice board, showing the three road blocks in the village, and the names of people who would be manning the posts. Naomi was marked for the western blockade, at the road where she, Richard and Ed had first arrived all those months ago. Strange. Of the three blocks, that was the least likely to be hit. Certainly not until the infected had travelled as far as Malton and started backing through the villages in the Wolds. She was one of the best shots in the village, and Mark tended to use her at the eastern blockade, where four single-track country roads converged to enter the village. That was the hot spot, and she had assumed Mark would want her rifle there. Instead she had been put to the backwaters, as if to keep her out of the way. She didn't know whether to be offended or grateful.

Her eyes flicked over the lists of names. She was angry to discover that not only had Richard been put down for night duty but that he would be remaining at the most dangerous point, the east. He was currently on a day shift there, and to go straight into a night shift was too much. He was going to be too exhausted to be adequately alert. Mark Andrews could be an imbecile at planning.

Karen had gone into the village hall. Naomi was alone on the road. She stuck her hands in her trouser pockets and ambled up to the church, lost in thought. She barely noticed the man who ran down the road. She slipped in through the church gate, and leant against the graveyard wall, staring at the church. Georgiana was crouching near the door. Long gone were the pretty dresses and the blossoming girl. These days she was to be seen trudging in baggy jeans and shapeless lumpy sweaters, regardless of the temperature. Her hair was lank and unwashed, begrudgingly tied up in a bundle at the nape of her neck. She wore a permanent scowl. She looked over in Naomi's direction, affronted by the intrusion into her private sanctuary, and raised herself, slouching into the church. Somewhere inside a door slammed.

Naomi tapped her fingers against the stone of the wall, like a drum roll. She realised she'd left her rifle in the corner of Ann Douglas' living room. She'd have to retrieve it before heading out on the next patrol. She'd go up to the eastern block first, see how Richard was getting on. She'd barely seen him since that first broadcast about the bombings.

There was something between a shout and a scream which interrupted her silent planning. Naomi casually glanced over her shoulder, up the road past the village hall. Out in the open a man and a woman wrestled. The man quickly gained the upper hand. Naomi's eyes widened as she recognised the woman as Mrs

Thomas, Georgiana's mother. She lost her balance and went backwards on her heels, held up only by the man's fistfuls of her clothes. The man went in as if to kiss her, which sparked off further screams followed by muffled cries. Her legs convulsed. He pulled away from the kiss, blood running across the woman's face, and he let her drop to the ground, sobs bubbling up through the blood. He looked like a child still learning where its mouth was. Food was smeared across his cheeks, dripping from his chin.

"Gordon?" Naomi whispered as she recognised the man. He was very changed. His hair was longer, his body thinner, wasted. His clothes looked like rags held together by the stains. Mud, dirt, or perhaps worse. There was something wrong with his stare. Although he'd always been one to make any woman uncomfortable, this was different. A hunger that was not to be satisfied with sex. He met Naomi's eye for a moment. There were blood splatters, burst vessels in his eyes. It was only a second, then he dropped to all fours and attacked Mrs Thomas with his hands and teeth.

The sounds of the wider surroundings rushed upon her. Naomi turned around to look up the village, horrified to discover a busy road full of running figures. Wretches she didn't know. All she recognised was that hungry desperation of the diseased and the mad.

"Jesus," she whispered, dropping to her haunches and pressing her back up against the wall. They had been funnelled to the village through narrow roads and the natural weave of the valleys, old glacier paths now filtering a nightmarish flood. It had come, and although expected, it had still caught them unawares. She had her hands on her face in shame. Her rifle was still in Ann Douglas' house. And what of Richard's house? She tried to think of how it had looked when she'd left. She'd definitely locked the front door, she remembered, because she'd almost forgotten and had retraced her steps back up the drive to lock the door. The step ladder was on the floor in the living room. It didn't matter, no one was there. Richard was at the eastern blockade. That was where they were all coming from. The wall had fallen.

Screams lifted up from the ground, some of terror, some of starvation and many of madness. All at once the swarm was upon them. Twisting against the rough stones, Naomi raised her body just enough to be able to peer back out onto the street. She gripped the stones to stop herself shaking, holding the gasps within her throat. A couple of houses up from Ann Douglas' property, there was a teenage girl in a maxi dress sobbing uncontrollably. "Anthony!" she screamed. "Anthony!" Her pitch was going ever higher. Incapable, she stood waiting to be rescued.

Naomi watched as Anthony appeared, darting out from behind a hedge on the opposite side of the road. He took a few steps out into the road, but he wasn't quick enough. A woman had run into the garden, and swung a punch, knocking the teenage girl to the ground. There was a moment when she could have scrambled up and run away; either that or defended herself, but instead she lay back, whimpering the boy's name and doing nothing for herself. The woman threw herself at the girl, sitting on her chest and pinning her to the ground. There was an ear-piercing scream as the woman ripped the girl's ear from her face. She stuffed the flesh into her mouth before her eager hands started to make short work of the once pretty face before her. Fingers up and down like sewing machine needles, every time plucking up morsels of flesh.

Naomi felt sick. Her view swung away, back down the road where Mrs Thomas lay inert and silent on the tarmac. Gordon had a knife. He was the civilised cannibal, and was butchering the corpse. Having slit up through clothes and abdomen to breastbone, he now had the cavity open. Glistening, organs and entrails were lifted out and brought to his mouth. Thick dark blood ran like warm treacle down his arms. Another figure joined him at the feast.

She had barely moved and yet she was breathing as if she'd been running for miles. She had to get to her rifle. Pulling a loose stone from the wall, forcing herself forward, she opened the churchyard gate. She couldn't stand and cry for help. No one was coming to save her. Fight or die. But she wasn't a hero and she certainly wasn't a match for these monsters.

Crossing the road diagonally, in a panic and not sure which direction to look, Naomi lobbed her rock in the face of a clearly infected man who was getting to close. There was a sickening crack of bone as the stone punched him between the eyes. He staggered backwards, fresh blood gushing down his face. There was a cut like a break in the earth at a quake snaking over his forehead.

She didn't pause. Her feet moved without thought. No hesitation, she was merely focused on that corner of Ann's living room where her rifle was waiting. The front door was open. Inside was the sound of a heavy coughing fit. Perhaps Ann was watching the horrors from her front window, breaking down from the sight of such monstrosities. Naomi stumbled thoughtlessly into the living room, never thinking to check her back, or make sure the room was safe to enter. Ann Douglas was still in her chair, hands clutching onto the arms as if a terrified patient facing a filling in the dentist's chamber. A lithe, slender young woman was crouched in Ann's lap as if caught in a lover's embrace. The noise of Naomi's arrival distracted her. Ann wasn't blinking. She dumbly stared at the ceiling, her feet tapping a dull beat on the floor. Her windpipe had been torn out. Naomi gagged on disgust. She had only been speaking to Ann a few minutes ago. The girl upon Ann had disturbingly pale skin, making an awful contrast against the lashings of blood smeared around her mouth. Blood in varying stages of congealing was pasted through her hair, pinning it to her skin in places, gluing it together in thick clumps. She opened her mouth as if to say something, but the virus had destroyed that part of her brain and words were lost to her; only sounds remained. A piece of meat fell out of her slack jaw.

The rifle was in the far corner. Naomi took a fire poker from the neat selection of brass fireplace implements, whacking the girl around the side of the head as she made for Naomi. It was a greedy move to get two food corpses lined up for a night of feasting. The girl staggered away, a hand to her head as if to check her skull hadn't fallen apart. The impact seemed to have knocked some motor sense from her. She wobbled drunkenly, bumping into the wall as she tried to attack Naomi again.

Naomi screamed, summoning the strength and blind fury to finish this. Using the poker as a pike, with two hands, she drove it into the girl's head, entering through the eye socket and pinning her to the back wall. A gruesome wall hanging to remember hard times by. The girl stood in place, convulsing. Her jaw dropped open, her body weakly vomiting, the last escape of infection. Naomi staggered away, looking at her hands which were now slick with dark, infected blood. Searching desperately around her, she wiped her hands on one of the settee seat cushions, then picked up the teapot. She poured lukewarm tea over one arm then the other, desperately scrubbing and wiping to get rid of the disease.

Picking up the rifle, she felt somewhat reassured by the steady, unflappable form of the weapon. Out in the hallway there was a noise as the man she'd hit with the rock made his drunken, half-blind way into the house. He was following the woman with the flaming red hair. Attracted by the colour.

Naomi opened one of the front window panels and scrambled out of the house, hoping that the bloody carnage in the living room would be enough to keep him out of the way. In her mind, the mantra *keep moving* was playing on endless loop. She wasn't sure where she was going. She hadn't thought that far ahead. She hurdled the low garden fence, fleeing through the neighbour's driveway, scrambling over the next fence and into the property where the crying teenage girl had died. She was still on her back, her head now a rapidly diminishing bloody pulp. No recognisable features remained. The thing on top of her had hold of her head, and was repetitively smashing it down onto the tarmac, trying to crack it open like a nut. It was no easy feat, for it was difficult to keep a good grip due to all of the blood and slime. It required all of her concentration, and she was oblivious to Naomi running along behind her, jumping the next fence, and disappearing from her vicinity.

Back on the road, Kenny, the looming giant of West Yorkshire muscle, was standing over a much smaller man. A bloodied and crazed specimen. Kenny used a similar tactic in whacking the man's head repetitively against a fence post to finish him off. He'd woken up from a lie in after a long night shift, only to look out of the front window to see they'd fallen into hell. Behind him another of the infected was coming. In its excitement it had tripped up over its own feet, and was rapidly dragging itself over the tarmac, aiming for Kenny's ankle. Whilst an ankle grab wouldn't turn him into supper, a quick bite would send him down the unavoidable road to death. Naomi paused, raising the rifle and aiming, leaning her body against a tree to steady herself, and fired. The creature's head exploded into crimson, the grabbing hands dropping inertly to the ground. Kenny looked around, oblivious to what had been behind. He dropped the now deceased man. "Naomi..."

She shook her head. She had to get to the eastern blockade. She had to find Richard.

The short journey to the end of the village passed in a blur. She had switched off emotion and was automatically pushing her way back up the stream of infected hoards that poured into the village. The strangers were in various stages of infection, all terrified and with a heightened sense of mass hysteria. Not all tried to attack her, many running past as if this were a race. The drama moved fluidly, a natural ballet. She did not think, merely moving against the shape of attack, swinging the rifle around to hit a roaring figure square in the face, pushing him over onto his back. As he moved to sit up and grab at Naomi's retreating figure, she turned on him again, the rifle in both hands to smash down like a shovel upon his skull.

Riots. The sound was perhaps the worst, if one didn't stop to focus on any one particular section of the gore for too long. She'd never realised that a simple human scream could take on so many connotations, from horror and fear, to the agony of the infected, the constant, insatiable hunger, the fury of those defending themselves, and the sheer pain of those who were perishing. Gun shots, running, bodies colliding into parked cars, doors, smashing windows, thrown stones and bricks, bodies desperately trying to break in. It was a nightmarish organic whirr.

She reached the blockade. She had managed this far without being bitten. The fact that autumn was upon them and she was wearing a reasonably thick jacket had saved her arms from many passing scratches. At the village entrance it was bedlam. Naomi felt her heart drop like a rock as she saw the stretch of dying refugees streaming down from the roads as far as she could see. They all homed in on the village, the promise of food and shelter putting new purpose and energy into their steps.

Naomi couldn't see Richard. She pushed against the people entering through the destroyed blockade. Beyond where the barrier had once stood, Martin, one of the hippies from Harrogate, was twitching in the road. A number of crouched figures surrounded his body, hands dipping in and out to feed. They'd lost control. All those stupid rotas of guard duty and unwelcoming barriers had counted for nothing in the end. None of it mattered.

"Naomi!" Richard was folded up a tree, shaded by the autumn leaves. He was furious to see Naomi suddenly running through the crowds of infected towards the source of the attack as if she was going to plug it single handed. What had she come here for? She couldn't help, and she ought to have remembered in these situations she just had to run. It was every person alone.

He was still alive. Naomi relaxed. Thank God. She forgot momentarily where she was until a woman ran into her, taking her by surprise and pushing her back into the village. The woman took a fistful of her hair, dragging her head back, and Naomi panicked. What the hell was she doing running through the village into the main throng of the infected? She screamed, swinging the butt of the rifle around into the woman's face. And again and again in a blind terror. What idiocy might have brought her to her own bloodied death? The woman let go of her hair and dropped to all fours. As Naomi brought up the rifle to bring it down on the woman's neck like the guillotine, the woman looked up at her. The whites of her eyes were virtually pure red, her skin was mottled and blotched. She managed a word as her fingers scrabbled in the grit. Moments of lucidity when she remembered being human. "Plurse."

Naomi paused, gasping for breath. Oh Jesus. Which of us is the monster here?

She heard Richard yell from the trees: "Run!"

Pushed forward by the constant stream of people, hands into her back and getting her moving again, she was caught back in the stream. This time she flowed with the rush. She was generally ignored, as if it were assumed she was already one of the infected. Ever forward, blinkered and terrified. She slipped out to the right and up the side road to the pub. Most of the invaders had missed this lane, instead following the natural lead of the main road. She ran to the pub, thinking she might be able to hide there, but the door was open and there were screams inside. Clearly not everyone had missed the side road. She loitered, hesitatingly, unable to think further than the immediate moment.

Jill stumbled out of Julia's cottage, where she had been living since arriving in Thixendale. She had a large rucksack on her back. She saw Naomi standing dumbly in the road, rifle held down by her side, watching the passing carnage as if it wasn't really happening. She hesitated, before darting forward to tug on Naomi's free arm, as if to wake her up. "We have to get out of here."

Naomi glanced behind her. Jill looked terrified. She doubted she'd even seen the worst of what was happening in the village. Memories of what she'd fled from, perhaps. She nodded, pulling herself together. The two women hurried down to the end of the road, and out into the field. Naomi looked back now and then to make sure no one was following. A few had tottered down the side road, but between the women entering the field, and the sounds of the pub, they had decided to enter the building. Naomi and Jill were able to leave the village without anyone in pursuit.

Dusk was falling as they kept up a steady jog. They moved up and out of the village, past copses of trees, fields, steep valley edges and over the tops. Gates and hedgerows where the wild flowers had been left to grow as they wished, now with seed husks and brown stalks, red berries and orange leaves. The light faded, shadows lengthening and colours merging into greyness. The sky was thick with clouds and when night came, there would be little, if any visibility.

Naomi fell into the role of leading, despite the fact that it was Jill who was the outdoors woman, the survivalist. Beyond getting out of the village, neither of them had a particular tactic in mind, no destination. Naomi could only think of one place to go. She did not know what they could do when they arrived, but as it meant putting more distance between them and the village, it seemed suitable.

They reached an L-shaped valley, a dale as the locals called them, and ran up the side of the shaft. Towards the top the path started to descend into the pit of the dale. Jill didn't want to go to the bottom. It felt safer on the tops. She could see for miles, at least when it was light, and she would know what was coming. Here they were falling into a bottle neck. If the hoards came this way, they would all be funnelled upon them.

"Where are we going?"

There were trees up ahead, and she could hear the trickle of water.

"Wharram Percy."

The name was familiar. They reached a line of fencing. Naomi opened the gate and slipped into the enclosure. Jill knew the name and spent a few moments trying to remember, to flick through the catalogue of her journey between roughing it in the countryside and eventually finding Thixendale.

They followed the path to the mill pond, over the wooden bridge and up to the graveyard. Here they came to the ruined church, full of shadows and cooling silence. Naomi wrenched open the door and they ran inside, past the roofed section to the open air, the gravelled earth underfoot. Naomi sank to her haunches at one of the unglazed windows, her back against the wall. Jill, breathing heavily, shrugged off her rucksack and crouched in the middle of the church.

"We can't stay here."

Naomi closed her eyes. This was it. The place to run to if there was trouble.

"If they come here we'll be eaten alive."

"They won't come here. The geography doesn't lead anyone here. They'll head west out of the village." Naomi opened her eyes and looked at Jill. "We just have to wait it out here and then..."

"And then what? Go back? Do you think there's going to be anything left there except corpses and the walking dead?" Jill was furious, at what exactly was unclear. "Thixendale is gone. We've got to get moving. Go deep into the countryside."

Naomi gazed at the tall rucksack Jill was hugging. Tightly packed, expertly packed, just as the day she had arrived at the village. At the first scream of the breach, she must have started packing her things. No, rather that the rucksack had always been made ready in case of emergency. She only had to get to the cottage, collect her belongings and she was ready to leave. It had just been chance that Naomi had been in the road at the time, and they had fled together, because company is always preferable, reassurance that one is not overreacting. "You were just going to leave."

"Of course I was. The village is gone. Staying in one place is dangerous."

Was this what it took to survive? Naomi wasn't going to see the year out. "But what about the others? What about Chad?"

Jill's gaze wavered from her face and she looked to the ground. "He's gone, they're all gone."

"You don't actually know that."

"You saw what was happening. The only reason we're still okay is that we ran away."

If that was true, what was she to do? A blood-stained jacket and a rifle were hardly enough to survive out in the wilds. Naomi shivered. Autumn nights were not ones to be sleeping outdoors. "How do you think you'll cope in winter?" she asked. "There'll be no food to scavenge. What little there is will be locked up. People won't want to give to vagrants."

"I managed before."

"Yes, and that was spring, summer. How are you going to cope with your little tent in the winter? What if we get a winter like last year? Weeks of snow, minus fifteen at night."

Jill didn't answer. Naomi shivered. She would just have to wait here until... until morning or something happened, she didn't know what. Only that she was going no further. This was the agreed point.

"Do what you like," she finally said, jamming her hands into her armpits for warmth. "I'm staying here. I'll go back in the morning."

A figure was jogging down the side of the dale, trying not to slip on the dew-slick grass. Both arms were stuck out and wavering like a reluctant tightrope walker. Naomi had her shoulder pressed to the unearthly cold stones of the church wall. The survival blanket, crumpled and twisted, hung off her body like a cloak. The rifle was balanced at the base of the window, relaxed but aimed in the general direction of the jogger. She couldn't tell in this weak early morning light who the figure was; or more importantly what state their health was.

The figure disappeared behind the line of trees. The path remained hidden from there until it re-emerged at the graveyard. At that point she would be close enough to see the whites of their eyes, or perhaps the reds. She glanced back into the interior of the church. Jill was in her sleeping bag under the roof at one end of the church, using the rucksack as a pillow. She had stayed the night out of an odd-formed duty towards Naomi. Naomi hadn't requested a thing of her. Perhaps she simply hadn't known what else to do. Despite Jill's noble sacrifice, it was Naomi who kept guard. Only Naomi who realised they were now three in Wharram Percy.

The sound of movement through unkempt, dying undergrowth crept upon the church. Normally English Heritage employed a part time site manager. Now winter would be the only one to tend the land at this historic site. The figure reappeared at the edge of the graveyard. Naomi's breath caught in the back of her throat. Richard. She moved to shout out, then stopped herself. Which Richard was this? One she knew or one slowing deteriorating from infection? A slow death he would try to drag others into.

He moved into the graveyard slowly, stepping around the graves, searching the area with increasing urgency. "Naomi?"

So he wasn't an incoherent monster yet. Naomi gripped the rifle, and stood up in the window.

"Oh, Jesus." Her appearance made him jump. He started towards the church. "Are you?"

She shook her head. "You?"

"No. I was stuck up that sodding tree."

Her grip on the rifle slipped. A saddened smile escaped onto her lips. She hurried through the church, her footsteps drawing Jill out of her slumber. Slinging the rifle over her shoulder, she came through the door and into the graveyard. Richard met her halfway in a bear hug, burying his face into her tangled hair. "You scared the bloody shit out of me, running amongst them like that."

Jill stood in the church entrance, watching the two embrace. No one had arrived here for her. She'd made no contingency plans with anyone. "How is the village?"

Richard looked away from Naomi. "Jill." He sounded surprised that anyone else would be there. "Are there many of you here?"

"Just me and Jill."

"It's pretty much over," he told them, not making it clear quite what 'it' was referring to. "There's just a few stragglers we're clearing up. Other than that, they've just headed back out the village. There's just the clear up to do."

"So there's still people...?"

"People left? Yes."

Jill returned to the church, quickly rolling up the sleeping bag and survival blanket, packing them away. As she left the building, Richard noted the large rucksack she was carrying.

"Are you coming back with us?"

She wondered if she would regret this. "I'll come and see what the situation's like."

Despite the distant sound of voices, of movement and of birds twittering in the background, there was an uncomfortable, desolate soundlessness upon the village. A dejected defeat.

They returned by the route Naomi and Jill had followed of the destruction yesterday evening. On the approach to the village boundary they could see signs of the clear up. People dressed in varying degrees of biohazard protection were working. Some were togged up in the professional gear the army had left for emergencies. The image of professionalism then disintegrated down to those who had created homemade versions. The supplies left by the army simply weren't enough for disasters of this magnitude.

On the walk back Richard had told them that the colonel had tried for hours to contact the army on the radio to get reinforcements, but there'd been no reply. Villages all across west Yorkshire had been attacked throughout the afternoon and night. Like a tidal wave of blood, the infected continued to roam the countryside, clawing and biting at whatever they came to. The army were pinpointing certain herds of infected, effectively wiping them out. It was an endless task. The original exodus from Hull had broken apart into so many sub sections, that there simply weren't enough soldiers to hunt down and exterminate them all at once. They were working their methodical way through the danger, but if the infected came to an unguarded village, civilians were on their own.

A figure in hooded overalls and mask stepped out of Julia's cottage, where Jill lived, and shut the front door. A diagonal line of paint was sprayed across the door. A careless, long, dripping red line. The mark of the dead. Replacing the can in a bag, the figure glanced up the road as the three stragglers returned to the village. The mask was pushed back up onto the figure's forehead, revealing the face of Mark Andrews. "Where the hell have you been?"

"I went to get Naomi," Richard said flatly, ignoring the scolding in Mark's voice.

Mark looked from Richard to Naomi. For a moment he looked as though he were about to break out into another angry tirade. He faltered, as if the words were breaking apart in his mind. It had been a long night. In truth he was thankful to see three more uninfected people. And that the two women had survived. "We've run out of proper protective gear," he told them. "Go to the village hall, we've got rubber gloves, electrical tape. Get protected as much as you can then come and help with the clean up." His eyes flickered to Naomi's rifle. "Keep your weapons with you at all times. We can't be caught off guard again."

Jill marched up to her front door, already possessive of her territory, despite the fact that less than twenty-four hours ago she had been prepared to leave the village without a thought. "What's happened in here?"

Mark looked back to the line he had painted over the door. "It's clear of living infection. All properties have to be checked: houses, sheds, garages, gardens. When they're clear of living infection, we mark a line on them. When the infection is removed, the property is crossed off." He swung an arm over the line, as if to paint on a bisecting line.

"Living infection..."

"To be blunt, anyone who is infected needs to be shot, whatever stage they're at. Then all remains need to be removed, blood splatters disinfected."

"You're just shooting people like rabid dogs?"

"This disease needs to be contained. We don't want yesterday happening again." Mark regarded Jill's well-packed rucksack. "Perhaps you missed the magnitude of what went through the village," he sneered. "But I know Richard was with us through the night. And I saw Naomi moving through the village when it first started. They'll know what I mean."

Jill glared at him, blood rushing to her face. She didn't like being told off. Although she wouldn't admit it, she did feel guilty for only coming back to the village now. She wouldn't defend her actions, but when the troubles were over, she'd realised she needed to come back to the cottage for somewhere cosy to spend the winter. As good as she was at living rough; winter was not fun in a tent, especially if it was going to be as bad as the last winter.

"So my cottage is clear?" Jill finally managed to ask.

"Of living infection," Mark said. "There's a body in the living room that needs dealing with."

Jill visibly weakened.

"All infected material is being gathered at the eastern blockade," Mark continued, referring to the junction where Richard had been yesterday. The point of entry. "Chad's digging a pit with the JCB on top of the hills. We'll drive all the material up there and burn it."

Jill tentatively put her hand on the door handle. If she was going to stay here, she was going to have to deal with this. "There's some cleaning stuff in the kitchen," she said. "I'll start on this."

Mark nodded. "I'll get a wheelbarrow."

Richard and Naomi left them, intending to head for the village hall. As they approached the cross road, Naomi found herself searching through the air for Richard's hand. The morning after felt even more terrifying than the tidal plague of yesterday. Figures in varying degrees of protective clothing trudged back and forth, carrying heavy buckets, pushing wheelbarrows, or in one case a couple of men pulling a small trailer usually fitted to the back of car. Up at the entrance to the village a great mound of carnage was building. Lifeless bodies piled like ragdolls. Bullet holes left gaping holes in heads. Faces had been torn off, expressions carried blood ravaged angry mouths. Limbs stiff like kindling. Glistening masses of flesh, buckets of gathered entrails, the results of litter picking. Heavily soiled clothes and sheets were in crumpled bails. They were only good for the fire pit now.

The oil-thirsty squeak of a wheelbarrow, a slender body flopped inside, legs and arms hanging over the edge, jolting, quaking with every turn of the wheel. Naomi watched it go by, mesmerised by the remains of the human head. The face had been completely torn off, and the cranium had been opened. There was a gaping bloody hole where the brain had once sat. A bloodied pulped remain of a head. The result of a macabre and sickening cannibalistic orgy. She recognised the now-stained dress that the body wore. It was the girl who had screamed for Anthony. She had stood in the front garden and neglected to defend herself. She had just waited for the man to fix her problems. Naomi felt weak headed, and breathed deeply, immediately regretting it. The smell was intensifying. Rotting flesh, blood, meat, iron. She felt Richard's hand tighten around hers. He'd missed the initial gathering of the bodies, leaving the village as soon as he could to look for her. He had jogged a circuit from his own home, to John's farm on the hill and across to George Farthing's farmstead, before remembering Wharram Percy. Nothing could prepare a person for this sight. For the smell. For the sounds. For the overwhelming atmosphere.

A gunshot in one of the houses echoed out into the street. Aside from the sounds the big clean up, of quite words of work, there was no conversation. A scream was heard, a second shot, then silence. A figure came out of a house and sprayed a diagonal line on the front door. The immediate threat was removed. As her eyes dared to flick over the village, she noticed more and more of these lines. They were all only single lines at present. Even when the bodies, the lumps of flesh and the soiled fabrics had been removed, there would still be the disinfection to complete. A fresh breakout could not be risked. This would take all day.

As they neared the village hall, the door to the church was wrenched open and Georgiana hurried from its sanctuary. As she reached the gate, she turned back to the church and with intense venom, screamed "Retards!" at the seat of God. She stumbled onto the street and rather dramatically stormed home. In all the movement, twisting and spitting, the shape of her body had pushed out against the baggy shirts and sweaters, those shapeless boxes that she had taken to wearing. Naomi realised that the girl was pregnant.

The door to the church hung open, and the noise of discussion seeped out. Naomi looked over at Richard. "I thought he'd said the village hall."

Richard shrugged. "Sounds like they're in there."

They walked up the path to the church and slipped in. Inside there was a sparse collection of villagers, most sat up at the front. Aside from a couple here and there, people were alone in their own personal section of pew. They all looked ahead to the front, where a man Naomi couldn't remember the name of, was up in the pulpit. His hands were fists, and he leaned forward and out of the pulpit like a figurehead on a ship. He reached so far forward that it was somewhat impressive that he didn't topple out into a heap on the cold stone floor of the church.

"Sinners!" the man screamed, his face puce, his fist slamming upon the pulpit as if the first item of the auction had just been sold. "We had led godless lives, and this is his wrath come upon us. We have taken the marks of God upon ourselves, and now we must repent."

This wasn't the biohazard protection point that Mark had sent them to. She was surprised that this hasn't happened sooner. In times of terror people turned to faith, and the insecure nutters forced their own warped version of religion onto whomever was prepared to listen.

"Naomi, Richard." Beverly, the hippy from Harrogate, appeared at the back of the church like an usher. The preaching paused and the villagers shuffled in their seats to see who had come to join the congregation.

"Have you been marked by God?" Beverly asked.

"Marked by...?" Naomi was bewildered. Beverly would have been the last person she'd have expected to turn to Christianity. The woman had always come over as a positive pagan. She remembered seeing Martin being eaten alive yesterday. Did Beverly even know? Had someone taken advantage of her grief? Naomi blinked, focusing on Beverly. There was something wrong, and the realisation seeped into her like an unearthly cold. The redness in the woman's eyes was not from crying. There were the first signs of blotches, of bleeding under the skin around the mouth. She looked to the rest of the congregation. They were all locals. They were frightened. More than the dumb horror of the cleanup crews, these people could hear a clock ticking. Their veins swelled with the HEMO 10 virus. She recognised them, people she had lived so compactly with these past months. Taken guard duty with, worked out in the fields. Part of a community collective that was disintegrating. She noticed Jean, and the retired solicitor Edward Ryan amongst the gathering. She shook her head. "We're not..."

"Sinners!" the man in the pulpit roared. "You've not been chosen by God to be saved."

"Saved?!"

Beverly's mouth turned to a bloodless flat line. "Get out."

Richard pulled on Naomi's arm, dragging her from the building. She couldn't think straight, still wheeling back on the idea that someone could believe being infected was being selected by an unseen, higher hand. As if you were one of the elite. As if sitting in a church and screaming about sin was going to save you. And the reaction when they'd realised Naomi and Richard weren't infected.

It wasn't jealously; rather disgust. As if they were two different races, sworn to hate one another.

The church door slammed shut and Richard bundled Naomi back to the street. "Everyone has their way of coping."

"Is the church empty?" Mark Andrews was marching towards them, accompanied by David, Kenny, and Linda, a bulky fifty year old who had been a secretary back in the old world. She was powered up by an industrious hobby of bread making by hand that had trained the strength of her arms to that of a pit bull. She was a hard worker but distinctly merciless, even back in the simple pleasures of administration and flour to concern her days. Recent events had only hardened her resolve. She carried a hand gun, and Naomi supposed she had the perfect mentality for dealing with the unpleasantness that had to be done. Her face was hard set, Mark looked particularly grim, but Kenny broke out into a grin when he saw Naomi. "Hey, Naomi," he said. He hadn't seen her since she'd shot an infected man that had been going for his ankles. She'd run off into the frey, and he'd assumed she'd have been lost, only that he hadn't seen her body yet in the clear up. It was a good surprise to see that she'd come out of it uninfected. "Good to see you made it."

She smiled weakly. "You too."

Mark was impatient. "Can we cross the church off our list?"

"There's a congregation in there."

"A congregation?" Mark sounded disgusted. "We have a clean up here; an entire fucking village to disinfect. Everyone has to help out with this. It is not the time to commune with God. I don't care what..."

"They're infected," Richard interrupted. "They're frightened and I think they're just looking for some comfort."

Mark pointed at the church. "It's full of the infected?"

Linda started up the church path.

"Wait," Richard started. "They're not dangerous. They're only in the early stages."

Mark ignored them and started after Linda, David trotting at his heels.

Kenny, something of a giant, stepped out in front of Richard and Naomi. "Guys, I know this is harsh, but they're not going to get better. We can't risk another breakout. You saw what happened yesterday. This disease turns people into psychos, and when they're in a group they just go nuts."

"There has to be a more humane way..." Naomi started.

Kenny sighed. "Normally I'd say yes. But we've been trying to hold the village all night. Since dawn I've been going around shooting the stragglers who didn't fuck off out of town with the rest of them. I've been gathering up half-eaten bodies, bits of guts, shit... we're all tired. I don't think nice is an option anymore."

There was a shot and the screaming started. The sensation of panic rushed from the church. Kenny ran up to the building to help the others as the shooting began in earnest. It was to be the final execution of the day. Nothing was sacred anymore. The shots flashed out against the stained glass windows. Naomi remained out on the road, transfixed by the church. She was intensely conscious of the fact she still had the rifle slung over her shoulder. She could have gone in there to help. She could play her role in eradicating the last of the virus from the village. Richard pulled her away from the church. "Let's go see how home has fared."

Richard's house survived better than others. The doors and windows had all been locked, and as luck would have it, no one had attempted to break in. There was just one body, face down on the patio around the back of the property. The man was dead, his neck broken. When they'd rolled him over and checked his eyes, his skin, it was clear that he had been infected. His corpse still was infected. The virus would be in his blood, even if his body had ceased to function. Richard took the body away in a wheelbarrow. Even though there were only a few drops of blood on the patio, Naomi set about scrubbing the entire surface with an intoxicating mix of bleach and water, which made her light-headed and grumpy.

They spent the rest of the day helping neighbours who were still alive clean out their properties. Houses now empty also had to be cleaned, for no one wanted to leave a potential health risk. Now that the village population had been cut so brutally, they might be able to take more refugees. If wandering strangers to the village could ever be trusted again after what had happened in the last twenty four hours. Naomi found herself working in Ann Douglas' now empty home, sanitising the blood soaked living room. The chair where Ann's ravaged body had been. The slick bloodstains down the wall where Naomi had finished off the stranger. All removed, the first tick crossed off on Ann's drive.

"I don't know what the hell had gone on in here," one of the villagers had said, making conversation. "I found a woman attached to the wall. The fire poker had been rammed through her head. It was stuck in the wall, Jesus, it took a bit to pull it out."

Naomi stared at the deep hole in the plaster. They'd peeled off a lot of the wall paper in the end and thrown out Ann's armchair to go on the fire. A section of carpet had been cut out where the two pools of blood had been. These were added to the pile for incineration. Everything else had been doused with bleach, then the doors and windows locked and the keys taken over to the village hall. Aside from the living room, the rest of the house had been untouched, tidy and clean, with a touch of lace and lavender, waiting for the old shopkeeper to retire for the night.

As dusk fell upon the tired, harrowed survivors, the bulk of the work was done. The last remains at the east were being taken up to the fire pit, and all houses had been cleaned out. If one disregarded the circumstances, it had been a particular success story of community spirit coming together.

Naomi didn't want to see the fire. She returned home. The air was chilled, but she'd not stopped all day and was still warm. She'd had to throw her jacket onto the pile for destruction. The fabric was blood splattered from her escape from the village. It had not improved with the clean up. She didn't ever want to see it again. Richard had driven up one of the last loads for destruction, so she went home on her own, feet set to automatic pilot. Fetching the step ladders from the kitchen, she climbed upstairs, pulling the ladders after her. She had turned the hot water on, heated by gas cylinders, which they tried to use sparingly. After today she felt justified in this little treat. She spent a good hour in the bathroom, in paranoia scrubbing every inch of her body, washing and re washing her hair to be sure there was no drop of infection resting on her. She spent a long time examining each eye to make certain there were no burst blood vessels; no first signs of sickness.

She went into the bedroom and drew the double curtains to keep in the heat and sat on the edge of her bed. The room was the warmest on the first floor, getting the most of the sun. There was no central heating these days. Any heat had to be retained, so everything but the bathroom and her room had been closed up on the first floor for winter. One room at the back was now used as a food store, although aside from what they had made or gathered themselves, there wasn't that much. All food was supposedly collective. They'd taken all the blankets, duvets and pillows and piled them on the one bed so that they would be able to sleep warm at nights.

Richard arrived back a couple of hours after Naomi. She listened to him rustle about downstairs, locking the front door and making sure all of the downstairs windows were secure.

"Naomi?"

She slipped out of bed and padded over to the open landing hatch. She rested the ladders against the edge to slide them down. Richard clambered up and drew the ladders back up, dropping the trapdoor in place.

"I put the hot water on."

"Good idea."

He looked exhausted. He was down to T-shirt and jeans. His shirt and jacket were missing. Probably too blood stained to be salvaged. "I think I'll go take a shower." Hot showers were a real treat these days. Usually they only had cold water.

Naomi nodded, and return to the bedroom. She sat down and grasped the edges of the mattress. What had happened? This shouldn't have been a shock. Months, seasons had passed since the HEMO10 virus had first erupted. They'd seen people die, countries fall, control disappear. They'd been sheltered in this little village, playing at guard duty, showing a lack of spirit to refugees, indulging in their communal farming. As if the world would continue, this would all blow over in a year or so. Things would go back to normal. Normality was gone, they were living the apocalypse, and things would only continue to worsen. They'd not taken a roll call, but the village population must have been halved at least. In one day. And now all the stupid protective measures they'd taken had ceased. The blockades weren't ever going to stop a hellish charge like that, and besides which they didn't have enough people any more to run the patrol rota. Anyone, anything would be free to run, walk, crawl through the village. People took their weapons home, locked the doors and watched suspiciously from upstairs windows. Tomorrow they were going to start boarding up the downstairs windows of the houses that were still in use. They were ready to meet the end of the world. One by one they would be picked off, torn to shreds, bloody limb dislocated and pulled from the trunk. Some would see the disease filter through their veins, others would starve. There was nothing good, nothing they could do for this to end. It would never end, only that with death they would be taken out of the continuation, one by one.

She stared down at her hands, which were shaking slightly. She could feel a knot in the centre of her chest. She knew that if she loosened it, it would release a desperate howl, a cry that she wouldn't be able to stop.

"Are you all right?" Richard stood in the doorway, steam curling off the surface of his body, still warm from the shower. Naomi was staring at nothing. The word for her stance was harrowed. Illuminated by a single lit candle on the bedside table. He could guess at what was going through her mind. The same things that had continuously tried to jump up and nip him as he'd worked tirelessly through the day. Everyone had lost themselves in the job to be done, but now that it was dark, they were left with their thoughts. People returned to their homes, locking the doors and checking that their guns, their clubs, their defences were close to their pillows. Wondering if there was anything good left. Any point. He was on the same page, but there were little shreds of hope to cling to. At least for some of them. He didn't know how some of the people coped when they sat alone at night, distinctly alone without any family, partners or real true friends. People like Mark Andrews, like Linda, perhaps even people like John Settle. John was genuinely liked in the village, but Richard supposed he still ended up in the same category.

Naomi smiled without conviction and looked as though she were about to cry.

"Come on." He walked over to her and crouched down, putting a hand around the back of her neck. "We're survivors. We came through this."

She put her forehead against his, closed her eyes and set her hands on his damp, warm shoulders. Survivors today, but what about next week? Next month? Just live day to day; even that was too long to consider. It would have to be just moment to moment. She felt those terrified shakes move up through her wrists again.

Stretching forward, she pressed her mouth onto his, hands moving across the top of his back. Richard responded, pushing back against her, drawing up her nightdress and pulling it up and over her head. They moved onto the bed, Naomi gasping as he entered her quickly, urgently, nuzzling into the side of her neck. She clutched onto him, and as she felt him come, the first tears came out of her eyes, and she couldn't stop. Richard crossed his arms and legs around her frame and rolled the pair of them onto their sides, pulling the collection of blankets and duvets over, so that they were lost in a cave of bedding. She sobbed into his shoulder. Even if she had felt up to talking, she couldn't have put this grief into words. He stroked her hair. "We'll get through this," he whispered. "I'm still here. You're still here."

"You won't ever leave me?"

"We'll always be together."

Any other year and people might have been pleased. This year no one wanted to see the snow. Snow meant cold temperatures and frozen pipes. The electricity had been turned off months ago. Most people didn't have central heating. In villages like this, some properties still ran off oil or gas cylinders, which they'd saved for the winter. Whatever they still had wasn't going to be enough if the winter continued in this fashion. It had barely gotten above zero today.

Today was the one day when the pipes could burst, frost could engrave the insides of windows and the walls become ice and no one would care. They were comfortably drunk and determined to hold on to some traditions, even if they had to staple their smiles in place.

With the taste of sloe gin still laced on her tongue, Naomi wobbled out of the bathroom and paused in the hallway of the old farmhouse. It was dark outside already, and when she touched the glass she realised the thin layer of ice was on the inside. Outside light flakes of snow drifted through the air. The world was draped in white, creating an eerie twilight where it would never be completely dark.

Naomi reached up to brush loose hair back off her face. Her hairstyle had progressively been falling apart through the afternoon. She and winced as the sharp spikes of the holly leaves bit on her fingertips. A sprig of holly was a stupid hair decoration. She was supposed to be a Christmas pudding. Fancy dress had taken on a more inventive air this year. She left the decoration in place and headed towards the staircase.

Down below in the main living room, lit by candles and an open fire, a select group of survivors were celebrating Christmas together. Food was sparse, but between them they'd saved up enough vegetables, pilfered enough eggs, found enough dried fruit, and plenty of alcohol to make the day go with a swing. There was even a cake that had been iced with a mix of icing sugar and water that had dried like rock. Party hats had been made out of coloured paper, and rather than the queen's speech, they'd listened to Gillian Nightingale on the radio. No one was actually sure if the queen was still alive. After the wireless entertainment, there followed a comedy sum of the year performed by Rab. It should have been depressing all things considered, but by the time they got to it, everyone was suitably drunk laugh at anything.

Naomi got to the bottom step and glanced up at the mistletoe suspended from the ceiling. A rather stupid touch considering the men outnumbered the women two and a half to one at this party. Herself and Jill were the only women attending. The others were Richard, Chad, Kenny, Rab, and of course, their dear host, John Settle, who had sent out hand written invitations including a list of things they would have to start collectively hoarding for the day. It was a waste of resources, but they had all needed today. It was an attempt at normality and a little morale booster. Fun could be had. The cow dung batteries were still a success, and were powering a little portable CD player that sang the songs of their lives. There was a roar of laughter from the living room.

"What are you doing hiding out here?" Richard was suddenly in the hallway. She was stood on the first step, and they were almost the same height. He glanced up at the ceiling. "You seem to have come to a halt below the mistletoe."

"It's a problem."

"Really?" His hands had slipped around her waist at some point and she pressed her hips against him. Grinning like a simple minded fool, she leant in to kiss him, her sprig of holly rolling forward and getting caught on his paper hat.

"You taste of gin."

"You taste of whisky." She pulled back and glanced to the front door. "Can you pass me that brown paper out of my coat pocket?" She pointed at the large red winter coat hanging by the door.

Richard stepped across and took the packet from her coat. "What is it?"

She shrugged mischievously. "Open it and see?"

"Oh no, you've not actually done presents have you?"

"Hey!"

He winked at her, as he ripped open the paper. A red scarf, long and in one basic stitch, with a few accidental holes speckled through, unravelled itself in his hands.

"I made that."

He stuck his thumb through one of the holes. "I couldn't tell."

"That's taken ages to do, for I am not a knitter and you should be impressed." It was her produce from wool and needles taken from Ann Douglas' home. She took the scarf and wrapped it around his neck, pulling on the ends as if to strangle him. "Wear it always and think of me."

"I will. Thank you."

"Shall we go back in?" She stepped down onto the ground floor; Richard swung her around so they were resting against the coats hung up in the hall.

"In a minute. I know this has all been back to basics..."

"You don't like the scarf?"

"I love the scarf." He reached into his back pocket, taking something out but keeping it concealed in his fist. "But I wanted to do something." He flicked up a smooth, flat stone, perhaps four or five centimetres across, held between thumb and finger. "This is a stone I picked up on the beach when I was in Papua New Guinea. Might have been a fishing weight. I don't know why I picked it up, but I carried it around in my pocket all over that island, all the weeks we were filming. And with a shoe lace and a bit of fancy knot work..."

She laughed as he revealed the extent of the homemade necklace. "That's very impressive." She accepted the gift. The stone tapped against the top of her chest as she knotted it up behind her neck. "Thank you."

"Come on, come on," Rab stormed into the hallway. "Never mind smooching in the coat rack. We're going outside to let the New Year in."

"But it's Christmas."

"We're still going outside." He led the way, a bottle of single malt in one hand, and stalked out into the snow. The others followed in varying degrees of eagerness, pulling on boots and coats. Footsteps crunched down into freshly laid snow, breath clouding out into the darkness. The lights from the farm house window were like a beacon in the cold, quiet countryside. There wasn't a breath of wind. The snow gently drifted down, catching on eyelashes and strands of hair.

"Should we really be strolling out making all this noise?"

"Aye, what if one of the undead gets us?"

"If those bastards turn up and want to eat me, they can fuck off," Rab declared belligerently, wobbling ahead through the snow.

There were still the infected that passed through but things had slowed. There hadn't been such a great attack as the one a couple of months ago. The visitations became sparser, and the crowds of the sick were much smaller. Perhaps the cold would kill off what little disease remained.

"It's not the infected we have the most to fear from," Jill muttered, pulling on her gloves. "The cannibals these days aren't driven by the virus, they're driven by starvation."

"That's just rumours."

"I heard it on the radio the other day."

"Yeah, well, it's not happening round here. This is the countryside. We've got plenty of food."

"Plenty of potatoes."

"Nothing wrong with tatties. I'd quite happily live on mashed potato and gravy for the rest of my days."

"Except there are no more gravy granules to be had after this tin."

"Oh, shite."

Rab stopped and turned back to face the group. "Let's welcome the new year."

"It's only Christmas day," Jill reminded him.

"It's the beginning of the new year for us. From now on, things are going to be great." He thrust up the whisky bottle into the air, as if to say cheers, before tilting it back, missing his mouth at first, to drizzle the peaty liquid in.

"You christening the new snow?" Kenny laughed.

"Aye, christening the snow, great plan." Rab unzipped his flies.

"I'm going to be sick," Naomi muttered, breaking off from the group.

"Are you of a sensitive nature?"

Reaching the side of a wall, she rested an arm in its snow-topped surface and leaned forward as the convulsions rippled up her throat. She vomited. Her Christmas cake, warm and steaming, splattered into the snow.

"Atta girl, Naomi!" Rab shouted as if she was being sick to get into the spirit of things.

All this good, wholesome living has turned me into a lightweight, Naomi thought. She'd never been a heavy drinker, but she could always manage a few drinks. Here she was, throwing up like a school girl who'd tasted her first beer. It certainly said something for underestimating the alcohol volume of homemade booze.

"Are you all right?"

Naomi wiped her mouth with the back of her hand, and glanced up as Richard walked over to her. She picked up a handful of snow off the top of the wall and swilled her mouth out, spitting it to the ground. "Yeah, fine," she sighed. "That sloe gin was potent stuff."

"We're not used to all of this good living these days."

"No." She rubbed her eyes. "I feel a bit rough. I think I'm going to go lie down." The plan had been for everyone to stay at the farm through to Boxing Day anyway.

"Come on folks," John was heading back to the building. "Traditions must continue. It's scrabble next."

"Scrabble, my arse," Rab muttered. He watched Naomi and Richard wander in together. Chad and Jill were also a little off from the main group. And then came the bachelors, John, Kenny and himself. The sexes weren't well balanced here at all. It was

Christmas and he was supposed to have good fun, a good whisky and a good shag. "Hey, John," he called out, following the others back to the house. "Why didn't you invite Karen?"

"Not particularly keen on her husband," John answered honestly. "And these days life seems too precious to spend it with people you don't like."

"Fair enough," Rab agreed. He stamped off the snow from his boots before going back into the warm farmhouse. It was a shame never the less, because Karen didn't seem that keen on her husband either. He could imagine she was spending a particularly grey day with the man. Thinking about him, he'd bet. Why did she not just leave the man?

The front door was slammed shut, bolted and locked. "All right people, the scrabble tournament will be commencing in five minutes."

Naomi started up the staircase again.

"Naomi, you're not away to your bed already?"

"I just feel a bit rough." She looked back at Rab. "Just for a rest. I'll be back down in half an hour."

"I'll hold you to that. If I have to play scrabble, no one else is getting out of it."

"Don't worry. I'll be back."

Naomi didn't wake up until daylight touched the ground. She rolled over in bed, bumping into Richard who lay gently snoring, oblivious in his happy drunken slumber. Grumbling, she slipped out of the bed, gasping as the chill hit her legs, and tottered over to the window. It had stopped snowing. The sky was as white as the ground. It would probably snow again today. A slight wind had picked up and it looked positively bitter outside.

Her stomach groaned and she felt a wave of nausea swell up. Whatever she'd thrown up last night wasn't quite finished with her. She took a boiled sweet out of her trouser pocket; something to distract her, and pressed her face to the window pane, feeling the ice rush through her skin. Christmas was over, and although they weren't quite at the end of the calendar, it felt as though it was the start of a new year. Her eyes swept over the white landscape, trees like black line drawings cut out against the uniform absence of colour. Fences and walls picked out the field boundaries. There was a small copse of trees in the distance, where a few birds, black and flapping, took to the air and filtered across the sky. The copse was a tangle of trees and bushes, the details merging at this distance. She was about to look away when something stepped out from the undergrowth.

Something or someone. She leaned into the window frame, squinting to try and focus better. A human figure shuffling, walking slowly, almost robotically. Like a drunk who had woken in a ditch after a good night's drinking, and was trying to wobble back home. No one would go to sleep outside in this weather. Coming from that direction she couldn't think who it might be. Certainly no one from the village, and definitely not George Farthing. The figure was too tall and slender to be George. A refugee, perhaps, she mused?

Rolling the sweet around in her mouth, clanking it against her teeth, a sugary sweet saliva boosting her early morning blues. She picked up her rifle from beside the door and headed downstairs. The house was silent, the remains of the merry making in the living room, the fire glowing pleasantly. Rab was stretched out on the floor snoring loudly, scrabble pieces scattered across him like snow. Naomi went to the kitchen and downed a glass of water, hoping that would finish off the after effects of the alcohol. Through the window she could see the figure making slow progress, cutting the corner of the field. They must have seen the farmhouse by now.

In the hallway she pulled on her boots. Shrugged her body into her winter coat, wrapping a black and white checked scarf around her neck. She tugged a woollen hat onto her head, fingerless gloves on her hands, and slung the rifle over her shoulder. Drew back the bolts, unlocked the door and left the building, careful to lock the door behind her. She paused in the yard, thinking that although she had her rifle, it wasn't the best method of defence these days. The village's supply of ammunition was getting low. As a half-hearted thought, she picked up a spade that was leaning against the wall. The snow slid easily off the metal surface. Hoisting it up, she propped it jovially on the opposite shoulder to the rifle, and walked out of the farm.

She wasn't sure what she had been expecting, or what she had planned to do, but somehow this had not been it. Cases of infection had decreased dramatically in the last few weeks. Between extermination, bombings and local executions and purges, a lot of the infected had been dealt with. Combine that with the weather and the lack of food, and the infected were less a force of apocalyptic destruction and more a hobbling collection of wretches, lethargic and half-frozen.

This man did not appear to be an exception. The breath steamed out of his mouth like a train at full speed, but his body did not match the eagerness. He moved slowly, dragging his left foot after him. He was dressed in a suit and a woollen coat, smart wear for a winter's day in the city, but out of place in the countryside. His hair, once gelled, was loose and tangled, leaves and other scraps of congealed items caught up between the strands. He soon clocked Naomi standing in the top corner of the field, and changed his course for her. As he neared, she could gauge the full extent of his infection. His hands were grimy, the finger nails black, as if he had been digging in the ground. In fact his fingertips looked positively rotten. It wasn't just surface discolouration, but rather something that went deeper. His coat was ripped at the shoulder seams, the top of his left arm showing through coat, jacket and shirt. It was bloodied pulp merged with woven fabric. Blood and grime were encrusted around his mouth. His eyes were red, his nose had been bleeding recently and his skin was blotched. He didn't speak, rather growled and gurgled, as if the noise itself would encourage him onwards.

He's a long way gone, Naomi thought, but he must be quite tough to have gotten this far. "You're infected, aren't you?" she called to him, not sure why she was attempting conversation with someone who had obviously lost his faculties a while ago. She perhaps wasn't all settled in her mind either, groggy and feeling ill after yesterday.

In response the man raised his hands and increased his pace towards her. He might have been coming for an embrace, but it was doubtful. She took the spade from her shoulder. "I think that's close enough."

The man ignored her. He continued to approach in his steady lumbering fashion.

Naomi reached out with the spade as he stepped forward and the edge of the blade gently met with his chest. He looked down at the blade, bemused by its appearance. She pushed, and he fell backwards thoughtlessly, a domino without a line to follow after. Helpless in the snow, he reached up at her, his right arm doing all of the work. Naomi calmly stepped down on his forearm, pressing his limb into the snow. She stared down at his ravaged face. If this had been the summer, and he had been well fed, he would have torn her face off by now. But instead he was starving and his body was so cold and undernourished that he could barley move. There was nothing that could be done for him. She placed the spade over his neck, resting just below his adam's apple. The steel edge grated against the beard like a blunt shaver. She put her right foot on the top rim of the spade blade, gripped the handle with both hands and directed all of her energy downwards. The spade broke through his skin and windpipe, splurges of deep red blood gushing out into the snow. There was some hesitation at the spinal column. She gritted her teeth and pushed her full weight into getting the spade to the ground. There was a sickening crunch as she broke through his neck to the other side, and the head was severed from the body. There was a slight gasp of surprise on his face as he stared up at the white winter sky, and life departed from his body.

The spade remained upright between head and torso, the red pool of snow spreading rapidly. Naomi stepped back a few metres and stared down at the body. No one would ever know, and perhaps there was no one left who cared. But at some point he had been someone's son, someone's lover, perhaps even someone's father. They'd never know where he had died, what had become of him. Just as all the others who had come through the village and been slaughtered. The rabid girl who had been tearing at Ann Douglas. The last thing she would have seen was a fire poker being rammed at her face. Then it was all over, life so simply extinguished. For some there was a funeral and mourners. For others a question mark no one cared to consider over a name on the last electoral register. Either way did it really make a difference? Such desperation to survive, the uninfected and the infected, a primeval instinct that drove everyone forward. It was just there. But what really was the point of it all?

She didn't know how long she stood in the field, reflecting over the stranger she had dispatched that morning. Only that it must have been some time, for she had lost the feeling in her feet, and hadn't noticed that it had started to snow again. There was a light film of snow over her hood and shoulders, loose strands of hair blowing out from the rim of her hat.

"Naomi?"

There were footsteps behind. She heard the voice, the question, but didn't turn around.

"Thank god for that red coat. You stand out miles off."

"Did he attack you?"

"Doesn't look like he'll be bothering anyone now." Jill stood at the head, hands on hips, looking down.

Richard took Naomi's hands, shocked by how icy the bare fingers protruding from the fingerless gloves were. "How long have you been out here?"

"Is she all right?"

"Naomi?" He put a warm hand to the side of her face. "He didn't hurt you, did he?"

The heat rushing through her skin seemed to wake her up. Her eyes focused again, and she was looking at Richard's face close up. He was baggy eyed, probably still a little hung over, with a week's worth of beard and scruffy hair that poked out from under his hat.

"I'm fine."

"Are you sure?"

"I've not seen one of these bastards for a few weeks," Rab was saying in the background, pushing a wheelbarrow through the snow. "Nice weather for a bonfire though."

"I saw him from the window," Naomi murmured.

"Are you guys all right to deal with the body?" Richard asked. "I think I'm going to take Naomi back, get her warmed up."

"Sure," John threw him the keys. "The aga's on, so you should be able to get some warm water pretty quick."

She was vaguely aware of the concerned expressions on people's faces as she was led away, like a mental patient that they had to go gently-gently with in case she might snap. She felt spaced out, the sickness or the alcohol or perhaps just the hunger and the cold having overtaken her. She felt as though she could have lain down in the snow and slept for the rest of her days.

By February barely a word on the virus was spoken. The news concerned itself with cannibalism, thuggery, thieving and raping. Organised crime ruled in disintegrating urban areas. Within the village they survived, but time and meaning dragged by. Heavily depopulated since attack, the patrol rota had been forced to an end. Wanderers were allowed through the village. Thixendale was just a long row of locked and boarded houses. In this unwelcoming atmosphere few lingered. Even those who were offered one of the empty houses rarely stayed for long. These days the kindness of strangers was viewed with suspicion. Ever fearful that the intention was to feed newcomers up and then put them in the pot. Rumours and urban myths were always a hundred times worse than reality, and although the village didn't witness any cannibalism first hand, they could only presume that there was never any smoke without some kind of fire.

Naomi had pulled herself out of her winter time depression. She had been verging on being positively catatonic at her lowest point. She had managed to pull herself back to a state of living. Melancholia remained like an unwelcome houseguest. Weeks dragged by and nothing seemed to get any better. Everyone had thought it would be over by Christmas. She remembered, in the times before the virus, that the January to February period had always been a bit of a depressive time. With Christmas and New Year over, but the dark nights and chills still reigning, there didn't seem to be anything positive to look to. This year it was only exasperated by the mess the country had fallen into, fuelled by malnutrition. Root vegetables and rabbits as a staple diet grew monotonous very quickly.

There were always people worse off. Karen had reminded her of this precious little cliche only that morning. Georgiana had waddled past, now a good six months pregnant. She seemed to be quite relaxed about her situation, more than could be said for Karen.

"I really don't think she understands how bad this could be," Karen muttered. She and Naomi were in the living room at

Richard's house, drinking weak tea and watching the slow traffic pass by on the street. The sofa had been pushed up to the window for a good view whilst the shutters were open. They had fleecy blankets on their legs to keep them warm. "I mean, even if she had a smooth, textbook birth, it's a first baby and I have no fucking painkillers to give her. I hardly think paracetemol are going to hit the spot."

"Don't we have morphine or something?"

"Mark's so loathe to hand anything out."

"I thought warm water was supposed to help."

"To a point. I'm going to need a team of helpers. Just to keep heating up pots of water." Karen sipped her tea. "And that's best case scenario. Jesus, I hope there aren't complications."

Naomi looked down at the dregs in her mug. "What will be will be."

"It's all very well living day to day, but Georgiana was an idiot. I could have dealt with the problem before it became a problem. If people would just admit and ask for help."

"Her mother seemed very protective." These days Georgiana didn't have anyone. Both parents were now dead. The locals had helped fortify the house, for Georgiana refused to move in with any of her neighbours. She seemed to be coping; in fact she was positively blooming at the moment, visibly swelling whilst the others grew thinner and greyer day by day.

"Kenny's got really bad toothache," Karen changed the subject, downing her tea. "He's been avoiding it for the last few days. My mix of cloves and oats hasn't hit the spot. Rab's going to pull it out with a pair of pliers. Kenny won't let him do it without medical supervision. As if I know the first thing about dentistry. He said to wait till ten. I think he's still hoping it would wear off."

Naomi shuddered and closed her eyes, feeling nauseous. She prayed to God she wouldn't have any problems with her teeth until the institution of modern dentistry was back on its feet.

"I'd better head off."

When Karen had left Naomi went upstairs. In the bedroom, she sat with her back pressed to the dormant radiator, and started to look through her belongings. There was a mish mash of belongings in her rucksack, most not of use anymore. She found it comforting to look through these old icons. Memories of better times would return to her. Little rituals kept her sanity, held the depression back. The first thing she pulled out made her gasp with surprise. It was the diary she'd started, written in a journal from John's wife's old possessions. She hadn't written in it for months, she realised as she flicked through the blank pages. It was a journal for posterity, the experience of hiding out in a village to ride out the virus. The novelty had worn off, and she hadn't thought of writing for a long time, but perhaps she ought to get back to it.

There was a MP3 player she'd not been able to charge up or use for months. A couple of empty jars, once having contained boiled sweets. She'd found the sweets in Ann Douglas' house after the woman had died. They were one of the few stashes that Mark had missed on his confiscation rounds. Those sweets had kept her going through the winter, a mix of the poor diet and lack of sunshine making her feel ill. The sugar had given her a necessary kick. She didn't know what she would have done without it.

Nestled on the crumples of a salsa dress was a teddy bear her mother had sent her in one of her more sentimental moments. Wedged down the side, almost under the dress completely, was the top of a cotton drawstring bag. She couldn't remember what it was. Pulling it out, she tugged it open and removed a couple of items: rolls of cotton, washed out and sanitised in cold water but now permanently stained. When the manufactured sanitary towels had run out, she'd made her own reusable ones, which had worked quite well. Replacing the rolls back in the bag, she set it on the floor and pursed her lips. It was as if that depressing little nag had just been verbalised. She couldn't remember the last time she'd had a need of her home made sanitary pads. Certainly not since Christmas. When had she last bled the previous year? She wasn't sure.

Her hands were shaking. Naomi closed her eyes, as if not seeing the shake would remove the fear. She was definitely thinking the worst. Women's periods would stop for all kinds of reasons, depression and stress certainly being capable of delaying a cycle. And that wasn't even getting onto the subject of malnutrition. She'd read stories of people who had lived in occupied Europe during the war. Some women's periods took a break, as if to say nothing fruitful would ever come whilst this horror was ongoing. These days the modern world had disintegrated due to a virus, and they lived in disorganised anarchy. It was enough to make any person's body switch off unessential bodily functions, put it on pause and wait for better times. This certainly couldn't be because she was, no, she would not even say the word, because it wasn't the case and she wasn't as stupid as Georgiana. Besides which, she would have noticed something, wouldn't she? Cravings or something. Everyone craved food they couldn't have these days. And she hadn't suffered from nausea; well, she had, but that was because she wasn't getting enough to eat.

Naomi put her head in her hands. "Fuck," she whispered. "Fucking fuckity fuck fuck."

"Naomi?"

She jumped at the sound of Richard's yell from downstairs. In a panic, she stuffed the cotton bag into the depths of her rucksack, as if he were about to rush into the room, see the bag, and demand to know why she hadn't been using it regularly. It's because I'm malnourished, she'd protest. I need more fish or green beans or maybe it's just the lack of sunshine.

"Naomi?"

Wiping at her eyes with the backs of her hands, she gave her hair a shake, straightened her jumper and tried to look casual. "I'm upstairs."

"You need to come over to the village hall," he called up. "You need to come and listen to this broadcast we've picked up."

He wasn't coming upstairs. Throwing her belongings back into the rucksack, she got to her feet, and looked indecisively at the rifle. She didn't feel the need to carry it around these days. In truth she'd wandered about a few days completely unarmed, until Mark had caught her bunking off and screamed at her. He was a pink-faced fury, the jowls of his face shaking like flaps since he had lost weight. She ought to have told him where he could stick the rifle. She certainly wasn't as retiring as when she'd first come to the village, but she'd been so taken aback by the sheer ferocity of his outburst that she hadn't known what to do. Picking up the weapon, she went out onto the landing to drag the step ladders back into place.

The colonel was departing as she approached the village hall. Gaunt, aged, he tipped his hat to her. "The Jerries planned it," he told her. "They're up to something. We're all counting on you. I've got to get back to the office. Another message to decode."

"Right," Naomi said weakly, watching him stride away. He seemed to think he was living in Bletchley Park, decoding intercepted messages from the Germans. She couldn't say whether it was dementia or simply that the pressure of the current state of the world that had sent him this way. Whatever was to blame, he seemed to be the happiest person living in the village.

Inside the village hall a small group of people crowded around the radio. All the key faces were there, for the population was not that big any more. David, John Settle, Rab, Anthony, Richard, Mark Andrews, Jill, Linda and Chad. A couple glanced up as Naomi entered, and Richard waved her across.

A woman was speaking through the crackles: "... Reservoir north of Leeds."

The message went to static.

"It's just rewinding."

"What's rewinding?"

"The message. It's on a loop. It's transmitting for about ten minutes every hour."

Naomi moved over to a desk to the side and sat down. She didn't need to be beside the radio to listen to the message.

The loop started again. "This is a recorded message to any survivors in Yorkshire. We are a small community based just outside Leeds. We have secured the streets of our compound from disease and crime, and we have full medical facilities and food supplies. We are requesting survivors to come and join us. We are organising the rebuild of Yorkshire. The army has barely survived, and the government, what is left, is a waste of space. We have to take this rebuild into our own hands. We need more people to help. I repeat, we have housing, medical facilities, food and protection. This message will be repeated on the hour, every hour. Please come. We will beat this together. We are located at grid reference SE 30793 41885, at Eccup Reservoir, north of Leeds."

The static returned, and remained so. The ten minutes' worth of transmission was complete, and the message relay had stopped until the following hour. Naomi pursed her lips and tried to replay the particulars of the message over in her mind again. What had happened to the army messaging service?

"What do we make of that?"

"I think it sounds a bit suspect."

"Suspect? Don't be ridiculous," Linda scolded. "It sounds like someone is finally trying to get something done, sort out this mess rather than hiding away at home brooding." Her eyes narrowed and her face soured as if she was thinking of someone in particular, but her gaze wasn't directed anywhere. The others avoided catching her eye.

"This needs to be investigated," Mark decided.

"I suppose we can't just disregard it."

"We can't continue in this fashion indefinitely. We're growing our own food, but we're very insular. If a crop fails we'd starve. Medical supplies are getting low, and facilities are none existent. We're simply not equipped to deal with a lot of conditions. In the long run that will severely affect the functioning of the village. We're already low on numbers," Mark continued.

"Georgiana's sorting that out," David sniffed.

"So what's the plan?" Jill asked. "Pack our bags and hike over there? It'll take days and none of us have been any distance from the village for a long time. We have no idea what it's like out there."

"We easily have enough fuel to get a Land Rover to Leeds and back," Richard threw into the pot. He was leant back against the desk close to Naomi, arms folded thoughtfully. He looked like he was mentally preparing for an expedition. Naomi stared at him, thinking that this wasn't one of his bloody wildlife documentaries.

"All right. Let's take a few provisions, guns, and get over there." Jill sounded decided. "There's no point us all stopping in the village to rot away."

No, Naomi thought, let's not do this. She could feel panic, controlled and pushed down in the pit of her stomach. She spread her hands out across the desk, shuffling through the drifts of paperwork. Even in the end of the world bureaucracy had found its place.

"No." Mark's rather definitive response surprised everyone.

"But you were just saying..."

"I mean yes, but not for everyone," Mark explained. "As you said yourself, Jill, we don't know the lie of the land between here and Leeds. What they've set up over there may not be suitable, or they may not be able to take us all at once. We don't want to empty out the village, leave it undefended, only to find that we need to come back. I think it would be prudent to send out a small party, two or three people, to check out the situation. They can come back and we can all make an informed decision then."

This set off mutterings, comments and chatter, people talking over one another. Richard had his hand to his mouth, thinking it over. "Normally, it would have been easily done in a day. But give it two days now..."

"Can we even drive there? Isn't there a ban on travel?"

"Do you think the army's still going to be bothered about that?"

"What's left of the army."

"All right, it's decided," Mark interrupted. "We'll send a party of three out to take a look. Now, who should go?"

You are very diplomatic all of a sudden, Mark, Naomi commented wordlessly, watching his profile as he looked around the gathering. David was staring tersely at him, either desperate to be allowed to go, or terrified he might be picked.

"Rab, how about you?"

"Me?" the Scotsman looked a little uncomfortable. The idea of moving onwards, to better living, rebuilding the country was all very gallant, but here in Thixendale they knew what to expect, found comfort in the familiarity. Out there it was a menacing blank. "I suppose I could go."

"Who else?"

Jill shrugged. "I'll go."

"No."

Anthony, one of the village teenagers, tentatively raised a hand. Looking to prove his worth. "I'll go."

"All right. One more?"

"Hey," Jill stepped forward. "How come it's ok for him to go but not me?"

Mark ignored her.

"I'll go with them," Richard volunteered.

"Excellent, we have our three." Mark looked particularly relieved.

"I want to go," Linda said.

"We have enough. We don't want a large party, and we need to keep enough people back here to defend..."

"Is this a private little boy's party?" Linda interrupted Mark. "I don't see why I can't go."

There was silence. Mark merely stared back at Linda. Normally in these circumstances he would have exerted his authority. Told her how he wanted things and that would be the end of the matter. He looked actually stuck for words, trying to gauge Linda.

"Yes," Jill backed her up. "We're a long way past the days of the little lady staying at home."

Everyone looked at Mark. "Very well," he decided. "There'll be the four in the group. Rab, Richard, Anthony and Linda. It's still quite early, you could set off now. You'll easily be able to get there before dark."

"What about me?" Jill protested.

"Four is enough." With a wave of Mark's hand, she was dismissed. "We'll get supplies ready here; Rab, go get the Land Rover ready. Richard, maps and navigational items. Linda, weapons. Anthony, you stay here and we'll get food sorted out for you to take."

After the weeks of inactivity and uncertainty, dragging through a cold winter, blowing heat onto cracked fingers and sitting down to another rabbit and vegetable stew, finally something was happening. People moved with more energy than they had in weeks. They looked hopeful. As if the lockdown in the village was finally to come to an end. Naomi felt sick. Even more so when she saw the determination on Richard's face. It was as if getting ready for another trip out to the other side of the world. Work to keep him busy, give him some worth and purpose. She scrambled up from the desk as he headed for the exit, knocking over the papers. Crouching down she carelessly shuffled them back up, pausing as she held together a disordered heap, glancing down at the list of inhabitants in the village; two hand written columns on the page. She didn't like the thought of records being kept on her at the best of times, but this, however innocent looking, made her uncomfortable. No one noticed as she folded up the top sheet, slipping it into her jacket pocket before tossing the rest of the paper back onto the desk. She hurried out after Richard.

He was striding across the road back towards their house. "Richard!" she shouted after him, breaking out into a jog.

Richard stopped and turned, waiting for her to catch up.

"Please don't go."

He broke out into an easy smile. "I'll be back tomorrow."

"I know you've been all over; can cope with roughing it better than a lot of us, but you don't have to do this."

"That's maybe why I need to go with them."

Something's wrong, she wanted to say. It would just have been dismissed as silly women's intuition.

"Naomi, we have to try this. We can't just stay here with our heads buried in the sand. There's a real chance for a future. If there's a community at Eccup..." he broke off, wrapping an arm around her shoulders and kissing the top of her head. "We'll be back tomorrow, day after tops; I promise." He pulled her into a bear hug. "Things are going to get better. I know this winter's been tough. I know it's hit you harder than some of the others."

He was thinking of her listlessness, her depression. She closed her eyes. This wasn't going to help.

"I can't sit by and let you get worse. We've got a real chance to better our situation."

"You don't even know how old that recording it. That camp could have fallen by now."

"We can't sit here and count the what ifs."

This was too easy. Too wrong. She felt her eyes welling up with tears, feeling ridiculous and emotional. The tightening knot in her chest said he mustn't go. "Richard, I..." what was she supposed to say? I think I'm pregnant although it's probably just the malnutrition and mental state I'm in. She didn't think she could even verbalise it to herself yet, let alone anyone else. And either way it would just push him on to try and better their situation. She did not want to be alone. She thought of that girl stood on the front lawn screaming Anthony's name until the woman had attacked her and ripped her face off. We're all ultimately alone. No one is coming to rescue us.

"You what?"

She took a deep breath, forcing calm upon herself. "I don't want you to go."

"I will be back before you know it. Go stay with Jill or Karen. It'll be one or two nights. Look, I've got to get things together."

He started for the house, but she pulled him back, kissing him full on the mouth, thinking that this would be the last time.

"It'll be fine, Naomi, really," he told her, a little amused by her intensity. He managed to untangle himself from her fingers. "These two days are going to fly by."

That had been the first lie. The time did not go quickly. The second lie was that it was not just a couple of days. Three days had passed and there had been nothing. She tried to keep busy because well-meant positive comments that three days were nothing to worry about were wearing thin. They should be home now. Something had gone wrong.

Naomi was in the bathroom, turning this way and that, avoiding one problem by focusing on another. She couldn't blame it on the angle of light. Her stomach was definitely taking on a bulbous look. Disgruntled, she tugged her top and sweater back down over her abdomen. Of course there were lots of reasons for a change in body shape. People got fat all the time, just not in times of starvation. There were conditions like rickets that gave those kids the pot bellied look, wasn't there? It could be a case of malnutrition, but until she got tested for the unspoken obvious, she couldn't settle the unease in her mind. She ought to go and speak to Karen, but the very idea gave her the shakes. Whilst the issue wasn't discussed she could deny it. She could pretend it wasn't happening.

Out on the landing, she sat on the carpet and listened to the radio. She was trying to find the transmission they'd all listened to the other day about the survivors' collective near Leeds. She should have written down the frequency, for it was impossible to find today. As electricity and telecommunications failed, people steadily went backwards. Radio had become a favourite method of communication. The airwaves were filled with broadcasts from journalists, bloggers, and anyone lonely and with enough know how to begin transmitting. It was a call to prove that they did exist. A sane voice in the anarchy. Of course, not all were sane voices, for with the pressures of disease, starvation and lack of shelter, people turned to what they could. There were an increasing number of religious channels – everything from the mainstream religions through to sects, cults, crazed conspiracy theorists and the barking mad.

Giving up, she turned off the radio. She'd have to go over to the village hall and get the wavelength off the army radio. Pulling on her boots and collecting her rifle, she hurried out into the crisp morning air. Locking the door, she headed over to the village hall.

The colonel was hunched over the radio. He glanced up at the sound of footsteps and smiled at Naomi, but said nothing. She approached the desk. A well spoken individual was reading through the inoffensive, standardised advice for people coming into contact with the infected. The radio was set on the government loop.

She pulled up a chair and sat opposite the colonel. "Do you know what frequency the Leeds' broadcast was on?"

He put a finger to his lips to motion to her to be quiet, before he continued writing symbols in the notebook in front of him. "I've got to decode all the messages."

The colonel was completely gone, she thought sadly. She ground her elbows into the table and propped her head up, listening to the dulcet tones of the government loop.

"Following the next warning, we will give a list of army-checked survivor camps. Survivors listening are warned not to respond to any unauthorised pleas for help or advertisements for collectives on the air waves. The following camps have been checked for safety...."

Naomi's brow creased. She'd not heard this before, although admittedly she hadn't listened to the government's channel for a couple of weeks. She tended to find they only broadcast the watered down facts, missing the essential advice and information because it was considered too harrowing and might cause a panic. Even now the spin doctors were employed. Writing out election-winning misinformation from their secret bunkers. People needed the harsh reality if they were going to survive. Not this polite drivel that suggested Downing Street was still in control.

"Could I change this to Gillian Nightingale?" she asked the colonel. He wasn't listening. He hummed absently to himself, the note taking discarded. Naomi reached over and changed the frequency, going for the numeric address for everyone's favourite journalist memorised.

"... in recent days the government have finally admitted that there is a serious problem, although they continue to insist on the baby approach of not giving people full information. People need to know what is really going on," Gillian ranted passionately. "In the last couple of months the number of private individuals broadcasting has dramatically increased. There are countless adverts for collectives and communes, groups of people claiming to have the answer and asking other survivors to join them. Whilst some of these are genuine, some well meaning although perhaps misguided, many are not. Survivors are strongly advised to only go to those listed on the government loop. These have been checked out by surviving army battalions. Those that haven't made it to the list are pushing people into extreme religious servitude; or worse still are being run by the criminal underground, where human trafficking is alive and well, and the slave trade is positively flourishing. Worse still are the cannibal groups, who driven by starvation and the madness from the pressures of the past year, are luring desperate survivors to their camps for butchery. One recent discovery, tipped off to the army a week ago; just north of Leeds, at Eccup Reservoir, was finally firebombed by the air force late last night..."

Naomi's nonchalant pose, head propped on cupped hands, fell apart as she recognised the name.

"Although the government are not releasing details, inside sources have revealed that this was a human slaughterhouse, victims hung and cut into slabs of meat either to be consumed by the gang, or sold on the black market..."

Gillian Nightingale continued, but Naomi didn't register the words any more. Cannibals at Eccup? It had to be a different place. Richard had gone there in good faith three days ago. He'd said they'd be back in two days' time at most. Something must have gone wrong. They couldn't have reached their destination. A roadblock, the army, locals or mechanical issues would have hindered them. They were struggling to get back to the village. Perhaps they had to walk back.

There was the slightest of sounds as a breath was inhaled. She swung around in her seat to discover Mark Andrews stood a few metres back. He was calm and very still. Everything was as expected. She had nothing to prove it, even to herself, just an uneasy feeling inside. "You knew."

A flicker of sourness moved behind his eyes. "I only heard about it last night."

A painful screech broke out as she pushed the chair back against the wooden floor. Her hands had started shaking, and she could feel the vibrations moving up her arms. The blood had drained from her skin, communing in her fury. "We have to go out after them. They could be..."

"There's no point," Mark told her flatly. "There's no point sending good after bad."

"After bad?"

"If they've survived, they'll come back. If they haven't there is nothing you or I can do." He grabbed angrily at her wrist as she made to leave. "There are precious few of us left here. We need to focus on our future. Don't do anything stupid."

She shook him off and hurried out of the village hall. Outside she gasped as if drowning, her body not sure if it was about to throw up or break out into distraught howling. She ran a shaking hand through her hair, looking blindly in one direction then the next, no idea where to run. Her eyes filled up and the bright colours of the spring morning became blurred.

"Naomi."

Mark Andrews appeared in the entrance, hands in the pockets of his dark green wax jacket. Watching her as if this was all part of an experiment. "You don't have to be afraid. I will look after you."

She was going to be sick. Shouldering her rifle, she headed for the meadows and woods, the steep green narrow valleys, the places where there were no people. Richard, Rab, Anthony and Linda were trekking back to the village even now. They'll have heard on the car radio that Eccup wasn't safe. They'd have turned around. She would have to go and meet them.

David answered the door warily. Not quite concealed by the shadows of the hall was the stick he held. It was possibly a baseball bat. His body language suggested he was too embarrassed to be openly armed. Whatever the reason, it seemed very unnecessary. It wasn't as though she was a stranger passing through, begging for food or shelter they didn't have spare. She wasn't infected. She was just one person. What danger did she pose to him? None. But then David was a bit of an arsehole.

He nodded to her. "Naomi."

"David. Is Karen in?"

"Yes." He paused, as if the question were to be taken literally; that there was nothing more required. "Why do you want Karen?"

The door was still only open ten centimetres. What business of it was his? She sensed she wasn't going to gain permission to enter until David had his answers. "I wanted to see her," she replied. "For medical reasons. I wondered if she had any pills."

"Pills?"

"Anti depressants."

"I don't think so, but you can see her. Yeah." He nodded to himself again as if it now made sense. "I'm sorry about Richard."

Naomi stopped half way in through the door, her stomach knotting. "What about Richard?"

He flustered. "It was a trap. They said so on the radio. A load of cannibals."

She had only just heard about it this morning. Bad news travelled fast. She regarded him coldly. "He's not stupid, he won't have gone charging straight in there without checking out the place first. He's heading back now."

"Oh, you've heard from him?"

Naomi glared at him. "Where's Karen?"

David locked the front door, plunging the hallway into darkness. The side window had been boarded up a long time ago. He led the way to the back of the house. Karen was slouched on one end of the settee. She looked thin, gaunt, and carried dark circles under her eyes. Her hair was greasy and unbrushed, matted together in thick bands. She looked to be in desperate need of those illusive make-me-happy pills.

"Naomi's here for some Prozac," David announced.

Karen gave him a bleak glance.

Naomi slipped past him and sat down in an armchair. David made no move to leave.

"Perhaps we could have a little privacy?"

"Oh, right." David left the room.

Karen rolled her eyes at the space he had just inhabited. "I heard it on the radio this afternoon," she said. "Eccup was a trap. I know it doesn't necessarily mean anything, but... Have you heard from them?"

Naomi shook her head. "Look, the thing I told David."

"It was a lie, I know," Karen finished for her. She leant over the end of the sofa and picked up a bag. "Did you come over because you're not sure, or because you want something doing about it?"

Naomi stared at Karen, a little dumfounded. She wasn't even sure herself if she was pregnant. There was no obvious bump, no dramatic increase in girth around her body that would make it undeniable. Once she'd calmed down from this morning's discovery, telling herself that Richard wasn't an idiot, and he was fine, it was just proving complicated getting home; she decided that she needed to know one way or the other if she was expecting. In her mind she'd still not gone any further than it being a medical condition. She didn't know how she felt about it, and all the future implications. Those kind of internal conversations would have to wait for now.

"I've been wondering about you for a few weeks."

Naomi looked horrified. That would be longer than she'd suspected herself. "But, how...?"

"It's my job," Karen reminded her. "How many weeks gone do you think you are?"

"I don't know, I don't even know if..."

"When did you last have a period?"

"I don't remember exactly. Late last year. I've definitely not bled since Christmas."

"I don't think there's any question about it," Karen told her matter of fact. "But if you want proof so you don't have any doubt in your mind, use this." She took a rectangular box out of her bag and threw it across to Naomi. It was a pregnancy tester kit. "It's the best I can do with the supplies I have here."

She tightened her fingers around the box.

"Have you thought about what you want to do?"

"Do?"

"Look, I don't know what your beliefs are; whether you're a pro choice or not." Karen unhooked her legs from the settee and leant forward, clasping her hands. "But if you want to get rid of it, it's a bit late for the morning after pill, if you know what I mean. Maybe we can bring on a miscarriage."

Naomi tightened her fingers around the box. She still hadn't admitted to herself that she was pregnant. But asking what she wanted to do about it? She didn't know what to say. This little piece of Richard was within her. What if he never came back? She would not allow herself to contemplate that. As she had told David, the Eccup trap didn't mean anything. He was coming back. Richard aside, her condition needed consideration now. This wasn't something that would just go away. This was another person. No, this was too overwhelming to think about. "I need to... check." She held up the testing kit as explanation.

"Ok." Karen curled back up onto the sofa. "But if you do want to do something, don't leave it too long." She stared miserably out into middle space. "This isn't exactly the best of times for babies."

"It has now been a week and a half."

Naomi's statement hung in the kitchen. It was fated to never receive a response, for she was still alone in the house. She had fixed a sheet of paper to the dormant fridge, and ticked off the days since Richard had left the village. A week and a half. She'd checked the maps. It was about 40 miles between the village and Eccup. Even if he had walked, he should have made it home days ago. Perhaps he had become caught up in a local drama on the way home. Another village with problems of its own. He had felt it only human to help out with before he continued on his way to Thixendale. Maybe one of the others in the group had become injured in the escape from the cannibal den, and it meant that they weren't able to travel very far each day.

She set the pen down on the kitchen work top. A hollow clink. Get home, Richard, she thought. This has been long enough.

There was a village meeting in ten minutes. To call it a meeting felt like a dramatisation as there were so few of them now. It had been so long since there had been a meeting requiring full participation. Perhaps there would be news about the group who had travelled out to Eccup. She needed some good news.

The tester kit that Karen had given her had only confirmed the foregone conclusion. Naomi was pregnant. Karen was also right when she had said that now wasn't a good time for babies. Having a family wasn't a subject Naomi had ever spent time pondering on. She was already thirty, and many friends had felt their biological clocks ticking in panic years ago. The baby question had never caused her a sleepless night. She was quite content with herself and her life as it was. Children had never been anything more than a vague perhaps for the distant future. The distant future back before modern civilisation collapsed. She still didn't know what she felt about this new turn of events, and had purposefully avoided Karen for the past week. She did not want to have to make a decision yet. Although deep down she was aware that the longer she avoided the question, the less of a choice it would be. Perhaps it was already too late to decide. An irrational internal belief stated that as long as she didn't discuss it, or openly admit to it, then it wasn't real. It wasn't happening.

She pulled on her jacket and moved to leave the kitchen, but stopped as her fingers touched crumpled paper in the pocket. Removing it, she unfolded the sheet and examined the writing. She'd picked this up in the village hall that morning when they'd crowded around the radio to listen to the distress call from Eccup. It had been on top of a collection of papers, and she'd slipped it into her pocket, like a kleptomaniac, not really sure why she wanted it, only that she had a need to take it.

It was written on lined paper, and contained two columns, two lists of names. Scanning through, she realised it was a register of the remaining village residents. It was a rather depressing fact that they all fitted onto one side of A4 paper. Judging from the order they were written down in, it looked as though the author had mentally started at one end of the village, and gone from house to house, noting down the inhabitants. Naomi and Richard were listed together on the same line, one on either side of the page. There were also a couple of people who were no longer with them. An old woman who had passed away in the night a few weeks ago was on the roll call. The death had been noted as a line had been cast through the woman's name. In fact a few lines had been drawn on the sheet; both Rab and Richard had been crossed out, despite the fact that they had been alive and well when she'd picked up the list. They were still alive and well, she mentally corrected herself. And what of the other names? Georgiana had a red line under her name. Naomi had two black lines under her name. Karen had a question mark. Jill had one blue line under her name.

It was a harmless enough list, but Naomi didn't like it. She crumpled it up and went to throw it away, then changed her mind, smoothing out the paper once again and putting it into one of the kitchen drawers. Just in case.

Jill was loitering outside the church gates as Naomi approached. Despite the sunshine and the early spring warmth, she was wearing a heavy coat and looked pale and wan. "Naomi, I need to catch up with you this evening."

"Sure. What's up?"

"Oh, I'll speak to you later; we've got to get in now." She wrinkled her nose. "Do you know what's going on? Something about the future. I don't like Mark at the best of times but he's getting weird."

"Lack of food."

Jill didn't look convinced.

The two women were the last to enter the church. It felt strange entering, almost a blasphemy, for the church was not used anymore. It stood closed and cold. An empty shell of worship with only the memories of the massacre to haunt the ailes. The interior had been cleaned out and sanitised, but a sense of peace had been lost. Naomi followed Jill down the centre aisle. When she had first come to Thixendale this church had been packed out at meetings. Now the entire village was present, and consisted of a small group up at the front. Mark wasn't in his usual place up at the pulpit, instead standing at the head of the gathering. There wasn't enough of a congregation to warrant the pulpit.

Jill went to the right where there was a space for her in the pew along with Chad and his parents. Naomi slowed down, her eyes scanning over the gathering. She spotted Karen right up at the front, slumped dejectedly in her place beside her husband. On her other side the Colonel sat, oblivious to reality. Just behind was Georgiana, rotund, her stomach resting in her lap as she picked at her nails. Kenny and John were on the back row to the left. John Settle shifted in his seat and smiled at her, patting the space at the end of the pew. "Naomi, come join us."

The pew creaked as she sat down, the chill snapping through her jacket and running down the length of her back. "Do you have any idea what this is about?"

He shook his head. "I think we're about to find out."

"Firstly, I'd like to thank everyone for coming," Mark started, making it sound as though they'd all made space in busy schedules to attend. "It's good to see the whole village gathered here today."

This really was it, Naomi thought. The remains of Thixendale.

"Before I get onto the main business of the day, I should say a few words about Eccup in case anyone hasn't heard. Last week we picked up a radio transmission about a new society that was being set up. A future for people, for us. We'd had hopes for it, and a scouting party headed off to check if our whole village would be welcome: Anthony, Rab, Richard and Linda. Sadly we have since learned that this transmission was a lure and I'm afraid the new society they spoke of was a lie. Although we're not able to get any confirmation either way from army sources who were there when they destroyed the site, I think after a week and a half we have to conclude that..."

"You've just written them off?"

Naomi closed her eyes, feeling sick. She didn't want to listen to this.

"Shouldn't we send a search party after them?" Kenny asked. "You don't know what, if anything happened to them. They might not have even made it to Eccup."

"No, they might not have made it that far. In fact they could be anywhere. But we have to face facts; they very well may be dead, and we can't send good after bad..."

"So that's it? Thanks for volunteering, but screw you, we're not coming after you?"

"What would you have us do?" Mark asked Kenny. "Look at us, look at the number of people here. This is the village in its entirety. We simply don't have the people to be sending out search parties, and even if we did, where would we search? They could be anywhere now, IF they're still alive. We have to consider this logically. Eccup was a trap and people who went there were killed. The place has been raised to the ground by the army now. It's forty miles away, and if they'd walked home, they would be here by now. Even if they walked – if they'd driven they should have been back the same day. It's been a week and a half and I think we have to be realistic."

"Jesus Christ."

"They were good people, they volunteered for the better of our village, but sadly it didn't work out."

Naomi lent forward. Mark had no idea if they were still alive or not. He couldn't just draw a line under their lives like this. She felt a hand touch her back. John leaned in towards her. "Are you all right?" he asked quietly.

"However, Eccup did get me thinking. About a future. About new societies. And perhaps this virus has in actual fact given us all a new golden opportunity to start again and create something good."

"Christ alive," Kenny muttered. "Do you think he's found God, now?"

"The wider world is a big unknown, but I don't think we need to leave to create a new society. We can do it right here. I know our numbers are depleted, but we have the knowledge, the talent, the abilities to do this. The virus seems to have died out. I don't think we'll see another attack like we had last year. It's cleaned out the world and reset the human race. It has given us a second chance."

"He thinks he's the second coming."

"We've managed to get ourselves this far, and it's almost been a year, I'd like to remind you. We have farmers here, we have builders, we have hunters. We have medical capabilities, and we've learned to make most of the raw materials around us for food. We can become self sufficient. We can make our own laws, defend our village, make this an Eden. Are you with me?"

People looked uncomfortably from one to the other; drained by the winter, baffled by Mark's enthusiasm. David sat at the front, his arms folded, nodding agreeably as if he'd bought into the scheme. But then, what else were they to do? They needed shelter, they needed food. It was working, in a fashion, and no one knew what it was like out there. Life had become very insular.

"We can create something, for us, for our children, for their children..."

Naomi looked up, glancing across the backs of heads. There were only two children under ten in the village, three if one counted Georgiana's unborn. And a fourth no one knew about.

"Of course, our low population is an issue, and whilst we can manage in the short run as we are; we have to consider the longer term. It's perfectly achievable; most of us here are of an age where we're still perfectly able to reproduce. We have the tools to increase our village."

He was nuts, Naomi concluded. Did Mark think shagging their way out of the situation was going to make life beautiful? A minimum quota of kids on every couple? All it would do was increase the number of mouths to feed, without increasing the number of able bodies who could work. They had precious few antibiotics and medical supplies. A drive to up the birth rate would put all the women at risk. Even if they had their babies without problem, pregnant women and women with the charge of infants would become burdens themselves. And she doubted anyone would want to volunteer for motherhood at the moment. They weren't bloody cattle; they were people and they were individuals.

"This can work," Mark continued. "To date I realise only Mrs Blackfriars has a proven track record..."

Track record. Were they handing in their CVs for suitability for staying in the village? Naomi glanced down the pew she was sitting on. Kenny was staring at Mark with something of horror on his face. She caught John's eye. He was worried.

"But Georgiana is soon to join her..."

As if women who had children were superior to those who hadn't.

A flicker of irritation moved over Mark's face. He could see people sharing worried glances. "And Naomi will be soon to follow."

John's eyes widened, both he and Kenny looking straight down to Naomi at this shocking revelation. Naomi lurched forward in her seat, feeling the blood rushing to her face. This was her secret she was still coming to terms with. How the hell could Mark Andrews be announcing it in the church? Up at the front Karen had now sat up properly in her place, and had her hand to her mouth, horrified at what Mark had said. She looked over her shoulder, searching for Naomi and fixing her stare. She hadn't told anyone. She looked back to her husband, who was still nodding and smiling, following Mark's train of thought.

Naomi couldn't stay to listen to any more of this. She moved to go, John catching her arm.

"Did Richard know about this when he volunteered?"

She just wanted to dissolve into her own tears. She shook her head. "I've only just found out. I don't know how he knows."

Mark continued with his good tidings at the front of the church. "I've written a small document on my vision for the village. There are copies at the exit. Please take one and read it through. I will help us towards to this future. I will lead us; but we all have our parts to play."

This wasn't a choice. No one was being asked. It was all so polite, but they were being told. This is what was expected of you.

Naomi hurried out of the building, ignoring the neat pile of Mark's visions waiting for distribution. They'd all decided that Richard was dead, and that her personal news was public property. This had nothing to do with anyone else. She didn't want to be a part of some loony fucking breeding cult.

Reaching the house, she fumbled with her keys, her hands shaking so violently that she couldn't get the right key in the lock. Convulsions tightened in her body, her neck in spasm. Tugging the keys from the door, she hurried around the back of the house to throw up in private. Slumping down by the patio doors, she pressed her back to the glass and closed her eyes. And tried to think of nothing.

Shortly afterwards both Kenny and John passed by the house. She heard them knocking at the front door and calling out for her, but she didn't answer. After that Karen came and tried the same thing. She sounded distressed, and promised Naomi that she hadn't told anyone. David must have been eavesdropping on their conversation; it was the only thing she could think of. When she didn't get a reply, she gave up and left.

Naomi pulled her legs up to her body and rested her head on her knees. Closed her eyes. How could this all get so messed up? Richard, just get back here now. Enough is enough and the joke isn't funny anymore. He couldn't be dead. The world had continued since he had left that morning. Nothing had changed. The birds still sang in the trees, the sun still rose at dawn. If he had died there would have been a sign. She would have felt something. He wouldn't just die as if he had never existed.

The air cooled as she was dipped into shadows. She wasn't sure how long she had been outside. Unfolding herself, Naomi looked up, disappointed to discover Mark Andrews standing over her. He had one of his pamphlets with him. He offered to her with an extended hand.

"You forgot to take one," he told her.

She took the papers, making no comment.

"I understand this is a hard time for you," he continued. "Especially in your condition."

Patronising bastard.

"The village will support you through this. You are one of the first, after Georgiana, to rebuild this society."

Patronising deluded bastard.

"I meant what I said the other day. You don't have to be afraid. I will look after you. I realise that this is Richard's; but there's no reason that you can't move on from that afterwards. You can go on to play a continually fulfilling role within the village..."

There was a slight crease in Naomi's brow. Thinking of Richard's name on the list, already crossed out.

"I am more than prepared to take you on..."

Abruptly she was on her feet and pushing past him. How could she have been so stupid?

Mark followed her around to the front of the house. He moved to follow her inside. Naomi blocked the way. "I have to lie down now," she told him, slamming the door in his face and listening to the reassuring click of the lock. To be certain, she drew the bolts, and hurried upstairs, heaving the ladder up after her. The virus might have disappeared, the refugees sparse, and the threats of marauders few, but it seemed those she had most to fear from were much closer to home.

Twelve days.

Naomi had remained in the house, safely isolated on the first floor. Mark Andrews had been walking up and down the village, spreading the good word. She had no desire to have to exchange words with him ever again. Around lunchtime he disappeared from the street, and she took the opportunity to get out and do what she had wanted to do all night. She wanted to talk to someone sane.

Sneaking out the back of the house, she hurried up the steep track to the top of the dale, painfully conscious that it was along this section she was very visible to the rest of the village. She didn't want anyone to see that she had left the house, and she certainly didn't want anyone following her. She was out of breath by the time she reached the top of the hill, the butt of the rifle bouncing against her hip. Red in the face, she hurried around the corner, and bent forward behind the cover of trees, trying to catch her breath. Her heart rate thundered in her ears. She could feel in her legs that she'd not limbered up that morning for such an immediate burst of physical strain.

When she'd regained her composure, she continued at a steadier pace, following the rough worn tracks across to John Settle's farmstead. The farmhouse was closed up and silent when she arrived, almost as if in mourning. It was a disturbing contrast to the bright sunshine. She knocked on the door and called his name, but there was nothing. She paced around at the front door, gazing across the fields and wondering where he might be. Perhaps he'd not heard. She'd check the house before she went over to the sheds and then the fields. The shutters were all fastened open, but she was surprised to see that in every ground floor room, the curtains were still drawn. Round the back, she took several paces away from the house to try and get a look at the upstairs. No movement. "John?"

It was perfectly reasonable to suggest that he was out working on the farm, but Naomi had the distinct feeling that someone was in the house, watching and listening but refusing to respond. She returned to the front door and banged heavily on it. "John? It's Naomi. I need to talk to you."

Inside there was the sound of footsteps. He was at home. The sound of bolts being drawn back, a key turned in a lock, and the front door cracked open halfway. John looked outside.

"Naomi."

She smiled, and moved automatically, expecting the door to be pushed open, inviting. John remained guarded, hands on the door as if ready to slam it back into her face at any moment.

"Is everything all right?"

"Not particularly."

"No, I don't suppose it really is since yesterday." She faltered. She'd never felt unwelcome here until today. "It was yesterday I was wanting to talk to you about. I thought I'd come and see you first, then try and get around to Jill's, then Kenny..."

"I wouldn't bother."

"Sorry?"

John's shoulders relaxed, and his stern gaze softened. He pushed the door wide. "Come in. I should at least let you know what's going on."

"What's going on?" Naomi followed him in, feeling a little nauseous. After Mark's deranged announcement yesterday, she didn't think she could face any more bad news. She watched as John relocked the door. "Why should I not bother going over to Jill's?"

"Because she's not there anymore," he replied simply, leading her down to the kitchen. "Jill left the village last night, for good..."

"She's gone?" Naomi moaned. She remembered when the plague of infected had hit the village. Jill had left with her rucksack. She'd been planning to abandon the village even then. She'd fled with Naomi, and after sheltering at Wharram Percy over night, she'd decided to come back. "She said yesterday that she wanted to speak to me. I got so distracted by what came out that I completely forgot. I should have gone over to see her. This is my fault."

"No, it's not. She stopped by here last night, along with Chad and his parents."

"Chad and his parents?"

John nodded. "They've all left."

"Left? But..."

They sat down at the kitchen table. "Jill's never liked Mark, but I think yesterday was the final push to get her moving. They don't want to be stuck in the village with all that nonsense kicking off, so they've packed up and gone. I don't know where to." He paused, looking down at the table for a length of time before meeting her eye. "She asked me to tell you she was sorry. They were going to ask you to go with them. That's why she wanted to talk to you. But after Mark's announcement, they didn't think that they'd be able to look after you. That you'd be a liability."

"A liability?" Naomi was horrified. "I didn't intend on getting pregnant. This isn't me joining in with Mark's sick plan..."

"That's not what I meant. Your mobility isn't exactly going to get better with this, is it?"

Naomi narrowed her eyes. She had honestly believed they were a good sub community of people that she could have relied on. Friends. She liked to think she wouldn't have thrown Jill to the dogs if the situation had been reversed. "I wouldn't have gone anyway," she said. "I've got to wait here for Richard."

John looked sadly at her. "Naomi, Richard's not coming back."

"Of course he is. It won't be easy trekking through the country with all of this going on."

"I think you've got to accept he's gone." He paused. "He's more than likely dead."

Her eyes beaded up with tears. She looked away to the windows, where sunlight filtered through the thin curtains. She had more faith. "So that's it, then?" She coughed. "Just you and me left?"

"Kenny's still in the village."

"Is he a liability as well?"

"Kenny doesn't think this is so serious. He thinks it will all blow over and come to nothing. Mark Andrews is just one man, he says."

"Well, he's right. Have you read that manifesto? It's complete nonsense. No one is going to agree to that..."

"People already are. Deluded or not, Mark Andrews gives over the air of authority, and people think they'll be safe under his wing. The older people aren't that bothered. They're too old to have children. They just want to be looked after. David's a little lapdog, and Karen's nothing more than a shadow that follows him round without thinking now. Annie Blackfriars actually said yesterday that she'd always wanted to have another baby. People will thoughtlessly give up all kinds of freedoms if they think it means that they're going to be safe."

Naomi's eyes dropped to Mark's manifesto, crumpled on John's kitchen table. "And what about you?"

A shadow of disgust filtered over John's face. "Survival at any cost? I don't think so. We ought to be free human beings, not breeding stock. Besides, the world's population hasn't vanished. There's lots of survivors globally, and places like Japan, Australia and South America haven't even been infected. There's more than enough people. Perhaps if we were the last surviving village in the world... but even then you've got to ask is it worth surviving for? The exploding human population was strangling the earth before the HEMO10 virus appeared. You can't help but wonder if the timing wasn't very apt."

"You're not suggesting this was manufactured?"

"Mother nature has ways of clearing out excess."

"So you're going to refuse to sign up to Mark's plan?"

"Yes but... refusal means leaving the village," John pointed out. "I'm cutting myself off from the village, as of now. The Farthings had the right idea. I will have nothing more to do with Thixendale. I wasn't going to answer the door, but then I thought I ought to explain things to you. You ought to know how everyone else stands on this, so you can make your own informed decisions."

"But the village relies on the farm for food."

"No," he shook his head. "There's not that many of them, and they have enough land down there to feed themselves. After this discussion, I am severing all contact with the village."

He includes me in that statement, she realised. I'm still living down there; therefore I am one of them. She'd never felt so alone. "But what should I...?"

"I honestly don't know what to advise you. You have to make your own mind up about what Mark is proposing. But you and Georgiana are in slightly more precarious situations than the rest of us."

Naomi felt numb. She wasn't going to get anything more here. How could relations from such a close knit group of friends fail so dramatically, just on the words of one local idiot? "I need to go and think about this," she said quietly as she stood up. "I'll see myself out."

But she didn't because John needed to make sure the door was properly locked and bolted after she'd left. She headed back towards the village, realising there was nothing left to do but go home and wait for Richard.

It has now been a month exactly, Naomi thought, since you left. They said on the radio that Swansea was bombed last night. For regeneration purposes: that was the explanation on the government loop. There was nothing to worry about. Gillian Nightingale, woman on the ground, holed up somewhere near Swansea, said that the bombing was to clear out the dross. The criminals had taken over the city, and between them and the cannibals and the lack of law enforcement, extermination was the easiest thing to do. They were planning a rebuild of the country and undesirable citizens weren't part of the scheme. How many more cities would go up in flames before they reached utopia?

She was lucky she was living in the countryside.

Standing at the mirror, Naomi turned side on and ran a hand over the pronounced bump of her abdomen. This morning it was covered by a black stretch jersey top. Jill had named this a liability, but in truth it was keeping her safe. Thank God Richard had left her with this little one. Expectant mothers had risen on pedestals in Mark Andrew's vision for the future, and they were to be looked after, little whims catered for. Both Naomi and Georgiana preferred to live on their own rather than move in with other residents, and if one pregnant woman was allowed to do so, there was no reason to stop the other. For now Mark left her alone. She wasn't sure what would happen after the baby had arrived, but she would figure something out. And in any case, Richard would certainly be back by then.

It was already light. No one appeared to be out in the village. It was the perfect time to sneak out of the house and go for a walk. She'd take the rifle just in case, but she probably wouldn't see anyone. She paused at the front of the drive, propping the weapon up against the fence as she zipped up Richard's coat. She could still just squeeze into her own coat, fully zipped, but she had reached a point where her extended stomach was starting to get in the way.

Naomi idly gazed about her, went to pick up the rifle, then stopped, realising she'd noticed something that was out of the ordinary. On the road heading out of the village there was a man walking steadily towards her. He looked like a tramp, with scruffy hair and beard and stained and torn clothes. He had been ambling along, but on catching sight of Naomi had picked up his pace, almost rushing.

She ought to have picked up the gun, warned him away, but there was something so familiar...

"Naomi."

Naomi squinted as he neared, as if trying to get his features into focus. "Rab?" He looked a mess. The long month had really taken its due from him, but he was back in the village. Still alive. "Oh, Jesus," she burst out, the implications of his appearance starting to filter through. "Rab. You've come back!"

They met in an embrace a little way from Richard's house, laughing and crying. Rab was almost shaking, grateful to be back with friends. Naomi clung to the solid physicality of his frame. This wasn't a dream. She strained beyond him, looking up the road. "Where are the others? Jesus, it's so good you're all coming home. We really feared the worst, after we heard the warning on the government loop." She couldn't stop grinning in expectation. "Did you hear about it before you got to Eccup?"

"Unfortunately not," Rab whispered.

"Unfortunately not?" Naomi uncertainly stepped back from the embrace. "Where are the others?"

"We realised pretty quickly when we got there that things weren't right. Fucking animals. They got Linda, but..." He paused. "We got away. The army levelled the place soon after we'd gone."

"And where's Richard?"

"I..." He looked at her, his eyes red-rimmed with lack of sleep. Every time he closed his eyes, the memories of that first week would return. Hell on earth. "Naomi, he's gone."

"Gone where?"

"He's dead."

"But you just said everyone but Linda got away," her voice was high in pitch, pleading, whining.

"We got away from Eccup, but we got trapped in Leeds. It was so bad there; the air force ended up coming in and blowing up the area. I got separated from Richard and Anthony; they didn't get out..."

"So you don't know..."

"Naomi." He ran a hand down her arm. "He was bitten. You understand. Bitten by someone who was infected."

"But the infection's dying out."

"It was rife in Leeds. That's why they bombed the place." He closed his eyes. "I hacked his arm off straight away, but I don't think it would have been enough. Naomi..."

"Oh, Jesus," she groaned, feeling nauseous. She staggered backwards, holding on to the fence for support. Rab had come all this way back just to tell her that Richard was dead. He couldn't be dead. She'd been waiting for him. There was nothing else to do but wait for him.

"I hadn't realised you were..." Rab nodded at her figure. Naomi was trapped in a bell jar, the outside world now muffled and blurred. Richard had been dead near on a month and the world had continued. She hadn't felt anything. There had been no change. No signal or sign to his passing. He couldn't end like that, a body lost beneath rubble. She'd never know for certain, an anti climax fading out but not concluded.

"Rab!" Karen's screech was like a bullet down the road. Naomi sank to her haunches, staring numbly at the tarmac. Karen, with a smile on her face, the first in a month, raced up from the village hall and threw herself at Rab, screaming with happiness. "You're alive!" she sobbed. "What took you so long?"

"I got pretty beat up trying to get out of Leeds. Some locals let me stay to get better. I was out of it for days."

The two stood, merged and reunited. Naomi folded herself up, arms crossed and over her knees, head on arms, all as a gently rocking foetus. She did not want to be here.

There was suddenly a lot of activity for such an unsociable hour of the morning. A flurry of footsteps hurried towards the reunion, speeding into a run for impact. Karen let out a scream. She was dragged by the scruff of the neck off Rab and cast off in a wide arc.

"What the hell do you think you're doing?" David shouted. It wasn't clear exactly who the question was directed at.

"David..."

"You are not supposed to be here."

"Look, David, I've just walked for fucking miles..."

Naomi looked up as David drew the handgun from his coat and shot Rab in the stomach. An echoing bang and a sickening thud as the bullet met with flesh like a punch, his skin and muscle curling around the entry wound like fingers. Internal organs were ruptured, long jagged lines breaking apart. His shirt was suddenly dark, an ink blot, and wet; saturation point was reached and the blood started to splatter on the ground.

"Rab," Karen screamed, running back to the Scotsman. David grabbed her elbow, drawing her back so roughly that she lost her balance and was dragged away the first few metres on her heels. She scrabbled around onto her feet, trying to break free. David removed his devastated wife from the scene. Rab gave a little groan, as if he'd been winded, then dropped to his knees like a great oak. His legs curled under and he sprawled out into the road.

"Oh God." Naomi scuttled across to him on all fours, without the faintest idea of what she could do.

Rab gazed up as she started to pull away his layers of ragged clothing, trying to get to the wound. "I'm really sorry," he coughed. "I tried to save him. I hacked his bloody arm off. I didn't know you were expecting."

"No one did then." Shit. He'd been shot at close range and it looked like a bloody cannonball had hit him in the stomach. There was so much blood pumping out. Her hands were slick and sticky, slipping over his abdomen. She had no first aid training. The most inept person to be first on the scene. He didn't stand a chance with her. Staunch the flow. Put pressure on the wound. Naomi looked distraught at Rab's stomach. She could see inside him for Christ's sake. Ripping off a large section of his shirt, she balled it up and pushed it into the wound, holding it in place and watching helplessly as it turned red and heavy, blood still pulsing up and out of his body.

"What the hell's going on here?" Mark Andrews, hair springing wildly, wax jacket thrown over pyjamas, stood at the foot of the scene, just out of reach of the rivulets of blood. He had a loaded shot gun in one hand.

Naomi looked desperately up at him. "Rab just got back. David shot him. I don't know what to do."

"David?" Mark sounded angry, turning to march back into the village the way David and Karen had just gone.

"Wait!" Naomi screeched after him. They couldn't all leave her alone. She didn't know what to do. Rab was going to die and it would all be her fault.

"Just you stay here." Rab whispered.

Naomi looked at him. Already the blood had drained from his face. His skin was a sickly white. This was going too quickly. "I'm so sorry. I don't know what to do."

"Just you stay."

At some point Kenny had appeared and calmly taken over. He'd looked at the rags Naomi was futilely holding down and realised that the situation was hopeless. "We can't leave him out here," was all he said, before picking up the feebly protesting Rab and carrying him back to the house. Kenny was a Yorkshire giant, but Rab was no slight man himself, and Kenny leant back into the weight, to keep propelling himself forward. Naomi took her rifle and followed, blood red hands gripping on to the barrel of the weapon for dear life. As they passed Karen's house, she made a vague gesture in that direction, thinking she might be able to get a little morphine or something to help Rab.

The house looked drained of all joy upon approach. The front door had been left half open as if it was hardly worth the effort these days. Naomi loitered at the threshold, uncertain of whether to knock, shout or just walk in. This was the house of a murderer, after all. Perhaps she was about to discover Karen's bullet ridden corpse. Someone was alive, for she could hear the sound of voices from within.

Deciding subterfuge would be best, she slipped in through the open doorway and crept down the corridor. She heard movement in the living room, and pressed her back to the wall, going no further, choosing only to listen.

"I don't know what the hell you expect me to do." Mark Andrew's voice cut sharply through the tense silence, his footsteps pacing back and forth. "We chased Gordon Cunningham out of the village for rape. What do you think they're going to want for murder?"

"It was early in the morning, no one knows."

"There were witnesses!"

"Haven't you got a control on Naomi yet? Karen won't say anything. I've dealt with her."

A pregnant pause, perhaps two men trying to stare each other down. David was the first to give way. "He wasn't supposed to be there."

"Sorry?"

"That was the deal. You promised me he wasn't coming back. It's all right for you, though, isn't it? Richard hasn't come back. He's been eaten by cannibals. But wee Jimmy..."

Naomi closed her eyes. She thought of that list she had taken from the village hall the last day she'd seen him. The population list, split according to sex, and Richard and Rab's names already crossed out. They'd already been written off. Get rid of the competition. If this is what we're surviving for, perhaps there's no point in surviving, she thought. Maybe John had the right idea all along.

Carefully padding back down to the front door, she exited and hurried across to Kenny's house. There wasn't really anything she could do; but at least she could go and sit with Kenny and Rab. Even if they were just waiting for the inevitable.

It took Rab two hours to die. Naomi had told Kenny quietly out in the hallway that Mark and David had been arguing over Rab's inconsiderate reappearance. Karen had been nowhere to be seen. Kenny had marched over to the village hall and taken what he could find. He'd found enough to deaden the pain, but not enough to finish Rab off, and neither of them could quite find it within themselves to take a pillow and press down on Rab's face. He'd lain like a ghost, and calmly bled to death.

When it was over, they'd wrapped him up in bed sheets and carried him over to the church. Kenny had set on digging a grave, whilst Naomi perched on a fallen headstone and watched the congealing blood-blossom appear on the sheets. The other villagers were awake now, and ventured from their houses. Some complained they had been woken early by what had sounded like gunshot. They saw the shrouded body, Kenny digging the grave, and asked who it was. Neither Kenny nor Naomi felt up to speaking. All the words left to be said had drained from their bodies. One man had threatened to come up and rip open the shroud to take a look inside, but a look from Naomi had proved the emptiness of his statement.

Mark Andrews had appeared at some point, and the jabbering had really started. At least it had distracted attention away from Rab's body and onto Mark. The villagers wanted to know who had been killed, who had done the shooting, what was going on. Mark was exhausted by the whole event. He had started to answer, telling them it had been Rab who had been killed, but this only sparked off countless more questions. He had feebly announced that there would be a village meeting tomorrow to discuss the matter.

He would have liked nothing more than to dismiss it as a mystery shooter, last seen running for the hills. An outsider, a foreigner. An unknown who was long gone. But Naomi had seen, and undoubtedly Kenny would know as well. David might claim to have his wife under control, but she was another potential breach. He couldn't understand why Naomi and Kenny didn't say anything. They were a pair of mutes working at the burial. He didn't suggest it had been an accident, for fear a lie would set them off. The angry truth yelled out could create a mob. He could completely lose control of the village.

Mark Andrews needed the time to plan. He was at a loss to find a solution. Some version of the truth ought to be told, but then justice would be required and he really didn't want to have to deal with David. The village population was too low, and to send another man of a good age away was pure insanity. Besides which, David had always been reliable, always in support of Mark and his leadership claim. He couldn't say that he could rely on any of the others quite as much.

There was the added problem of the rat backed into the corner. If people found out that David had murdered Rab and demanded vengeance, David may cling to anything to save himself. He could drag others down with him. Only this morning he'd already pointed out that Mark had promised the Rab issue had been dealt with. They'd neglected to mention they'd already heard on the government loop that Eccup was a trap. Instead they'd played the Eccup relay message, deliberately encouraging Rab and Richard to leave, to venture forth and look for the new community. Anthony and Linda had been unfortunate collateral damage; especially Linda who had been another of Mark's supporters. Mark could deny it all if David started to tell all. He could call it the last words of a desperate, condemned man. But the seeds would have been planted. It was already dangerous, because he didn't know how much Karen had overheard. She'd been somewhere in the house when he'd gone over to talk to David.

He stayed up through the night, drinking coffee and trying to find a solution. He had accepted that he would not get any sleep until this situation was resolved to his advantage. Damn David, and his spineless, weak-willed character. Why should Mark and the village suffer because David hadn't been able to keep his wife happy?

As light crept back into the dale, there was a knock at his back door. Apprehensive, Mark checked through the unboarded section of the kitchen window, relieved to see it was just Karen. She didn't look as though she'd slept either. Her left eye was surrounded by an ugly bruise. She had a cut lip which had bled onto her chin in the night. David's poor behaviour clearly continued. Perhaps Mark would be better off without him. Why not throw him to the dogs?

"Karen."

She glanced at him. He wasn't sure if she was glaring, or it was just the exhaustion. "David asked you to meet him at Thornyhaugh."

"Thornyhaugh?" Mark didn't sound impressed. It was a ruined farmhouse, four or five miles from Thixendale. On top of the hills, it had taken the brunt of the winter winds, chilled air and snow blizzards. Just a pile of rubble these days, it had been abandoned decades ago, and had never had the comfort of a modern road to its door. The old cart ruts had long since been ploughed into fields. He would have to walk there, but the distance could be covered in a couple of hours.

"What time?"

"As soon as possible."

"He's already there?"

"He left in the night."

"Running away with his tail between his legs," Mark scoffed, as if nothing better could be expected.

Karen scowled at him in distaste.

"Don't worry," Mark assured her. "First, I must go and sort out your husband."

It was a fine morning for a hike up through the dales and to the tops of the hills. Mark's mind was too distracted to appreciate the scenery. The commander of tactics, he was working through the possibilities of what David was going to say to him, and what he could counteract with. If he was really lucky, David wouldn't be coming back, and then he wouldn't have to worry about David revealing how they'd planned to get Rab and Richard out of the village.

Up on the tops a lot of the fields hadn't been planted for this spring. The local farmers saw little point in producing an excess that the army would just take without payment. Even if they'd had a mind to feed the nation, the seed merchants had gone and there was no supply of seed. Nothing to sow. The land was covered in weeds.

Thornyhaugh, the old farmhouse, was a pile of stone in the corner of the field. Little was left after useable pieces had been recycled into stone walls and other farm buildings in the area. A couple of trees grew up through the plot. They were well established specimens. The trees and rubble cut the corner of the field off from crop production. What was missing from the scene was David.

Irritated, Mark opened the gate by the ruins and stepped into the field. Had he grown tired of waiting and just set off? Perhaps Karen had been told to go and tell him straight away, but she'd left it a few hours before going to Mark.

His eyes scanned over the field, sunlight striking a fluttering piece of white catching his eye. A fence post had been hammered into the centre of the field, and upon it a large white piece of paper had been nailed. Muttering to himself, Mark stalked out over the field. It might have been nothing, but as he neared he saw his name written on what turned out to be a large envelope. A message from David. The coward had already fucked off into the blue yonder. At least it would leave Mark a little freer to give his explanation to the village this afternoon. This mess could still be salvaged.

He ripped the message down from the post, and opened the envelope. He ought not to have expected any better of David. Inside there was a single sheet of paper, folded in half. Pulling it out, he opened it to its full extent and peered down at the single sentence in bewilderment.

'David hung himself at half past two this morning.'

How curious, he had thought, that they could be so specific about the time; before a sharp pain in his right knee had sent a gasp and all other thoughts to the atmosphere. He'd lost hold of the paper, and staggered, moving all his weight to the left. He lost his balance and toppled onto his side into the weeds.

"Jesus Christ," he swore loudly, reaching down to massage his aching knee through his trousers. He was horrified to feel the wet, pulpy mess, slippery and at body temperature, beneath his hand. He looked down at his leg, and the pain increased as if the volume had been turned up. It looked as though his knee cap had exploded out of his leg.

"Shit." He pulled himself up, screaming as he tried to stand on his right leg. He had to get out of here. He had been an idiot not to consider that this could have been something other than a meeting to discuss their options. He looked around the field, his breathing ragged, but he was the only person there.

He roared as agony shot through his left knee cap, a slick shower of crimson spurting up on impact, glittering in the sunshine. He tumbled onto his back, staring up at the sky, gasping for comfort. If it had taken him about two hours to walk here, how long would it take him to drag his bleeding body back home? It didn't matter, for he would not try. The message was perfectly clear. He wasn't welcome there anymore. He closed his eyes and waited for the final headshot. It never came.

At the far side of the field, over the stone wall, Naomi sank down onto the grass and stretched her legs out, straight like pins. She rested the warm rifle across her legs and breathed easy for a moment. It wasn't much to avenge either Rab or Richard, but it would have to do. She wouldn't kill Mark, for she wanted him to have a long time to think about what he had done. She didn't want him coming back to the village either, and figured a man with no knees wasn't going to get anywhere. He could spend what little was left of his life with his thoughts and his pain. Perfectly alone.

May. Naomi had been in Thixendale for a year. It felt like a lifetime. It was all so far divorced from how things had been when she'd first arrived. She stood and clung to the armful of bloodied sheets, no idea what to do next. Opposite her, Karen, pale and wan, awkwardly thin and bony, was thinking, her eyes flitting across the room as she engaged in her internal conversation. She held her hands together, nervously tapping fingers against palms. Naomi assumed these things were never meant to happen without a bit of pain and blood, but Karen's demeanour wasn't exactly encouraging.

Georgiana had gone into labour. She'd started having contractions in the night, but hadn't gone to fetch Karen until the morning. She'd heard that it could take hours before a woman was ready to give birth, and had preferred to be alone. Naomi was a little in awe of her bravery, or sheer foolishness, but had agreed to go with Karen. No one else had seemed willing. Not that there were many people left in the village. Kenny had turned green at the suggestion. The Colonel was away with the fairies and the Blackfriars pointedly wanted nothing to do with the people they blamed for the disappearance of Mark Andrews. Naomi and Karen were on their own.

Karen was nodding at the landing, suggesting they needed to have a conversation out of earshot.

"What's going on?"

"It's breached."

Naomi peered at her. She had never been particularly interested in babies or mothers before now. "What does that...?"

"Normally, your body gets everything ready. The baby's moved into position, you know, in a vertical position, ready to be pushed out," Karen whispered. "Georgiana's baby is still flat out on its back. It's not coming out."

"But she's giving birth."

"I know, but nothing's coming out."

"So what do we do?" Naomi felt sick. Karen had estimated her own pregnancy at around five months so she still had enough time ahead of her, but this wasn't the kind of thing she really wanted to see in her condition.

"Normally, in this situation, a caesarean. But I don't do those, the surgeon does. And even if I could operate, we're not in suitable conditions. The infection risks..."

"We can't just leave her to it."

Karen shook her head.

"Jesus, does this happen to everyone?"

She shook her head again. Folded her arms and unfolded them again. "If we don't do something soon, the baby will die, and then maybe Georgiana. We have to try and get the baby into position now, manipulate it. I've been trying to do it..."

"That's what you were doing on her stomach."

"It wasn't working. I'm going to have to be brutal, a bit medieval. I need you to do what I was doing on her belly. The head's to Georgiana's left. You can feel the baby when you push into her. You need to push the head down, feet up."

Naomi looked horrified. She couldn't do that. "And what are you going to do?"

"Grease up."

"Grease..." Naomi glanced back into the bedroom where Georgiana was puffing away, red faced, and as drugged up as they dared let her be. Grease up: Naomi realised what she was referring to. Thinking of snippets of countryside programmes, sturdy-armed farmers doing the necessary with a cow or sheep in trouble, helping nature on the way.

"If I can get a hold on the head..."

Naomi's blood volume dropped and she felt herself sink towards the wall. Karen clung on to her arm. "I'm really sorry," she whispered desperately. "You shouldn't be in here. But I need your help. We have to get this finished now."

They tried once, but failed, and Georgiana passed out with the agony, things going in the wrong direction as her body was entered rather than exited. Naomi and Karen had retreated to the hallway for a brief respite before Georgiana woke up and they went back to her. They tried again, but by the time they got the child out, the cord's strangle hold had been too long and too tight and the baby was dead. Georgiana was barely conscious, weak like a heavily induced opium addict, yet her body worked industriously, pumping blood out, soaking sheets and mattress. By the next morning, mother had joined her child.

Numbed, Naomi had padded out of the house, pulling her jacket on over Sheryl's flowing maxi dress she was wearing. She sat down on an upturned bucket on the verge by the road in front of the hedge. Her hands were caked in rust brown congealed blood. She watched the sunlight move over the tarmac. Listened to the birds twittering in the early morning. She wondered how much longer she had left to live, and if she'd be able to take as much punishment as Georgiana. Georgiana had just been a teenager, with unknown reserves of energy and resilience. Naomi was in her early thirties. She was probably classed as an old mother. Her eyes filled up, and she tugged on her jacket sleeve, covering over her hand, to wipe at her eyes. Crying wasn't going to help anyone, but she'd come to the point where she really didn't know what else to do.

And it was at one of her lowest moments, when there seemed to be no hope, that it came down, roaring, out of the sky, and landed in the road before her.

It, or rather they, were two military helicopters, twin towers of rotating blades slicing through the air. The noise was deafening, war drums announcing their arrival. Naomi stared down the road, wondering if the Colonel hadn't been mad after all, and these were the reinforcements that he had chattered on about. The engines started to whir down when the helicopters were safely on the ground. The blades slowed so that it was possible to make out their individual form with the naked eye. The side doors opened and a handful of military men, aged before their years, jumped out, armed and suspicious. They were followed by a particularly well groomed man, also in combat gear. In stark contrast to his comrades, his clothes did not look as though they had seen action. In fact they looked like the designer versions, better intended for lounging on weekend getaways, posing by the Range Rover and hoping it would be dry so that he wouldn't get mud splashed on his boots.

She couldn't even start to imagine who or what they were, but she was too tired to care. This village was dead and they were just a few scraps waiting to die. She would have looked away and given them not another thought, but a final figure stepped from the front helicopter. He was thinner, older, unkempt, with shoulder length hair and a wise old beard. There were lines around his eyes she didn't remember, but he was still recognisable.

One of the soldiers said something quietly, but Rudi waved his comments aside and headed towards Naomi. He slowed when he saw her arms. It was tentatively assumed that the worst of the outbreaks were now over, but with the world expanded to an unexplored mass of little communities, enclaves and islands, no one really knew what was surviving where.

"Naomi, you're not...?"

Not what? She caught sight of her hands, then shook her head tiredly. "No, I'm not infected," she sighed. "This isn't even my blood. It's Georgiana's."

He stopped a couple of metres from her. "And how is Georgiana?"

"She's dead." She caught his eye. "She died in childbirth last night."

Not really the year for getting pregnant, he thought, but Georgiana might have been a close friend. Making smart comments in retrospect wasn't going to help. He was relieved to find that Naomi was still alive, and surprised by how well she was looking. "And you're well?"

"Surviving."

Screw worries of infection and other diseases. Rudi marched up to her, just grateful for a thread of life before the HEMO10. She was a friend from before who was still alive. Naomi stood up as they met in a tight hug, old flatmates from university days. "Hello friend." He held onto her, almost crushing the breath from her body, just to be sure this was real.

"And you've been here all this time? I've not been able to get through the last few months. I think the telephone exchange went down."

"I know. All we've had is the radio. And what about you, still working hard in London?" Naomi stepped back and zipped up her jacket. It was a little chilly still.

"I got transferred to Edinburgh a couple of months ago."

"Scotland? I thought they'd locked down the border."

"They're starting to take in refugees. We got our labs moved up there as we were considered of strategic use." His voice drifted off as he stared down at her changed body shape. In other times it might have been rude to comment, because she simply might have been putting some weight on. But gluttonous times were over. People survived, but that was just it: they existed and muddled through, but the good, idealised life, if there ever had been one, was over. "Oh, Naomi, you're not expecting as well?"

She grimaced. "Still a few months to go. I could have done without last night."

"Were you attacked?"

She gazed at him. Dear old big brother Rudi, sheltered, naive and a little out of touch at times. A lot of women probably were pregnant now after rapes. Georgiana was one such example. With law and order nonexistent and terror driving people, basic urges were hard to control. People changed into monsters. "No," she answered quietly. "Just a little careless."

"And the father?"

Her throat stuck. "Dead."

"I'm sorry, I..."

She brushed it aside. That was enough for the first time admitting how things were. Acceptance might take a little longer. "What I'd really like to know is what you're doing here?"

"We're on a reconnaissance mission," he explained, sounding as though he'd picked up a bit of jargon from his military friends. The result of too many grave conversations in the backs of trucks and helicopters as they travelled over the country, quite safe in their motorised transport and behind their automatic weapons. "We had to get some equipment, some samples. Touch base with London. We're heading back now and I managed to persuade them to make a stop off in Thixendale. I needed to see if you're all right."

Naomi shrugged. "I'm not sure about all right. But I'm still alive."

"Are there many people in the village?"

"Barely anyone. Most were killed. We had a plague of infected rush through after Hull was bombed. Then some people headed off to try and get help..." she coughed, keeping her composure. "And of course there's been a few natural deaths, a few suicides. Other people have just upped and left. I don't know what happened to them."

"You can't stay here."

"I don't have much option. I don't suppose York is any better, and besides, how would I get myself there?"

"Come back with us. You can't stay here on your own, especially with this." He gestured to her stomach. "You'll have to go through quarantine, we all do, but then you could go to your mother's. You'll have access to full medical care."

"I guess," Naomi started uncertainly.

One of the soldiers joined them. Naomi knew very little of military ranks, and wouldn't like to guess what position he occupied in the army, only that he gave off an aura of being in charge. The one who made decisions. Judging by the heavy lines engraved into his brow, frowns of tactical planning haunted his days. Perhaps in his forties, he was all iron and sinew. Tensed, ready to react, and yet relaxed enough to suggest that there was nothing any of them could do that would surprise him. "Is she coming?"

"Yes."

"I..."

The man looked to Naomi. "We've not got a lot of space; so if there's a lot of survivors I wouldn't broadcast this. We can take a max of four people; no luggage. Small rucksack, bag or whatever per man. That's it. I want to get out of here in thirty minutes, earlier if possible."

He made it sound as though they were deep in enemy territory, where the locals were hostile and savage. Naomi gestured vaguely at the house behind her. "I should tell Karen."

"Thirty minutes."

"We need to bury Georgiana." Karen's voice interrupted negotiations. The group turned to look at her. She looked like a bloodied butcher fresh from her work.

"And who is Georgiana?"

"She's dead," Karen said, as if the fact Georgiana needed a burial could have left them in doubt. "She and her baby are upstairs."

The man sighed, twisted and nodded to two of the soldiers. "You two. Get shovels, get digging. Church is over there." He looked back to Naomi. "Anyone else to ask?"

"We should say something to Kenny."

"Kenny is?"

"He lives just down there." She pointed down the road, pausing as she spotted Kenny loitering at the edge of the front garden, watching proceedings without trying to draw attention to himself. "He's just there."

Another soldier was dispatched to go and speak to Kenny about arrangements, to see if he wanted to be evacuated.

Naomi wondered if there was anyone else to speak to without creating a rush. Not that there were enough people here for a panic. The Blackfriars wouldn't speak to her these days. The colonel was mad and probably wouldn't want to get on board for fear of letting the enigma team down. John Settle had been good on his word and had not been seen these last couple of months. On the occasions when Naomi or Kenny had gone up to the farm to try to talk to him, they'd been met with silence and closed windows. They didn't even know if he was still living there or even alive. She could understand how his disillusion had driven him to this isolation, unable to give the world any time, but it also felt like a personal slight, as if she hadn't quite come up to his required standards.

Rudi touched her arm. "Where are you living? Shall we go and see if there's anything you want to take?"

Naomi touched the smoothed flat stone hung around her neck, and thought that there probably wasn't anything else of significance. "All right," she nodded. "We can go take a quick look."

They walked together down to Richard's house. Naomi unlocked the door. Rudi followed her in, depressed by the sight of boarded up windows, the torn out staircase, and cold, chilled rooms. It was post apocalyptic living. There was a stepladder propped up where the staircase had once been. Naomi gestured upstairs. "I'm just going to go wash my hands, grab a few things. I'll be five minutes."

Rudi nodded vaguely. "I'll wait down here."

In the bathroom, she cast aside the jacket, no longer required, and scrubbed at her arms. When she felt suitably clean, she went to the bedroom, emptying her original rucksack out onto the bed. What did she have to take? There were keys to her old flat in York – pointless now – but she couldn't help herself and flung them in, followed by Richard's own house keys. Her salsa dress which she pushed to the bottom along with her memories connected to it. She took a few clothes, trousers she couldn't quite fit into these days, gloves and hat, archery wrist guards. She'd have to leave the bows here. A small stuffed bear, a couple of CDs and her MP3 player, unused for months, a couple of pairs of earrings and rings. A paperback book John had leant her that she'd never returned, along with her journal. That would do. She pulled on a woollen cardigan, followed by her winter coat, and left the bedroom. She'd never come back here.

For old time's sake, she moved the step ladder and propped it up in the kitchen. "Rudi?"

"I'm in here."

She went to the back of the house, where Rudi was in a little box room, Richard's old travel study. There was a number of photographs on the wall, dramatic scenery, land never touched by the development of man. Jungles, waterways, mountains. And in a couple Richard made an appearance, an eager, enlivened glint in his eyes, filled up by the adventure. Rudi looked over at her. "Is this him?"

She couldn't quite bare to speak. She nodded.

"I think you should take these with you." Rudi started to take the pictures down, opening up the frames and removing the photographs.

Naomi wandered up to the bookcase, running a finger along the spines of travel guides and maps of the world. Atlases and information on cultures and customs. It was all obsolete now. She took down one hard backed jotter that was lying haphazardly over the top of other books, flicking it open. A hand written journal, in Richard's handwriting. She paged through to the front. Papua New Guinea. Before the world had ended.

"These should fit in the back of that." Rudi passed her the photographs. "Stop them getting crumpled."

Naomi slid the photographs in the back of the journal, and squeezed it into her rucksack, pulling the zip to. "We should probably go now."

Outside a couple of soldiers were carrying a roll of tousled, stained sheets across the road to the churchyard. Georgiana. She'd be buried, a definite known ending, which was better than most people got, but there'd be no service. What was there to say? She'd died too young, it wasn't fair. As if fairness had existed before the virus. Rudi put Naomi's rucksack in the first helicopter, before going to speak to the commander. The styled man in fashionable combat gear strolled over to her, smiling and flashing his white teeth as if he were about to try and sell her a helicopter.

"Hey there, so you're the girl we stopped off to collect. Naomi, right?"

"Yes."

"I'm Guy," he offered a hand. "Guy Riddell, I work for Zanprotean."

She numbly shook his hand, bemused that anyone thought they worked for anyone else these days.

"And I hear you're expecting. Congratulations you," he tinkled. "You know, meeting you, seeing a village, where survivors are living, it's really shown me that we're doing good work. This journey's really worth it. People's lives are going to get so much better. I understand in present circumstances it's better for you to come to Scotland. You want the proper medical treatment. Medical supplies, treatment... that's what we all rely on. Something like this happens, and it reminds you of the basics, the essentials. The thing everybody wants."

He's definitely trying to sell me something, Naomi thought.

"We're going to bring hope."

"I'm sorry, I've not heard of Zanprot..."

"Zanprotean," he flashed her a smile. "You will."

"They're a drugs manufacturer." Rudi had reappeared, his voice a little monotone. It was noticeable that he did not share Guy's enthusiasm. "They're developing a vaccine."

"Ah, ah, ah." Guy waggled his finger at Rudi. "Developed, I think you'll find. We're ready to start healing the world. We're going to get us back on track, get economies moving again."

"Oj, Riddell," someone in the background shouted. "Do you want this or not?"

"Excuse me," Guy said. "I have to see to this."

Naomi looked at Rudi. "Get the economy moving?"

Rudi grimaced. "Everything comes at a price. Even the end of the world. Zanprotean are currently negotiating with the Scottish government..."

"Negotiating what?"

"Price."

"Price? You mean there's a vaccine but no one's getting it because someone has to get paid first?" Naomi started furiously. "I would have thought money was a little obsolete these days."

"I don't know whether the vaccine is fully developed. I don't think they've run enough clinical trials, the data sets...." Rudi drifted off, judging by Naomi's expression that she didn't want a science discussion right now. "The HEMO10 virus clearly wasn't a big enough kick to stop the human race being greedy. Whilst most of the world has spent the last year dying, uninfected nations: Australia, Japan, New Zealand, South America... they've been researching the disease. They've been working on vaccines and cures. Well, there's no cure, the cell damage seems to be irreversible, but a few independent labs claim to have developed vaccines. There's a company in Paraguay that's manufacturing already. The Americans have bought up their entire production for the next two years."

Naomi rubbed her eyes. "I don't understand this. Wouldn't they need cases of infection in order to have something to research?"

"They've been sending in task forces, teams to collect samples. A lot of teams have died or been held hostage by the locals, but some got back."

"So these countries have been sending in teams to get samples; but not taking any refugees. They just left people to the end of the world, so they can crack on in their labs and develop vaccines they're going to sell back to us at over inflated prices? What are we going to pay them with, grains of sand? Or will they run up a tab for us so that we can live in abject poverty for the next hundred years, clearly indebted to our isolated saviours."

"Naomi, calm down."

"Do you think this is all right?"

"No, of course I don't. But this is the way the world is now; the way it's always been. What's right has never come into these things."

"I guess not." She folded her arms and watched as the soldiers returned from the graveyard.

Karen followed them, her arms now washed, and her clothes changed. She'd only made this much effort because she'd been told there was no way Scotland would let a blood slathered refugee in through the border. She didn't have any personal belongings with her. She hadn't wanted to take anything. In truth, she wasn't particularly bothered about fleeing to Scotland, but at the same time she didn't care if she never saw the village again.

Kenny had also decided to leave, and was already in the second helicopter. The pilots were back in the cockpits, starting the engines. The blades began to whir, around and around, faster and faster until the blades vanished.

"We'd better get on board."

Naomi let Rudi help her onto the helicopter. There was an empty space inside, with rows of seats at the front. She sat down next to Karen, who was vaguely staring out of the window. She pulled on her seatbelt as Rudi got in next to her and the doors were slammed shut. The engines revved up, and there was that surreal moment when her thoughts remained on the ground, but she could feel her body being taken up into the air. Leaving. The sun was particularly bright this morning. The blades of the helicopters kicked up clouds of dust that swirled and billowed down the road. A couple of villagers, curious enough to have watched the last half hour through their windows, but not dare approach the military, came running from their properties, realising now that a chance at evacuation had been lost.

They rose up out of the village, the remaining locals becoming dolls, and then dots on the landscape. The billowing wave of dales cutting through the Wolds became dramatic from the air. It was a quiet, natural landscape, with no electricity, low populations and nothing but darkness and starlight at night. Naomi leaned up against Karen, getting her last look at Thixendale as the helicopters started to pull away. Goodbye, she thought. Goodbye to all of you.

www.ingramcontent.com/pod-product-compliance
Lightning Source LLC
Chambersburg PA
CBHW070118260626
47160CB00004B/1522